OUTSTANDING PRAISE
NO DEFENSE

"*No Defense* is a winner."

—Kate Lehrer

"The care Wallace takes with LuAnn's characterization enhances this well-paced legal thriller, as do flavorful Southern voices and a bracing dose of romance."

—*Publishers Weekly*

"This page-turner of a novel is refreshing for its uncommon perspective, as opposed to the usual legal novel that focuses on lawyers."

—*Booklist*

"A powerful first novel."

—*Library Journal*

NO DEFENSE

RANGELEY WALLACE

St. Martin's Paperbacks

Lines from "The Ballad of the White Horse" by G.K. Chesterton appear courtesy of Ignatius Press.
Lines from the "Sesame Street Theme" appear courtesy of Sesame Street, Inc.

NO DEFENSE

Library of Congress Catalog Card Number: 95-31437

ISBN: 0-312-96169-3

Printed in the United States of America

A Wyatt Book for St. Martin's Press hardcover edition/November 1995
St. Martin's Paperbacks edition/April 1997

St. Martin's Paperbacks are published by St. Martin's Press, 175 Fifth Avenue, New York, NY 10010.

10 9 8 7 6 5 4 3 2 1

For Jim

The thing on the blind side of the heart,
   On the wrong side of the door,
The green plant groweth, menacing
   Almighty lovers in the spring;
There is always a forgotten thing,
   And love is not secure.

—G. K. CHESTERTON

ACKNOWLEDGMENTS

I am especially grateful to my editor, Bob Wyatt, for his belief in my work and his invaluable contributions to this book, and my friend and agent, Leslie Breed, for her loyalty and tireless efforts on my behalf. I am also indebted to Joyce Renwick for her insightful suggestions and guidance, and Ruth Noble Groom for her help and encouragement. Special thanks to Holly Wallace and William Nealy for their moral and technical support. Finally, thanks to my husband, Jim Denvir, whose patience and hard work have made this book possible and whose comments have made it better, and my children, Daniel, Jamie, and Emma for teaching me to take risks and for their love.

No
Defense

PROLOGUE

I hurried down the wide marble hallway of the new county courthouse planned by and named after my father; the clicking of my high heels on the marble floor echoed behind me, skipping a beat when I hesitated in front of the massive wooden doors to Courtroom G. I took a deep breath, bracing myself, then I firmly grasped the brass handle on the right and pulled the door open.

Once inside the spacious courtroom, I tried to stare straight ahead and ignore the blur of people watching me. I willed myself not to bite my lip, a nervous habit I'd had as long as I could remember, one that had been mentioned by some reporter in one of the articles about my family after my father, Newell Hagerdorn, the mayor of Tallagumsa, Alabama, and the leading candidate for governor, was indicted for murder.

The courtroom spectators seemed to be seated according to their sympathies, reminding me suddenly and absurdly of a wedding celebration where the bride's family and friends take the left section and the groom's family and friends the right. The organizing principles here, however, were my father and the crime with which he was charged.

The first three rows on the right side behind the prosecutor's table were occupied by the dead boys' mothers and their supporters, a rectangle of black in a sea of white.

Members of my own family—my mother, Gladys, my sister, Jane, and her husband, Buck, as well as my husband, Eddie—sat just one row back from that group.

As far as I could tell, the rest of that section was filled with reporters, many of whom I could now identify by name. Ben

Gainey, from the *Washington Star,* was there, of course. This was, after all, his news story, his coup, the kind of story young reporters dream about. Since reopening the fifteen-year-old unsolved civil rights murders and marshaling piece by piece the evidence that ultimately led to my father's indictment, Ben Gainey had ascended to the now familiar role of reporter as hero.

It was not enough that Ben had rooted around in the past that had been buried with our town's infamous crime and come up with my father. Far worse—as more than a few news articles had pointed out—was that my relationship with Ben, my involvement in his work, and my participation in his investigation had been critical to his success.

And so I suffered under the unbearable weight of my own guilt as I approached the defense table, kissed my father good morning, and wished him good luck. Ever calm and cool, he reached for and patted my trembling hand. The sharp contrast between his composure and my distress suggested I was the one on trial here, not him.

I sat down in the first row of seats behind the railing separating my father and his lawyer from the crowd.

A few people reached over the back of the pewlike bench and patted my shoulder, offering comfort.

Someone behind me whispered, "We're with you, LuAnn. Don't worry, hon."

I turned around and forced a small smile. Members of the sheriff's department, the mayor's office, and our many other champions and friends filled the rows on the defense side of the courtroom.

To my disgust, Lucas Terry, the imperial wizard of the Knights of the Ku Klux Klan, and some of his deputies sat in the back row. At Terry's wave, I felt my face redden and I quickly turned away.

The night before, after finally getting my six-month-old twin boys to sleep—no easy task, as they were teething—I'd fallen into bed exhausted but sleepless at the prospect of what the next day might bring. I started to cry. I'd cried plenty lately but had tried hard not to fall apart in front of my four-year-old daughter, Jessie. She must have heard me, though, because she appeared in the bedroom doorway wearing the *Star Wars* T-shirt my husband, Eddie, had forgotten when he moved out.

The T-shirt was a ridiculous fit, so long the hem dragged the ground with each step and so wide the short sleeves reached her wrists. Still she'd insisted on sleeping in the shirt every night since her father left.

Jessie stood still and watched me cry. Her golden brown hair fell around her shoulders, and her green eyes were open wide, filled not so much with fear as curiosity.

"Take a deep breath," my daughter ordered, mimicking my advice whenever her emotions got away from her. "Breathe in slowly, Mommy. Slow-ly."

I did as I was told, caught my breath, and somehow controlled my crying. Then I patted the bed, and Jessie ran across the room and jumped up next to me. I gathered her into my lap and kissed her lightly on the forehead.

"Are you sad?" she asked. She spread her father's T-shirt over her toes.

"Just a little. Now that you're here, I'm fine." I wiped the last tears from under my eyes and smiled.

"Why were you crying?" She ran a finger along my cheek.

"That's a long story," I said.

"Tell me."

"It's late."

"Please," she begged. She tugged at my nightgown.

"Let's see," I said. I set her on the bed, stood up, and crossed the room to the bookshelves. A sudden wind heralding the predicted early fall burst through the open window as I passed. I slammed it shut, shivering slightly.

On tiptoes, I reached up to the top bookshelf, pulled out the blue and gold photo album that contained bits and pieces of our lives over the last year, and brought it back to the bed.

Jessie and I lay on our stomachs over the photographs. She opened the album, which looked heavy and large in her small hand, then I flipped past the pictures taken during the winter months of 1978. When I reached the April 1978 photos from the dedication of the Newell Hagerdorn County Courthouse, I stopped.

I pointed to a picture of Jessie. "Oh, look at you in your sailor dress. I bet you've grown an inch in just six months."

"I look like a little kid there," she said in her most mature four-year-old voice.

"Remember that day, Jessie?" I asked her. "We were celebrating the opening of your granddaddy's new courthouse. I guess I'd say all of this mess started that day."

"You mean the twins?" she asked profoundly, pointing in the picture to my bulging eight-and-a-half-months pregnant belly.

"No." I laughed. "Hank and Will are messy, but we love them. Right?"

Jessie made a face and stuck out her tongue. As many times as I'd explained it to her, I had no doubt that she held the twins accountable for our move from Atlanta, Georgia, to Tallagumsa, Alabama, and for her father's leaving us not long thereafter.

I turned the album page and stared at the photograph that had been printed in all the Alabama newspapers the day following the courthouse-dedication ceremony. Mother and Daddy, my sister and her husband, and Eddie, Jessie, and I were standing on the top steps of the courthouse, the water from the fountain arcing in the background, all of us smiling—even Eddie, who hadn't been thrilled to be in Tallagumsa that day.

Although the ceremony dedicating the courthouse hadn't been nearly as happy as it *looked* in these pictures, if I had known what was to come in the months ahead I would have savored those hours. Perhaps then I would not have been so willing to turn all our lives upside down.

CHAPTER ONE

J ust hold the scissors right there by that pretty red
ribbon, Mayor," Scotty Scott said. "A little
higher. Right there. Good."

Scotty, the photographer for every official Tallagumsa event
over the last fifty years and the skinniest man in town, moved his
tripod and camera a few feet, balanced his sunglasses on top of
his crew cut, and squinted into the viewfinder.

"Now smile, Newell," he said. He snapped a picture of my
father standing next to the dedicatory ribbon strung between
two of the courthouse pillars and tied in a huge bow.

"Open the scissors," Scotty said. He took another picture.
"Now cut that sucker! Sure hope the courthouse don't fall
down." He laughed at his own joke.

Daddy laughed too, somehow managing to look dignified
and fun-loving at the same time. His dark hair was gray just
around the temples. His green eyes sparkled. Ever the politician,
for the dedication of the courthouse he'd worn a navy-blue suit,
red suspenders, and a white dress shirt. Thin red and white diag-
onal lines striped his yellow tie.

While Scotty completed my father's individual photographs,
the rest of the family waited its turn to join him. Eddie, Jessie,
and I were on the east side of the steps, where Jessie had ample
room to run and play without getting in the way. I waited sitting
down: Eight and a half months pregnant with twins, no one
dared begrudge me this breach of etiquette. My sister, her husband, and my mother stood talking among themselves not far
from Scotty.

Most of the people who'd attended the morning dedication had gone ahead to the reception at the Tallagumsa Steak House, two blocks down First Avenue. A dozen or so people lingered on the steps, talking with each other and watching Scotty in action.

"Stand next to your name over there on the wall, Mayor," Scotty said as he carried his camera across the courthouse landing. He took three pictures of Daddy standing under the brass letters that read: "Newell Hagerdorn County Courthouse."

"I don't know if I can take much more of this!" Eddie complained to me. "The way everyone's acting you'd think we were in the White House Rose Garden with Jimmy and Rosalynn Carter and not at some podunk county courthouse affair."

I looked up at Eddie from my seat on the sun-warmed granite steps. He was leaning on one of the courthouse pillars, smoking a Salem and staring wearily at my father and Scotty. Tall and good-looking, with straight black hair and gunmetal eyes, he was still in good shape from his years on the college track team.

Eddie had tried to abort this trip, arguing for the last few days that he couldn't possibly take a day off with his workload as political cartoonist for Atlanta's *City Paper*. After I made it clear to him that Jessie and I would come whether or not he did, he stayed up until three in the morning to meet a newspaper deadline, then grudgingly accompanied us on the two-hour early-morning drive west to Tallagumsa for the ceremony.

The new Greek Revival courthouse, built to serve a population of almost one hundred thousand people, took up a full city block of the small town of Tallagumsa. It could be reached on any side by climbing two steep flights of stairs to the massive landing, which led to the entrances. On the west end of the landing was a large square fountain in which the water rose up out of the mouth of a bronze fish hovering above a sparkling pool of water. A bronze statue of Confederate veteran Elijah Ellis bore a sword skyward, guarding the east end of the landing.

Jessie hopped over to where Eddie and I waited. With each

hop, the pleats of her sailor dress flew up, then floated back to cover her tiny thighs.

"I'm hungry," she announced, pulling on my sleeve.

"As soon as the pictures are taken we'll eat at the Steak House. Come here, sweetie." I kissed her cheek and handed her a penny from my pants pocket. "Throw that in the fountain and make a wish, but be careful not to get in Scotty's and Grand-daddy's way." She hopped off.

"I have a wish," Eddie said. "That this will be over and we can go home."

"You never like being here, do you, Eddie?" I asked.

"Nope." He looked down at me. His intense gray eyes blamed me for having dragged him here. "Especially when it's some trumped-up celebration in honor of your father."

He took a final draw on his Salem, dropped the butt, then stepped on it, grinding it into the granite, where it left a dark smudge on the pristine stonework.

"It's not just for him," I said. "It's for the whole county." At Eddie's skeptical grin, I laughed despite myself. "I know you think that's pompous and stupid sounding, but that's the point of Daddy's whole career—to better this county and this state."

"That's why the courthouse is named for *him* and why we're waiting for *his* pictures and why we'll go listen to *his* speech. Not for the good of Newell Hagerdorn—no, of course not—but for the good of us all. You just can't see past his act, can you?" He sat down next to me and kissed my neck. "But I love you anyway."

"I love you too," I said.

I looked around for Jessie, who'd thrown her penny into the fountain and then disappeared around that side of the building. "Jessie," I called.

She reappeared, walking slowly, as if each step were too much for her to bear. "Can we go now?" she asked. The diversion offered by the penny toss had lasted about two minutes.

"Sorry," I said, as sympathetically as I could.

Her face flushed bright red and she began to cry. "But I'm hungry and I'm tired!"

"At least it isn't hot," I said.

Although it was barely April, in Alabama we'd had our share of April scorchers. In fact it was a perfect spring day, the temperature in the midseventies, the blue sky dotted here and there with innocuous white puffs. A mild breeze carried only the suggestion of warmer days to come.

"Why don't I take her over to the park?" Eddie stood up and wiped off the back of his jeans.

The dogwood trees, azaleas, tulips, and daffodils in the park, nourished by two weeks of rain in early March, were in full bloom. Built at the same time as the courthouse with private Garden Club funds raised largely by my mother, Gladys, and my sister, Jane, the oasis of green had beckoned to Jessie all morning.

"That'll take too long," I said. "We all need to wait here, Jessie—Scotty said so. I know it's hard to get up so early and then just hang out here doing nothing. I have a great idea! How about this? As soon as we finish, you can get a candy bar at the Steak House—any kind you want *and* before your lunch." I crossed my heart. "Only a little bit longer. I promise."

I tried to sound soothing as I pulled her toward me and hugged her, but she pushed away from me, ran around the legs of the Confederate soldier, and sat down at the base of the statue's marble pedestal.

"Next time we come here, LuAnn, you're going to have to bribe me too," Eddie said.

"LuAnn, y'all can come on over," Scotty called a few minutes later. "Gladys, Jane, Buck—everybody who's family right here, on the top steps of the courthouse with the mayor."

"At last," Eddie mumbled under his breath. "Jessie," he called. "Show time."

She walked over to us.

"See?" I said. "I told you it wouldn't be long." Before getting up I wiped Jessie's tear-smudged face with a Kleenex from my pocket. "One of these pictures will be in the newspaper, so try to look happy. Both of you."

"Let's go, let's go, Annie Hall," my brother-in-law, Buck Newton, hollered as he bounded toward us in his slightly rumpled suit. He wiped the sweat from his wrinkled forehead, pushing a handkerchief back across his balding head.

I held out my arms to Eddie, who groaned as he pulled my unwieldy pregnant frame up to a standing position.

"Coming, coming," I said.

"Annie Hall" was Buck's attempt at a humorous reference to my outfit—a white maternity shirt, polka-dot tie, black vest, baggy pants, and a floppy man's hat—as well as a compliment on my looks. Unfortunately, any physical similarity between the movie character and me was far more apparent when I wasn't on the verge of giving birth to twins.

My dark brown hair was pulled back in one long braid down my back. Hoping to give my face some of the definition it had lost as puffy cheeks replaced high cheekbones, I'd recently added a thin layer of bangs that almost touched my dark eyebrows.

Though Buck tried to hide it, there was an undertone of irritation in his voice. I knew my clothes bugged both him and my sister, Jane. Not long ago Mother too would have taken the time to make an unflattering reference to my appearance, but around the time Jessie was born she began to look past me. Why bother with me, clearly a lost cause, when she could try to mold Jes?

Buck crammed his handkerchief into his back pants pocket and slapped Eddie on the back.

"Y'all are quite a pair," Buck said. "Annie Hall and—who do you think you are, Eddie? Clint Eastwood? Or the Marlboro Man? Couldn't you borrow a suit from a friend, big guy?"

Eddie had on Levi's, Frye boots, a dress shirt, and a tie. He was not a hick dressed up to go to town; but an individualist who refused to wear a suit to the courthouse simply because he was supposed to.

The three of us walked toward the rest of the family.

"Why do you worry so much about how LuAnn and I look?" Eddie asked. "At least I don't look like a lawyer, Buckie boy."

"Well, I am a lawyer," Buck said.

"No shit," Eddie said. "Not something I would brag about if I were you."

"Y'all don't start in on each other," Mother pleaded when she heard Eddie and Buck exchanging the usual insults. "We all want the pictures to turn out well, don't we?" she asked sweetly.

"Yes, ma'am." Buck hitched up his pants to just below his bulging stomach and tucked his loose shirttail in.

"Good," Mother said.

Over the years my mother had taken the art of being a political wife to new heights, submissive to the point that when standing next to my handsome father she seemed to fade away. Daddy had just turned sixty. Mother was fifty-seven, but she looked older than he. With her thick blue-framed glasses, short curly gray hair, and pale wrinkled skin, she looked like the grandmother she was. She and Jane shared thick ankles, which I had been spared, and large breasts, which I had missed out on. For the ceremony Mother had chosen a navy gabardine skirt, a white silk blouse, and a red, white, and blue scarf around her neck. A small gold American flag pin held the scarf in place.

"You go in back, LuAnn, Jessie in front of you, and Eddie next to you, on the left," Scotty ordered. "Newell, you and Gladys stand next to LuAnn, and Jane and Buck should be next to Gladys, on the right here.

"It looks good," Scotty continued from behind his camera. "Smile!" He took two pictures. "Now y'all come on over next to those main doors, the middle ones."

"Maybe you should sit, LuAnn," my father said as the group made its way to the front entrance. "Are you all right standing so long?" He looked up at the sun, which was almost directly overhead. "Is that sun too much for you?"

"I'm just a little tired, Daddy."

"A little? A little? You look totally exhausted," he said. "Pretty as a picture, dear, but tired. I'm worried about you. I want you to know that. When the babies come, something's got to give. Where you live, how you live, it just won't work anymore. You're not college kids anymore, and I'm not going to let you kill yourself to prove some stupid point."

Eddie looked at me and smiled—not a real smile but an "isn't that typical of your father intruding in our lives" smile.

"We'll survive, Daddy. We always have," I said, although I wasn't so sure.

"You haven't always had three children under the age of four, no help, and no money." My father grabbed my upper arm and stopped walking to emphasize his point. Everyone else stopped with us.

"You know how he loves to take care of you," Mother said lightly.

"And how she loves to be taken care of by you," Eddie added with a slight edge to his voice.

"Why doesn't Jessie come stand next to me for this one picture since our outfits match?" Jane asked when we were assembled in front of the entryway. She stood with her lips pursed and her hands on her ample hips, waiting for an answer.

"Scotty was in charge of these pictures last time I checked, Jane," my father said sharply, shaking his head.

Jane pretended not to hear what Daddy had said, but I caught the hurt look in her dark brown eyes. She quickly turned away and busied herself with running her right hand across her bouffant hairdo.

"It's okay," I said. "Go on over next to your aunt Jane, Jes."

Jessie, who adored her aunt Jane, hurried over and stood in front of my older sister. From a distance, anyone who didn't know better would have assumed that they were mother and daughter. Save for the minor differences in dress waists and shoe heels, they were dressed in almost identical outfits, down to their navy velvet headbands.

This was not a coincidence. Just a few days earlier, Jane had sent Jessie the matching outfit specifically for this occasion. If Jane's doctors ever managed to get her pregnant and keep her that way, I wondered whether her fierce attachment to my child would abate.

"Oops," Scotty said. He snapped his fingers. "Everybody relax a sec while I put in some more film." He removed a roll of film from the camera, leaned over, dropped it in his black camera bag, and took out a new roll. He was about to reload the camera when he stopped to talk with a man I'd never seen around Tallagumsa.

"Now what's Scotty doing?" Eddie asked. "Let's go, how 'bout it? Chat on your own time, Scotty!" he yelled.

Scotty shook hands with the stranger. The man was almost as tall as Eddie and slightly bigger-boned. He had sandy blond hair, dark eyes, and a pleasant smile. A camera hung from a strap around his neck.

In a small southern town it wasn't hard to tell who fit and who didn't, and this man didn't. His khaki pants and burgundy polo shirt weren't made of polyester or a double knit, and his hair—like Eddie's, just long enough to touch his back shirt collar and cover the tops of his ears—was considered fashionably long in Birmingham or Atlanta but didn't conform with Tallagumsa notions of style.

"Y'all don't mind if this reporter fellow takes a few pictures too, do you?" Scotty asked us.

"Happy to have him," Buck answered for everyone. "Right, Mayor?" he asked my father.

"Where you from, young man?" my father called out.

"Washington, D.C.," the man said. "I write for the *Washington Star.*"

"You aren't one of those fellows Woodward or Bernstein, are you? You know, from the Watergate thing?" Buck was thrilled at the prospect. "Come to think of it, you look kind of like Robert Redford."

"Wrong paper, Sherlock," Eddie said.

"I think it's more likely he's that reporter friend Junior Fuller's been talking about," my father said. "Ben something or other."

"That's me. Ben Gainey." He gave us a little salute. "Is Junior around? He said I should meet him here, but I'm afraid I'm a little late."

"He's at the reception already," Buck said, "at the Tallagumsa Steak House down First Avenue, that-a-way." He pointed to his right.

"Lucky Junior," Eddie said. "I'll be dreaming about Steak House food tonight; I'm obviously never going to get any today." He folded his arms across his chest and looked annoyed.

"Mr. Gainey, I'm Buck Newton," Buck said, "and this is the future governor of the great state of Alabama, Mayor Newell Hagerdorn. Looks like Paul Newman, doesn't he? Don't you think that'll be an asset in the next election?"

"Buck!" my father interrupted: "How many times do I have to tell you not to talk about that?"

"That you look like Paul Newman?" he asked.

"You know damn well what I mean," Daddy said, seething. "It's not the time or the place."

"Just trying to help." Buck grinned, oblivious to how mad Daddy was at him.

Buck had been my father's campaign manager in the last mayoral election, and he relished the possibility of running his gubernatorial campaign.

"Pleased to meet you, Mayor." Ben Gainey hurried over to shake my father's hand. "Junior's told me all about you and your town. I'm looking forward to interviewing you for my book if you have the time."

"Happy to oblige," Daddy said. "Just let us know. We'll do anything we can to help you."

Like most successful politicians, my father was able to sound sincere regardless of his true feelings. He'd told me earlier that day how concerned he was about this reporter friend of Junior's portraying Tallagumsa in an unflattering light.

"You're at the top of my list, Mayor Hagerdorn," Ben said.

13

"Not that it's unusual, but is everybody here going to suck up to your father all day long?" Eddie whispered to me.

"Stop talking, y'all, and smile," Scotty yelled as soon as Ben Gainey rejoined him. Ben raised his camera to his eye, and he and Scotty snapped several pictures. In between photos, we talked.

"Who is that guy, Newell?" Eddie asked.

"A friend of Junior's from law school who's a reporter now. He's writing a book about the New South and thinking about featuring Tallagumsa in it," my father said. "If he decides to write about us after visiting this week, he'll move here next month."

"That would be incredible good luck," Buck said. "He could give us a big step up—I mean, give you a boost, sir. Bring national attention to your campaign."

"Come on," Eddie said incredulously. "He wouldn't know the real South if it walked up and bit him. I can look at him and tell you he's just another South-basher come to air all our dirty laundry and remind the rest of the country what racist hicks we are. No reporter comes to this town to write about the state college. They come to write about Jimmy Turnbow and Leon Johnson. That'll really do you a lot of good, Newell."

"Goodness, Eddie," Mother said. "You must have gotten up on the wrong side of the bed today."

"I'm sorry, Gladys, but I'm tired of this Yankee holier-than-thou attitude toward the South. They've got plenty of their own problems. I've had enough of this South as a bastion of evil crap."

"You've done a lot of cartoons critical of the South yourself," I pointed out.

"As a Southerner, I'm allowed," he replied.

"Just one or two more shots," Scotty said. "Go over to the fountain and sit along the edge. Don't jump in, Jessie," he joked.

We dutifully crossed the landing to the fountain and sat one by one along the broad ledge.

Daddy detoured toward the Confederate statue, took his

14

jacket off and hung it on the soldier's bent left arm, then joined us.

Smiling, we all looked toward Scotty and Ben Gainey.

"Mr. Gainey's not interested in our past, Eddie," Jane said after the first snapshot. A gust of wind blew the collar of her sailor dress up over her face. She forced it down with her palm and continued. "Junior said he wants to focus on all the progress we've made, the changes, the good things. And he does too think the state college is important."

"I'll believe it when I see it," Eddie said.

"Do I detect a note of jealousy?" Buck asked. "I bet you'd give away LuAnn to be the political cartoonist at the *Washington Star*."

"I'm not his or anyone's to give away, Buck. And leave Eddie alone, would you," I said.

"I for one think we've put those dark days behind us," Mother said.

"I hope not."

"Oh, LuAnn," Jane said. "What is that supposed to mean?"

I couldn't see Jane's face since she was in front of me, but I was sure from her tone that she was grimacing.

"Cross your left leg over your right, Gladys. And smile, Jane!" Scotty said, confirming my suspicion.

"Just that lately everyone seems so anxious to sweep the civil rights movement under the rug and pretend nothing horrible happened here or anywhere else in the South," I said. "I don't think it's right. I also don't think it's smart or productive."

"I agree with LuAnn's last point one hundred percent," my father said.

"Big surprise," Jane said, too quietly for Daddy to hear her.

"Everybody look that way and smile." Scotty pointed at the fountain.

As we complied with his request, Scotty and Ben Gainey raced to the other side of the fountain and took the last few more pictures.

15

"So, what are y'all sitting around for?" Scotty finally asked. "Get on over to the Steak House—everybody's waiting on you."

"Ever thought about comedy as a line of work, Scotty?" Eddie asked.

"No. Have you?" Scotty replied, grinning.

CHAPTER TWO

M y family and I, and the few remaining strag-
glers from the courthouse dedication, made
our way down First Avenue toward the Tal-
lagumsa Steak House. When the light turned red, I grabbed Jessie's hand and tensed for the dangerous confrontation that
crossing streets in downtown Atlanta had become. I looked both
ways. Two cars were making the turn; both stopped. The
woman in the first car smiled and motioned us to walk ahead. I
relaxed and released Jessie's hand.

How nice it would be not to have to worry at every downtown intersection about life and death. One day in Atlanta, on
the way to Jessie's day care, I had to jump about two feet back-
ward, jerking Jes along with me to avoid being crushed by the
speeding car that turned right into us. I couldn't imagine that my
children would ever be old enough to cross Atlanta's busiest
intersections alone.

Of course, in defense of my fellow Atlantans, I understood
that these Tallagumsa drivers were so much more courteous and
less likely to try to kill a person, at least in part, because they had
less cause to be rude: There was no such thing as a traffic jam
here, and the concept of a rush hour was ridiculous.

When I left Tallagumsa for college in 1969, I'd hated its
molasses-slow pace of life. Back then I dreamed of men and
women in designer clothes rushing from one momentous meeting to another, hailing cabs, passing through the revolving doors
of towering buildings, and waiting in front of elevator banks that
would take them to the sixty-fifth or seventy-second floor,
where they would conduct business of earth-shaking impor-

tance. I fantasized about packed expressways and busy down-town streets. I desperately wanted a city full of strangers who didn't know everything about me *and* my family, who'd pass me on the street and not recognize me, a place to get lost when you wanted or needed to be left alone. I wanted challenge, action, excitement, and anonymity.

What I once found romantic about city life, however, I now found inconvenient, unsafe, tiring, or simply irritating. A recent string of unsolved burglaries in our Atlanta neighborhood worried me whenever we left our apartment, and a walk through downtown Atlanta left me longing for clean air, peace and quiet, and open spaces.

We walked two and three abreast the two blocks to the Tallagumsa Steak House. Mother and Jane were in the lead; Buck and Ben Gainey were close behind them. Jessie, feeling a bit frenzied from the courthouse-dedication ceremony, the waiting and the posing for pictures, ran up and down the sidewalk, circling us and the parking meters in a series of giant figure eights. She sang over and over the only lines she knew from the "Sesame Street" theme song: "Sunny day chasing the clouds away. Can you tell me how to get to Sesame Street?"

Smoking a Salem, Eddie followed a few feet behind my father and me. At least he wasn't muttering to himself or, worse, shouting in anger like the Glad Bag Man near our Atlanta apartment.

The Glad Bag Man was an elderly homeless man who kept his belongings in a green plastic garbage bag that he somehow balanced upon his head. He passed the day screaming at all who passed his park bench. His verbal barrage of curse words and stream-of-consciousness conspiratorial plot lines tying together hell, President Carter, UFOs, and Patty Hearst had given Jessie more than one night of bad dreams.

The next time Jessie ran past me I stretched for her hand, caught it, and interlaced her fingers with mine.

"Sunny day chasing the clouds away. On my way to where the air is sweet. Can you tell me how to get, how to get to Sesame Street?" I sang along with her, helping her with the missing line.

Jessie tried to skip, but I pulled her back and pointed at my belly. I looked chagrined, letting her know how sorry I was that skipping just wasn't possible right now. She accepted my limitation, and we sang together, swinging our arms back and forth, until we reached the doors to the Tallagumsa Steak House.

The Steak House was the largest restaurant in the county and the only one with a AAA rating. Open six A.M. until twelve P.M. every day of the year except Christmas, the popular immaculately clean, family restaurant, was known for fresh, delicious food; nothing too fancy, just good solid home cooking.

The restaurant occupied a two-story building in the middle of the block between the SP Drug Store and Bowe's Department Store. On the first floor were two dining rooms. In the front dining room, from which diners could see anyone who passed on the street and where the majority of the seating was in Naugahyde booths, the atmosphere was always informal. In the more secluded back dining room, where lunch was served under the same bright fluorescent lights, nighttime brought tablecloths, candles, and, by Tallagumsa standards, a measure of intimacy. The top floor consisted of one long, large carpeted room, perfect for banquets and parties, divisible into two or three smaller areas to suit any occasion.

As I passed through the Steak House foyer, walking by the Lions Club plastic gum machine, the orange *Birmingham News* dispenser, and the black *Tallagumsa Times* tray, I felt my present collide with my past. I had worked, dated, and celebrated every significant event of my life, from my first horse show to my wedding, here.

Inside, the smell of fresh coffee, pies, biscuits, and sweet rolls enveloped me. I looked down the wall booth, a single continuous green Naugahyde booth running almost the length of the front dining room and separating that dining room from the hallway to the back. Green plants grew out of the planters framing the top edge of the booth. The wall booth ended like a giant upside-down L at a corner booth where the owners, Mimi and Howard Bledsoe, could usually be found, watching over the restaurant's activities.

Neither of the Bledsoes was in their booth, and for a second I worried that they'd sold the Steak House. I'd recently heard from Mother that they were thinking about selling the place and retiring. Mimi's arthritis was getting worse, and Howard wanted to travel. I sympathized with their reasons, I understood that one day I would come here and someone else would be sitting in their booth, and I knew my heart would break when that day came. I was saddened last year when my parents rented out the family home and moved to a fancy new wood-and-glass house on Clark Lake; I needed more than ever for the Steak House to endure unchanged.

Estelle, my best friend since first grade and the Steak House hostess, was perched on the stool behind the check-out counter. Her petite figure was barely visible behind the old cash register. Estelle's blond hair was in the same pageboy cut she'd worn since high school. As Buck always said, she was "as cute as a button."

Estelle saw us, squealed "LuAnn," sprang off the stool, and flittered over to greet Eddie, Jessie, and me; the rest of my family was already upstairs.

"Y'all are here! Y'all are here!" Estelle cried. "Look at you." She patted my stomach. "You look wonderful!"

I turned to hug her in a sideways embrace, the best I could manage with my stomach. "Only a best friend would say that," I said.

Estelle hugged Jessie, then Eddie; her head just reached his chest.

"Jessie, go on and get your candy bar from behind the counter," I said. "Then you can go ahead upstairs if you want."

Jessie looked to Estelle for official permission.

"Help yourself," Estelle said.

Jessie walked around the counter and slid open one of the glass cabinet doors. She surveyed the array of candy bars for a moment, put her hand into the cabinet, almost took a Hershey's Bar, hovered briefly over a Nestle's Crunch, and finally landed on a Three Musketeers. She grabbed it and ran upstairs calling "Granddaddy! Glady!" "Glady" was her name for my mother.

"I've been excited all day!" Estelle clapped her hands several times.

"I didn't know *you* cared so much about the courthouse," I said.

"That's not all that's happening today," she said.

"Oh, no! There's more? What else, Estelle?" Eddie loosened his tie and scowled. "I can't take much more."

"Can't tell," she teased. "I'll come upstairs in a while and visit with y'all."

She went back to the cash register to ring up the long line of customers filing out of the back dining room. They were mostly women in their fifties and sixties, who, I assumed, were passengers from the tour bus outside on their way to the Grand Old Opry in Nashville.

I looked around the front dining room. Several people, customers and friends from over the years, waved to me. I waved back.

"Hey, Chip," I said to the short stocky man in one of the front booths. He'd been the county prosecutor until last year. "How's Betty?" I shook hands with him and talked briefly to people at four other tables, then joined Eddie, where he'd been waiting near the cash register.

He looked irritated as he took a few packs of Steak House matchbooks from a countertop bowl and put them in his pocket.

"What is it, LuAnn? What is it with you and this place, this town, these people?" He glared at me. "Every time we come here, I get the feeling it's 1968 and you're homecoming queen again. I thought you and Estelle might start up with one of your cheerleading routines just now. And if you weren't so pregnant, I know we'd have to stop on the way out of town and watch you ride your horse. You love this. All of it. You just can't let it go."

Before I had a chance to respond, Mother appeared at the top of the stairs, fiddling with her American flag pin.

"Are you two ever coming? Your father's waiting, LuAnn," she said.

"Coming," I said. Happy to avoid another argument with Eddie, I turned away from him and walked up the carpeted stairs and down the hall toward the party sounds: laughter, talking, silver clinking against china.

The room was full of people—at least one hundred, maybe more. Someone, probably Estelle, had decorated the room with red, white, and blue helium balloons.

The room dividers were pushed into the wall, leaving one large open area. Straight ahead, the buffet lunch was being served off four banquet tables pushed together and covered with tablecloths. The centerpiece was a bouquet of white gladiolus in a crystal vase. On each of the fifteen round tables placed every few feet and surrounded by six chrome and leatherette chairs was a single red rose in a stem vase. Near the doorway was the bar.

To my right, at the far end of the room, was the speaker's dais. Above and behind it hung a huge photograph of my father's face. Ever since Buck and a few state Democratic party officials decided to push him as the next governor, any event involving my father resembled a political rally.

I'd heard about, but never before seen, Daddy's new campaign picture. I studied it, trying to see him as a voter might. Honest but not dull. Attractive but not vain. Self-assured but not too cocky. Governor Newell Hagerdorn. That sounded good to me.

Standing with Daddy and Ben Gainey near the speaker's dais was my high-school love, Junior. A former star of the Tallagumsa High Tigers football team, he was six foot five and brawny, his large crooked nose and thick neck souvenirs of long

22

workouts and spirited high-school games. We had been boy-friend and girlfriend beginning in the ninth grade and our senior year had been elected homecoming queen and king. I'd never regretted ending our relationship when we went our separate ways in college, but I still had a soft spot in my heart for this gentle giant.

Much to everyone's surprise, Junior had returned home recently as the county prosecutor after nine years out of the state, seven in college and law school and two at the Department of Justice. Rumor had it he had national political aspirations.

A few of the helium balloons had floated down from the ceiling, and Junior held one in each of his beefy hands. He tossed one balloon into the air, then another. Falling, they cast shadows like fat ghosts across the wall.

Eddie caught up with me at the door. "You're in luck, Queen LuAnn: There's your king, Junior Fuller." His tone was mocking.

"Please stop being so mean, Eddie," I said, pulling him back out into the hall. "I know you don't want to be here, that you wish you were still in Atlanta, but could you possibly pretend you're not miserable. Please!" Tears welled in my eyes and I leaned against the wall. "You're making me crazy."

He sighed deeply. "I'm sorry," he said. "You know I get deranged whenever we come here. You don't act like yourself, and it scares me."

"I think you're the Mr. Hyde here, Eddie, not me." I sniffed.

"Maybe I am. But you're so drawn to this place, so absolutely and totally happy here, that I can't help but take it as a slap in the face. I feel like an intruder." He lit a Salem with one of the Steak House matches. "And it doesn't help that people here think of me as a loser—Eddie, the political cartoonist. Doesn't he have anything better to do? When's he going to get a real job? That's your father's opinion, I know."

"It is not his opinion, and no one thinks of you as a loser. They know you're an artist and a journalist, that you've been published in the *New York Times*, that you're almost syndicated." I sniffed again. "Could you get me some Kleenex?"

He went into the men's restroom a few yards away and came out with a wad of tissue.

"They also know I don't support you and all these children you keep having, that your father's been sending us money," he continued.

I took the tissues and put all but one in my pocket. *"I keep having?* Excuse me! I had a little help in that department! And who do you think knows about the money? Nobody! You're getting paranoid, you know that, about everything."

"You don't think Buck and Jane know? Junior too? How much you want to bet?"

"Junior has no idea where we get our rent, Eddie."

"And Estelle? What about her?"

"Come on, Eddie. This is stupid. The money is between me and Daddy, so let's drop it. This is Daddy's big day, and he wants us with him."

"Every day is the mayor's big day around here as far as I can tell."

"I guess we'll have to talk about this later. I'm going in now," I said. "You're welcome to come if you stop acting this way. Otherwise, feel free to make your usual escape: Go hide in the kitchen with Roland and talk to him while he cooks."

"I can't—Roland's in there too, by the bar." He pointed with his thumb in that direction.

I heard Roland's deep heartfelt laugh before I saw him. He was talking to the waitress serving the drinks. Roland, recently made the Steak House chef at age thirty, was a small, thin man and one of the few Tallagumsa-born hippies. Freckled from head to toe, he wore his long red hair pulled back into a ponytail. His sense of humor and his respect for Eddie's work made him one of Eddie's favorite people in town.

"I thought he cooked every weekday afternoon," I said.

"I guess they turned him loose for the big event. Look, I don't want to go downstairs anyway, LuAnn. I want to stay here, with you and Jessie." His hands were outspread in front of him.

I clasped his hands in mine and kissed him lightly on the lips. "A truce?" I offered.

He kissed me back. "A truce."

"Do I look okay?" I asked.

He took a stray piece of hair and pushed it into the root of my braid. "Beautiful," he said, draping his arm across my shoulder. Together we walked into the reception.

"A drink might hit the spot," Eddie said, turning quickly in the direction of the bar.

I reached for him and caught his forearm. "In the middle of the day?" I said. "Don't, Eddie. You're cutting down, remember? You promised."

"Come on, LuAnn. I deserve it. You want Eddie happy?" He grinned and shook his arm free of me, then ordered a scotch on the rocks. He took a gulp. "You'll get Eddie happy."

CHAPTER THREE

After the buffet lunch and the speeches, only the family and a few friends and guests remained at the Steak House. It was almost three in the afternoon. Jessie lay sleeping across three chairs I'd pushed together against the wall. Telltale evidence of her Three Musketeers Bar spotted the front of her white sailor dress. Eddie and I sat on either end of our daughter, I at her head, he at her feet, nursing another drink. The rest of the family relaxed at a nearby table, rehashing the events of the day. Ben and Junior were off at a corner table, chatting.

I was so tired from the day's activities that I was tempted to push together enough chairs to follow Jessie's example, but I knew my swollen body lying there wouldn't be a pretty sight. Instead I slipped off my shoes and propped my swollen feet and ankles up on a chair I'd placed in front of me and watched my shirt pop up here, then there, in an undulating dance caused by the twins in motion.

I don't know where the babies found the room, all scrunched up in there, but often when I was very tired and still, as now, they would go at it. A fist, an elbow, a knee. Sometimes I simply relaxed and watched the show. Other times I responded, rubbing whatever was poking out or gently pushing it back in. It was an odd but satisfying means of communication.

Their activity brought home, as it sometimes did, that there were two babies in there, *inside me,* two babies who would very soon be Jessie's brothers or sisters. I knew this, of course, as an objective fact, but at another level pregnancy and childbirth seemed too incredible to be true and had been no less amazing when only Jessie occupied the same space. After she was born, I would often stare at her for hours, marveling that she had lived as part of me, that she had grown into Jessie inside of me. This most common of human experiences seemed at the same time both preposterous and miraculous.

My father put down his cigar and lightly tapped a spoon against his beer glass. His navy jacket was draped over his chair back, revealing his trademark suspenders. His own likeness loomed behind him, the green eyes Jessie and I had inherited from him staring out at us.

"I imagine y'all are all tired of hearing me talk, and I'm tired of talking, but I have one more announcement." He reached around, pulled some papers out of his inside jacket pocket, and unfolded them in front of him on the tablecloth. He put a clean butter knife on the top of the document and a salt shaker on the bottom to hold it open.

"I have here the deed to the Tallagumsa Steak House," he said.

I looked at the others, confused at the non sequitur. What did the deed to the Steak House have to do with the new court-house?

Estelle, who was helping two of the waitresses bus the cluttered dining tables, caught my eye and winked at me.

"And it says here that Mimi and Howard Bledsoe have sold the Steak House to . . . " He cleared his throat. "Let's see now, sold it to . . ."

He pretended to search the papers for the name, moving his finger along each line and obviously exaggerating the delay to create suspense. He stopped reading, loosened his tie, and ran his hand back through his hair.

"Ah-hah," he said, reading again. "To Ms. LuAnn Hager-dorn Garrett."

"What?" I asked, astounded. My feet fell to the floor; I sat up at attention, more alert than I'd been all day. "What?" I said again.

I wasn't the only one in shock. Eddie, Buck, Jane, and Mother couldn't have looked any more dumbfounded had I just delivered the twins on the table next to the remains of prime rib, baked potatoes, and Brussels sprouts. Only Junior and Ben seemed unruffled.

"I don't know what to say," I said.

"That's unusual," Buck said.

" 'Thank you' would be just fine," my father said jokingly.

He walked over, handed me the deed, and kissed me.

The deed was dated five days earlier: March 31, 1978.

"Everything's set up. When you get to town y'all can stay in the old house where you grew up," he said. "The renters are moving away this month and the house is full of the new furniture we bought when we moved to the lake. I've arranged for Jolene to come days to look after Jessie and the babies. Your horse, Glory, has been waiting a long time for you to come home." He smiled, looking pleased with himself.

Howard and Mimi Bledsoe followed close behind Daddy; he shook my hand, she hugged me. Eddie stood up, leaned over, and snatched the papers out of my hand. He walked over to the bar, filled his glass with the equivalent of a triple scotch, and studied the deed.

"But, Daddy . . ." I began. I was bewildered by this turn of events.

"You probably need to think about it, honey," my father said. "Talk with Eddie. You don't need to say anything today." He sat down again next to Mother. "I know you'll do what's best for you and the children."

"Well, I have something to say," Mother declared, her usually pale, placid face a bright pink. "What on earth do you think you're doing, Newell?"

I was shocked at this rare display of boldness on her part. She always agreed with Daddy and, if she didn't, would certainly

28

never let on. I loved her because she was my mother, but I loved her more as an extension of my father, the role she'd played, without deviation, for as long as I could remember.

"I'm taking care of my family, Gladys, just doing my job," he said, dismissing her concern.

Mother walked over to the bar and held out her hand to Eddie. He gave her the papers and looked at me, his face showing a mixture of confusion and anger. Then he turned away, shaking his head slowly.

Jane's reaction was equally unenthusiastic. She scooted her chair back from the table and, frowning, asked, "How could you possibly run this place and raise three small children? Why even bother to have them if you're going to take on something like this? If I had one—even one—you wouldn't find me anywhere but at home with him . . . or her."

"I work *now*," I pointed out.

"Some people like to work, Jane," my father said. "You have never been one of them, that's all."

"That's true," Buck said, laughing.

"If Daddy told you I was a bank robber, you'd agree with him, wouldn't you?" Jane asked petulantly.

"I would not, Jane," Buck replied, sulking.

"And I do too like to work," Jane said. "I run our home and I do tons of volunteer work: the Junior League, the County Hospital Board, the Garden Club, the Church Guild. Who raised all the money for your new courthouse park, Daddy? Me and the other Garden Club girls, including Mother, that's who."

"I know you do your share, Jane, just like your mother, but some people like to have real jobs," Newell said. "LuAnn needs to do more than the kind of ladies' club stuff you do. And she's too smart and too good to work for other people. This is a great opportunity for her to quit those pissant jobs she's had to take in Atlanta and have something of her own."

I hadn't complained that much, but my father knew me well enough to know how unhappy I was with my work now, a mishmash of odd jobs: giftwrapping at Rich's Department Store, sitting for neighbors' kids, waitressing at the Steak and Ale. I was working toward a graduate degree in psychology but at the rate I was going—with work and Jessie and soon the babies—I would be a grandmother before I got my M.A. and, with it, any chance for a challenging job.

"You remember Liz Reese, LuAnn," Jane continued ominously. "She started her own business when her son was young and then her husband killed himself."

"She had a daughter, Jane," my father said harshly. "And that's not why her husband killed himself. Stick to the Junior League and don't go yapping about things you know nothing about."

"You'd just think that if you are blessed enough to have children you'd want to be home with them," Jane said. Her last few words were barely audible. She crossed her legs and, resting her elbows on her knees, dropped her face into her hands and started to cry.

Jane had lost a little more perspective on the subject of children with each of her four miscarriages, and I didn't blame her. It was a horrible fate for any woman, especially one like Jane, who believed her sole purpose in life was to have children. I worried sometimes that the ease with which Eddie and I reproduced had increased her suffering and contributed to her growing bitterness.

"Liz Reese was just about the best mother I've ever known," Newell said. "If you and Buck ever have children, Jane, you'd better pray you're half as wonderful a mother, half as devoted, as Liz Reese was to her daughter. And your sister is doing a damn fine job too. She just needs more help so she can do something with her own life."

"Who is this Liz Reese anyway?" I asked. "She doesn't live in Tallagumsa, does she?" I was relieved to move to a subject other than the Steak House deed.

"She did," my father said. "After her husband, Dean, blew his brains out, she and her daughter moved away. She's the founder and owner of Miss Reese's Pies."

"You're kidding," I said. "She's *the* Miss Reese! Wow! I read all about her in *Newsweek* last year. But I don't recall her mentioning anything about Tallagumsa."

"She was only here a year. She left town as fast as she could and never looked back," Mother said from across the room, where she stood next to Eddie at the bar.

"Just the way you should, LuAnn," Eddie said. "Follow her example and run."

"How can you even consider this, LuAnn?" Eddie asked as soon as we got into the car to drive home.

"Can we talk about it when you're not drunk?" I wedged myself behind the wheel of our old Buick Skylark and pulled out of the parking space. Eddie was in the front seat and Jessie in the back. I drove west to the end of the street, circled the block, then picked up First Avenue going east out of town.

"I'm not drunk," he said. "Maybe I was, but I'm sober as a judge right now. We are not moving here."

We spoke in angry, loud whispers, hoping that Jessie, who had waked up when Eddie carried her from the Steak House to the car, wouldn't hear what we were saying.

"Did I say we were?" I asked.

"No, but I know how your mind works."

After a brief silence, he spoke again. "We could sell the Steak House and keep the money."

"No, we couldn't."

"Why not?"

"We either run the Steak House or we thank Daddy and give the restaurant back to him. I guess he'd sell it to someone else."

"*You* sell it. Your name is on that goddamned piece of paper. You own the place!"

"I'm well aware of that."

"I can't believe you'd even for one second think about raising our children in Klan country, redneck heaven."

"What happened to the gallant defender of the South ready

31

to die for her honor in front of that reporter?" I asked. "Or did you just not like *him*?"

"As I said then, I'm allowed to give constructive criticism because I'm a Southerner. Same as family secrets, you know, they should be kept in the family."

"You're hardly an expert on family secrets," I said. I knew that was below the belt, but I couldn't help myself. "Everyone in Tupelo knew each and every time your father was out on a binge. Your mother made sure of that. And you aren't that far behind him drinking-wise, Eddie."

"This isn't about me and my father, LuAnn. *Your father* has been trying to get you to move home since the day you left. He thrives on being surrounded by his admirers, and you're one of his most devoted. He's probably thinking of the campaign coverage he'll get—the dashing mayor, his very beautiful adoring young daughter, and all those precious grandchildren. Don't fool yourself. This isn't for you or the kids. It certainly isn't for us. It's for him. Just like everything else he does. And he hadn't even told Gladys! What kind of marriage is that?"

"He wanted it to be a surprise."

"More like a nuclear detonation. You saw your mother. She was stunned. You know what she said to me? That he had no right. Those were her words: 'No right.' From a doormat, those are pretty strong words."

"It's his money."

"Bull. He wouldn't have any money if it weren't for your mother, but you'd never know it, the way he acts."

"Do you hold that against him too, that Mother's family had money and his didn't? That's ancient history. What else did Mother say to you?"

"That taking the restaurant and moving to Tallagumsa would be the biggest mistake you could make."

"Look, Eddie, he offered us a business and a house and a wonderful baby-sitter—Jolene, who raised me and Jane." We stopped at a red light and I looked at him. "This would mean no more day care. Can't you step back even for a second and see how generous he is?"

"Manipulative, you mean. Controlling, you mean. And then there's the rest of them. I couldn't live in the same state as your sad, frumpy sister and her fool of a husband. Buck can't prostrate himself enough when it comes to your father. And what's all that celebrity crap? Paul Newman? Clint Eastwood? The Marlboro man? He's so full of it."

"That's just how Buck talks. It's his way of complimenting people he likes. Besides, you do look like the Marlboro Man," I said.

Eddie shrugged and smiled slightly. "Love is blind, I guess."

"You're even more handsome than the Marlboro Man," I said. I had vague hopes of charming him out of his anger.

I looked in the rearview mirror. Jessie had fallen asleep again. The light changed. I stepped on the gas and drove in silence for a few minutes.

"Stop!" Eddie shouted. "Turn right here."

"Why?"

"Just do it," he said.

I turned right onto Old Highway 49, a two-lane highway rarely used since the expressway was built. "This is the long way home. There's nothing on this road, Eddie."

"How quickly they forget."

"What?"

"The memorial, the tree."

My shoulders sagged. "What do they have to do with anything?" I asked quietly.

"You used to believe they had to do with everything."

"I meant, why go there now? Jessie's asleep. I'm tired."

"I want to remind you of what the people here are capable of."

"Sometimes lately I think you're losing your mind. The town did not kill them, Eddie."

"I guess those boys shot themselves that night."

"*Someone* shot Leon Johnson and Jimmy Turnbow. It wasn't me or anyone I know. I grew up here with a lot of fine people. Look at me. Am I a bigot?"

"When we met, I had my doubts, but I saved you from all that, taught you some of the things they don't teach people around here."

"Don't flatter yourself."

"Come on. You were an incredibly naive country girl who'd never even met a black person who wasn't your maid or gardener, LuAnn. Not one. You had no inkling of the world outside the narrow-minded one of Tallagumsa, Alabama. Who got you involved in the civil-rights movement? Who got you interested, active in the antiwar movement?"

"It was 1970, Eddie. I think I might have found my way without you."

"Are you claiming that organizing the memorial fund for Leon and Jimmy was your idea?"

"I didn't say that."

"Here we are. Pull over."

"No!" I shook my head and set my eyes on the road ahead, determined that we wouldn't stop at the memorial. "This has nothing to do with our problems, Eddie. It's past four now; I want to get home. I'm not interested in thinking about tragedy right this minute."

He grabbed the steering wheel and turned us sharply onto the side of the road.

I slammed on the brakes.

"What happened? Where are we?" Jessie asked, waking up. "Are we home?"

"Daddy needs to stop. Everything's fine," I said.

Our car stopped not far from the huge old pine tree that bore a large barkless gash a few feet from its base. The tree. No one had expected it would live after taking the full force of a head-on collision fifteen years ago when, not long after Martin Luther King's "I Have a Dream" speech, two young black men were shot driving to the state university a few hundred miles to the south. The school was under a federal court order to integrate, and had they made it there, Jimmy Turnbow and Leon Johnson would have been the first black students to attend a white Alabama college.

They never got there. Leon was shot in the head and died instantly, crashing his car into the tree. Jimmy was shot crawling away from the wreck.

"Let's get out and look at the memorial," Eddie said. "Maybe it will jar your memory."

"No, thanks." I locked my door and left my seatbelt on.

"I want to see," Jessie said.

"You're really being a shit, Eddie," I said.

"I think it's important to see the tree and the memorial and remember what happened here, because I know you and I know you want to take your father up on his offer—the restaurant, the house, Jolene. I understand that the Steak House is an opportunity for *you*, but moving here is the wrong opportunity for *us*. You can't just pretend that Tallagumsa is the perfect little place to live and raise a family; it's not. You can't ignore all the bad things that have happened here. Didn't I hear *you* say something along those lines today? Or was that just to irritate Jane and Gladys?"

"Maybe you don't know me at all anymore if you think I need to listen to this stupid little lecture," I said. "My point was that I want to honor the past, but that doesn't mean I can't look to the future, that I can't see how much has changed. The county has doubled in size over the last fifteen years, and look at the state college. Teachers from all over the country would not be here if Tallagumsa was the town it used to be, if Alabama was the state it used to be. That's why that reporter Ben Gainey is here. The New South, Eddie."

Eddie got out of the car, came around to my side, and waited.

I gave up, got out, and unhooked Jessie from her car seat.

We all walked to the tree.

On this lonely stretch of roadside, the dirt closest to the road gave way to clumps of grass and dandelions. Old beer cans cluttered the landscape. Down the road a ways was a house, a barn, a shack, and more farmland. Adjacent to the tree were several acres of land that had recently been turned in deep furrows for planting, probably corn or alfalfa. In the distance were the green foothills of the Cumberland Plateau.

Jessie picked a dandelion, blew on it, and watched as its seeds sailed away, carried into the air by a light breeze.

Near the tree was a large commemorative iron plaque on two waist-high steel posts. I didn't have to examine the raised metal letters on the plaque to know what they said. A young college student home for the summer in 1972, I'd organized the effort to raise the money to purchase and install the memorial.

The simple but compelling inscription had been suggested by Leon's mother: "Leon Johnson (1943–1963) and Jimmy Turnbow (1944–1963). They had a dream."

CHAPTER FOUR

I was a college junior and Eddie a senior when we moved in together. In 1971 living together was still regarded by most of the adult world as "living in sin." In the college community, however, it was common, and with our friends Hildy and John, we moved into one of the furnished apartments owned by Violet Crawford and her mother, Iris Ann Crawford. Over the next two years, Hildy and I exerted enormous amounts of energy hiding the true identity of our roommates from our parents.

Unlike our parents, Violet and Iris Ann didn't give a hoot about marital status. The sole qualification for moving into one of their five decaying Victorian homes in the Little Five Points section of Atlanta was a southern birthright. "Where were you born, dear?" was the first question Violet, a frail, elegant woman in her fifties, asked each of us when we answered the newspaper ad about the apartment. A good portion of the former Confederacy was represented by the four of us, and at the end of the interview we were invited to join the other college and grad students who rented their units.

The Crawfords had subdivided their houses into apartments with an eye toward minimizing cost and maximizing rent-generating units. The result was that each of the furnished apartments was peculiar in one way or another. In carving up the house we lived in, they'd transformed the dining room by adding a closet, a dresser, a vanity, a bedroom light fixture, and a double bed, then advertised the unit as a two bedroom. The front door of the apartment opened into a living room, which was not unusual. But all the other rooms—the kitchen, the bathroom, the other bedroom, the truncated hallway—were accessible only through this ersatz bedroom. Hildy and John and Eddie and I were so happy to find an apartment we could afford and a landlady who would have us that we gladly overlooked this design flaw. We drew straws to determine who got stuck with the walk-through bedroom and who got the bedroom with privacy. Eddie and I won. Six years later we were still in the same bedroom.

Jessie now occupied the walk-through room that had once been Hildy and John's. There was no third bedroom for the twins, who would have to reside in bassinets in the corner of our bedroom until we figured out something better. Knocking out the flimsy wall that separated our apartment from the second floor, the stairs, and the hallway and taking over the entire house was Eddie's latest plan for handling our impending space needs. I saw several flaws in this approach: He hadn't broached it with the Crawfords; we didn't have the money to pay for the extra space; and the upstairs was home to Adrienne and her six cats.

Adrienne, the only one of the Crawfords' present tenants older than we were, was a thirty-year-old flower child, a veteran of Haight-Ashbury's Trips Festival and Be-In, who had arrived here via Sweden and Drop City, Colorado. All Violet and Iris Ann cared about, though, was that she'd been born in Charleston and that her mama's maiden name was Davis. It turned out that they actually knew Adrienne's mother's brother's wife.

Adrienne made ends meet answering phones at Radio Free Georgia a few blocks from the apartment and doing astrological charts for friends and friends of friends. Not long after she moved in a year earlier, she did my chart in exchange for a pair of Grateful Dead tickets a co-worker at the *City Paper* had given Eddie. Eddie and I briefly toyed with the idea of going to the concert, but felt too old, too tired, too married, too busy.

So I gave the concert tickets to Adrienne, who was a Dead Head, and one evening a few weeks later she invited me upstairs to look at the ten-page astrological chart she'd prepared. In her living room, by the light of the thirty or so candles she preferred to light bulbs, I read about houses, squares, past lives, retrograde planets, and ascendants.

Somehow Adrienne had gleaned from this star and planet data that I was idealistic, romantic—though I would have only one true love, she predicted—impulsive, proud, energetic, and hardworking. I put those attributes in the positive category. On the somewhat negative side, Adrienne had writen that I was stubborn and loyal to a fault, that I held a grudge far too long, and that I should learn to let well enough alone.

It was dusk. The muted light of Adrienne's candles illuminated her second-floor windows as Eddie, Jessie, and I pulled into the driveway. After the initial argument and the detour to the tree and the memorial, neither Eddie nor I had spoken of the possibility of moving to Tallagumsa and taking over the Steak House. I had the sense, though, that my father's offer had become a living, tangible thing. I could almost feel it hovering over us in the car, as we walked up the front steps, and as we stood on the front porch.

While I searched through my purse for the front-door key, Jessie sat in one of the wicker porch rockers and Eddie, his tie stuffed in his shirt pocket, raised the lid of the small metal mailbox hanging to the right of the front door. He pulled out a bunch of mail. A Salem hung from the corner of his mouth while he shuffled through the pile: two bills, a magazine, a catalog, and a letter. He put everything but the letter back in the box.

"Here it is!" he said, holding up the letter to his face as if he might be able to read what was inside without opening it.

"Universal Media?" I asked.

"Who else?" he said. *"They* write me, *they* ask for all my latest work, *they* tell me how great syndication is, and then *they* ignore me for a month. But here it is. At last."

"Open it, Eddie," I said, laughing. "Come on, come on, come on!"

He stood there studying the envelope. His jaw muscles tightened.

"Don't you want to know?" I asked.

"Yes, and no."

"Well, give it to *me* then." I put my hat, Jessie's toy bag, and Eddie's jacket on the empty porch rocker, took the envelope and ripped it open. How our lives would change if Universal Media made Eddie a good offer. I began to read. I didn't have to read too far. I sighed heavily and looked at him. He could see the rejection in my face. I wished that I hadn't opened the letter, but I had been absolutely sure the envelope carried good news that would make Daddy's Steak House proposal irrelevant.

"Let's go inside," I said dully. I inserted the key in the lock, turned it, and pushed open the front door. "Come on in, Jessie."

Jessie leaned back as far as she could in the rocker, then rocked forward forcibly and flung herself out of the chair.

I shook my head. "You're gonna fall right smack on your face one day, young lady."

She ran past us into the apartment.

Eddie hadn't moved from his spot in front of the mailbox. He took a drag on his cigarette and looked at me, not a trace of feeling in his eyes. "I give up," he said.

"Oh, Eddie, come on. You've only tried two syndication groups in two years. You can't give up—you're too good and you know it."

"Maybe not," he said. "Maybe they know something I don't." He leaned against the wall and stared out at the street.

"The *City Paper* loves you, and you have a fan club of devoted readers," I said. "Just because Universal Media doesn't appreciate you proves they're stupid, that's all."

"Stupid or not, it means I have to get a second job just so we can stay even. And 'even' isn't exactly where I'd hoped to be by now. I noticed in the Sunday paper that they're looking for people to do caricatures out at Six Flags over Georgia." He grimaced.

"We're not that desperate, are we? Come on, that's like a joke job, Eddie."

"Maybe I am a joke," he said.

"You are not, but you're acting like a martyr. If you're so worried about our future, then we should just go ahead and move to Tallagumsa." I regretted raising the subject again but pushed ahead anyway. "You can write there as well as here. The paper doesn't care where you are, they've told you that before. You could use the top floor of the house as a studio. Oh Eddie, you'd have the time and the peace and quiet to concentrate on your work. You're always complaining about both. Why won't you at least think about it?"

"Because I don't want your father to determine the course of my life," Eddie said. "That's why." He stomped out his cigarette on the porch as if he wanted to kill it.

"Then I guess I can look forward to many more years of crappy, low-paying jobs and crummy apartments and never finishing my degree. And Jessie and her siblings can look forward to being brought up in day care. I'm thrilled."

"Your father is managing to make me look like the bad guy here. Don't you see that, LuAnn?"

"All I see is . . ." I stopped myself before I said what I was thinking. "Come on, please, let's go inside. It's been a long day." I took the bands out of my hair, unwound the braid, and shook the hair loose, ready to go to sleep as soon as I saw our bed. Then I picked up the cigarette butt, as well as the items I'd deposited in the rocker, and walked inside the apartment behind Eddie.

"It looks so clean," he said, surveying the room. "You didn't clean this morning before we left, did you?"

"You know I didn't," I said. I looked around. It only took a few seconds for me to figure out what was wrong. "It looks clean because it's empty. Our stereo, our TV, and the two lamps Mother gave us aren't here."

"Shit," Eddie said. "Jess! Come here!"

She ran back into the living room, responding to the urgency in his voice.

"Let's go outside for a minute," he said.

"Why?" Jessie asked. "We just got here."

"I want to see if Violet's outside, sweetie," I said, even though I knew Violet and Iris Ann were in Augusta all week. "I need to tell her something."

I lied to Jessie because I didn't want to tell her what had happened. How would she react when she learned that someone had come into her home and taken her family's belongings? Most of my life—and certainly when I was her age—I'd had an unshakable sense of safety and security. How dare someone take that away from her?

We walked through the side yard single file, well trained by the Crawfords not to step on their carefully planned perennial borders.

From the vantage point of our backyard I could see that the back door into the mud room was wide open. We tried the back door to the kitchen. That door too was unlocked.

Biting on my lip, I walked out toward the swing set Daddy had given Jessie last year. I sat on one of the two U-shaped plastic seats and began to cry.

"What's the matter?" Jessie stood in front of me, her hand on my left knee.

No one answered her.

"What happened, Mommy?" she insisted.

Because it would be impossible to keep the burglary a complete secret from her, I tried to cushion the blow. "Somebody took some things out of the apartment without asking first," I said. I wiped the tears off my cheeks with a tissue from my pocket.

"We think," Eddie said.

"Oh Eddie, what else could have happened?" I asked. "There've been a bunch of break-ins around here, we leave town for the day, and our stuff is gone. How would you explain it?"

"Well . . ." he said.

"Were they bad guys?" Jessie asked. Her eyes grew larger. "Are they inside?"

"The Crawfords must have seen something," Eddie said.

"They're in Augusta, remember?" I said. "Oh, no! I guess you'd better check their house."

Eddie trudged from our yard to theirs and pulled on their back screen door. It didn't budge. He went around the house, tried the front door, and checked all the ground-level windows. There were no signs of forced entry. That at least was good news. It was unpleasant enough to imagine the reaction of Violet and Iris Ann to our loss, but I knew they'd be heartbroken if anyone had stolen their silver, one set of which Iris Ann claimed her great-grandmother had hidden from the Yankees during the War Between the States.

Jessie turned her hand into a gun and ran down the path between the two houses. "I'll shoot the bad guys," she said. "Bang! Bang, bang!"

"Where did you learn to do that?" I asked, shocked. I'd never seen her pretend to shoot a gun. She played house, dress up, horse show, and tea party, but never guns.

"At day care," she yelled.

"Terrific. Maybe we all should go get real guns," I said.

"Don't be ridiculous, LuAnn," Eddie said. He kicked one of the thick wooden legs that balanced the swing set. "I don't understand why, when their house is full of silver"—he waved in the direction of the Crawfords'—"and enough rich people live around here, why in the world did they choose ours? Anyone can tell we don't own anything valuable. Did you forget to lock the door this morning?" His tone was accusing. "Or maybe you arranged it to make Tallagumsa look better to me."

I glared at him from my swing seat.

Jessie solemnly handed me a bouquet of the Crawfords' treasured pink and yellow tulips she must have gathered from their garden.

Under the circumstances, I couldn't reprimand her. "Thank

43

you, sweetie. Why don't you go play in the sandbox, Jes," I said instead. I didn't want her to listen to how furious I was at Eddie.

"In my dress?" she asked, astonished at this breach of my own rule.

"It's okay, this one time."

She ran off. Normally I wouldn't have allowed her to play in the sandbox dressed up. Sand would be embedded in every seam of the sailor dress, under her shoe insoles, and in her tights, but by that point in that day I didn't care.

"You're right, Eddie," I said, my voice rising. "Those seemingly innocent busboys at the Steak and Ale are really criminals. I promised them all my tips if they'd pull off the job. Who's being ridiculous now? Goddamn you! I didn't know Daddy was giving us the Steak House until—"

"*You,* you mean," Eddie interrupted. "He gave *you* the Steak House." He pointed at me menacingly.

"But it's for all of *us*! And I didn't know about it until today, at exactly the same moment you and everyone else found out. You act like there's a conspiracy between Daddy and me or something. There's not. I was as surprised as you were. But you're right: Tallagumsa looks better all the time!"

"See? You've made up your mind." He paced back and forth in front of the swing set. "I know you have."

"I really haven't, I swear. Would you please just think about Daddy's proposal? That's all I'm asking. We can discuss it later, rationally, calmly."

"You're just humoring me."

"Oh, stop! I don't want to argue with you while we're standing outside our burglarized apartment, you're furious at the whole world, and Jessie is nearby."

"Why shouldn't I be furious? The world sucks," he said.

Jessie suddenly jumped up out of the sandbox, ran over, and grabbed my arm. "Did they take Lily Lee?" she wailed, referring to her favorite doll.

"I'll go in and check on her and everything else," Eddie said.

"Get Jessie and me a jacket too," I called. With the setting

44

sun's waning warmth blocked by the tall row of cedars in our backyard, the temperature had dropped to the low sixties.

Eddie walked in the back door of our apartment.

"What if Lily Lee is gone?" Jessie worried.

"I promise they didn't take her," I assured Jessie, confident no one would. Lily Lee was the ugliest, rattiest doll I'd ever seen, and Jessie adored her. When Jessie received Lily Lee at the age of four months, Lily Lee was a lovely little baby doll. Since then, though, she'd been colored and painted on, thrown up on, and glued on and to various objects. After every abuse, I'd done my best to restore her, but some of her hair and most of her eyelashes had fallen out, and the blue of her eyes was smeared across her plastic face. Lily Lee was safe from even the least discriminating burglars.

"The vacuum, the radio, the blender, those are the only other things I noticed missing," Eddie said when he came out of the apartment. He carried a beer in one hand and Jessie's jacket and doll in the other. I didn't worry him about my jacket.

"Sounds like they needed home furnishings," I said. "Maybe they were newlyweds." I smiled at the absurdity of this notion.

"Is Lily Lee all right?" Jessie asked.

"She's fine, honey," he said, handing her the battered doll and the jacket. "So are all your Barbie dolls. I called the police, LuAnn."

"The police!" Jessie cried. She pointed her finger gun into the air again and ran around shooting it. "You're dead," she yelled. "Bang, bang!"

"I think I'll check with Adrienne, see if she saw or heard anything," I said. "Why don't you swing with Daddy while we wait for the police, Jes." I thought I'd better warn Adrienne, who wasn't particularly careful about keeping her drugs—a lot of pot, some acid—out of sight.

I held out my hands to Eddie. "Ooh!" I yelped as he helped me up from the swing. My hands automatically reached for my stomach.

He looked at me quizzically.

"It's nothing," I said, even though I wasn't sure what the sharp pain meant. Maybe the contraction was different from those I'd felt over the last month, maybe not.

Focusing on my body and the pregnancy for the first time in hours, I realized how incredibly exhausted I was. The day had made more than its fair share of emotional and physical demands: the trip to Tallagumsa, the dedication, the gift of the Steak House, the trip to the tree and the memorial, Eddie's rejection letter, and now our house burglarized. Enough! Enough! Enough! I wanted to pull a cover up over my head and forget about everything for at least twenty-four hours, but instead I walked slowly around to the north end of our front porch and rang the side-door bell.

I could hear Adrienne walk down the stairs to her front door. When she opened the door, two cats rushed past, under the hem of her billowing floor-length skirt. She didn't seem to notice them. She was high. Very high. Her eyes were all pupils, dilated as fully as they could be, perfect black circles. Her pale freckled face was framed by naturally curly shoulder-length strawberry-blond hair. She looked otherworldly, a wraithlike Orphan Annie with a joint.

"We're back," I said. I gave a little wave. "Just wanted to let you know and say hi."

"I didn't know you left," she said. Another cat walked slowly out the door past us.

"I told you yesterday, remember?"

"Oh, yeah," she said. She showed no signs of concern about her flagging memory, only curiosity. "Where'd you go again?"

"Tallagumsa, Alabama," I reminded her. "And someone broke in our place while we were away," I said. "They stole some things, the TV, the stereo, I don't know what all."

"Wow!" she said. Her expression reminded me of Jessie's when I'd arrive at day care with a surprise toy or cupcake.

"You didn't hear anyone or anything odd?"

"I was at work. Then Bryce was here and"—she shrugged and grinned—"we were busy, you know?"

46

"Eddie called the police," I said. "They'll be here soon. Maybe you ought to go over to Bryce's for a while."

"Thanks," she said. She opened the door and left, walking down the street without her purse, her shoes, or a care in the world. I could hear her singing "Sugar Magnolia" as she turned the corner.

CHAPTER FIVE

At the sound of police sirens approaching our apartment, Jessie dragged the toes of her new patent-leather shoes in the dirt beneath her swing and came to a standstill. She let go of the swing ropes, covered her ears, and squeezed her eyes closed until the police car stopped out front and the sirens wound down and jerked to a stop, then she ran around the side of the house to greet the policemen.

A sharp pain gripped me, filling the silence. I reached for my stomach. Again, my abdomen was as hard as stone. According to my watch, fifteen minutes had passed since the last contraction. Although it didn't necessarily mean anything—during the last months of both pregnancies I'd had lots of contractions off and on, some almost as piercing as the last few I'd felt—I knew that I should go to bed or at least sit down in the living room and prop my swelling ankles on the footrest.

I stared at the back door to the apartment as the last vestiges of the warm sunny day disappeared and darkness engulfed us. I just could not bring myself to go in *there*. After all my worrying, Jessie didn't seem to be particularly bothered by the burglary, but it had shaken me and left me feeling unusually vulnerable. Waiting right where I was in the backyard took all the energy and courage I could muster.

Jessie ran back around the side of the house. "Two police are inside," she announced as she climbed back into her swing.

I pushed her back and forth. Her long golden-brown hair flew out behind her when she went up in the air, and her shoes pointed to the stars. My eyes followed in that direction. I looked for the familiar constellations of my childhood. Only the brighter ones, like Ursa Major, Leo, and Gemini, were visible thanks to the uninhibited growth of downtown Atlanta, which was leaving in its wake a dull haze that increasingly interfered with a clear view of the night sky.

When I was not much older than Jessie, before I'd learned to read, my father and I had studied the night sky most evenings after dinner on the side-porch swing, while Jane and Mother sewed or worked on some church thing or other at the kitchen table inside. I could easily imagine Eddie and Jessie on the same porch in the same swing, "star hopping," as my father had always called it.

Eddie was wrong, though. I hadn't made up my mind about moving. I was being pulled in that direction, but I had doubts and reservations. If anyone had asked me a few years ago whether I'd ever return home to live, I would have laughed. Plain and simple. As much as I loved my family, Jolene, who'd helped raise me, my horse, and my old friends, Tallagumsa belonged to my past, not my future.

But my future was not falling into place quite the way I'd imagined. I had always assumed I'd finish graduate school and teach or do research, Eddie would be a respected political cartoonist, his work appearing in every major newspaper, we'd buy and renovate an historic home, and then, perhaps in our early thirties, we'd focus on children and raising a family. In my future, we lived happily ever after.

It was hard for me to believe that my dreams could be worn away by reality in much the same way the sand castles Jane and I had built together as children were worn away by the tides. During family vacations in Florida, Jane and I often spent our mornings constructing elaborate sand structures. In the afternoon, after high tide had destroyed our work, I was shocked to find that a lump of sand had replaced that day's masterpiece. Jane (or "Sis," as I called her back then), older and always the pragmatist, took the loss in stride. I, on the other hand, stubbornly refused to accept the inevitable.

One such occasion had been preserved for posterity by a photograph Mother took during a Gulf Coast vacation when I was five and Jane eleven. In the picture, Jane and I are standing on the beach in our bathing suits. I am sobbing, my head on her shoulder. Her arms are wrapped around me, consoling me. Next to us are the remains of the castle we'd worked so hard on, and in the background is the tide, rushing in to take even more of our creation away from us and out to sea.

Could the Steak House be just another sand castle?

With the next contraction, I felt something inside me give. A rush of warm liquid flowed down my legs. Ready or not, my future was here to claim me.

As I had before giving birth to Jessie, I focused on this moment, after which my life would always be different. This time around the scene before me was one of moderate chaos. Jessie was swinging and laughing, giddy from lack of sleep. Eddie and the two policemen, one a small black man, the other a fat white man with a thin black mustache, were huddled outside the back door, talking. The stillness was periodically broken by the squawking and screeching of the police radios. More stars had appeared, though not enough to suit me. I shivered and touched my sopping-wet pants leg. Yuch.

In contrast, the day preceding Jessie's birth nearly four years ago had been slow-moving and quiet. Eddie and I had been sitting in this same backyard reading, the summer sun hot and wonderful overhead. I had marked my place in *Dog Soldiers,* Eddie's favorite novel of the year, closed it, and willed myself to know the look and feel of the moment because I had understood that very soon our lives, Eddie's and mine, would be transformed forever by the birth of our first child.

This time, three would become five.

"Eddie," I called.

"One sec," he said, without looking over.

Eddie conversed easily with the officers, matching their questions with questions of his own about police training. The policemen might have assumed that Eddie was interested in joining the force, but I knew better. Eddie loved to talk to people from different walks of life—firemen, construction workers, plumbers, painters, mailmen, lawyers, doctors, poets, singers—anyone who would answer his questions about the details of their work, details he somehow remembered and worked into his political cartoons days, weeks, or even years later.

I gave out a yell. Although I was standing behind Jessie and the swing set, the contraction gripping me was so powerful and intense that for a moment I was sure she had somehow swung all her weight smack into my lower back. Jessie, as far out in front of me as the swing could take her, turned around and looked at me, concerned. "Eddie!" I screamed.

He looked over.

"I think we better get to the hospital," I said. "Now!"

All three men, two of whom had certainly been trained for more serious emergencies than this one, stood stock still and stared at me as if I'd spoken to them in ancient Greek. After a moment, during which each digested the information I conveyed, everyone sprang into action.

Jessie skidded to a stop and took my hand. Eddie rushed to my side, a look of disbelief on his face. The black policeman offered to radio for an ambulance.

"Thanks, but Eddie can drive me," I said. "Can't you, Eddie?"

Eddie nodded.

"We'll escort you then," the white policeman said. "Which hospital?"

"Emory," Eddie said. "We have to drop Jessie at her friends.' At Abby's, right, LuAnn?"

"Right," I said. "It's on the way."

"What should I do now?" Eddie asked. He sounded mildly frantic.

"Call Abby's mother and Dr. Powers," I said. "And I'll get my stuff."

Everyone went inside—Eddie, Jessie, the two policemen, and I. In the bedroom, I changed my pants, underwear, and socks and packed. Jessie followed me each step of the way, so closely that I had to move cautiously lest I step on her. Then we packed her overnight bag, a small pink duffel with pictures of ballerinas on it.

"Mommy, do you want to take Lily Lee with you?" Jessie asked in a small voice, holding out her doll to me.

"That is the sweetest thing you've ever said, Jessie." Tears filled my eyes. "But I think she'd like to be with you at Abby's. Thank you though, honey. Thank you so much." I sat on the edge of her bed and opened my arms to her. She tried my lap, gave up, and we snuggled side by side. "Daddy will pick you up at Abby's as soon as he can, and then you can come visit me at the hospital," I assured her.

I'd hoped to get a gift for Jessie to give her when she visited the hospital, but hadn't had time. Eddie would have to pick something out for her.

Jessie didn't know—though I'm sure she sensed—that this was a moment in her life after which things would never be the same. I felt guilty for that.

As we approached the hospital, our police car escort close behind us, I thought back to when Jessie had been born. The thing I remembered most about that day, besides Jessie of course, was how I'd felt about Eddie. I'd been warned that during labor I might hate him, scream at him, accuse him of horrible crimes, but instead the day Jessie was born I fell in love with him all over again. What a marvelous feeling that was. If only we could repeat that experience now, when we needed so much a reminder, a sort of refresher course in the intense feelings that had brought us together in college.

★   ★   ★

My freshman year I'd known all about Eddie Garrett the way you know about someone famous, but I didn't meet him until my sophomore year. He was known as a wild man, almost a legend at age twenty. Part of his fame was based on the fact that one of the political cartoons he'd done for the school paper had been published in the *New York Times*. But there was more. He rode a motorcycle, he rarely went to class but always made straight *A*s, his best friend, Sam, was black, he dated women from the city, he played pool, he was the star of the track team, he wore cowboy boots, and he spoke—along with Sam—at just about every civil rights and antiwar protest, both on and off the campus.

Eddie turned up one evening at an out-of-the-way hospital snack bar where on any given night five to thirty students studied. A few doctors and nurses dropped in for junk food out of the machines, but usually the small room served as a college hangout, an extension of the library for those who liked to eat, drink, or smoke while they studied. I preferred the hospital snack bar to the modern college library because it had windows that opened, as well as a small patio area good for study breaks and star hopping.

That evening Eddie and Sam sat two tables away from me. I couldn't help but watch Eddie and listen to his conversation with Sam. While I'd seen him before, up close I was struck by his compelling good looks, his steel-gray eyes, and his wonderful but infrequent smile. When he did smile, he looked like he was about to do something that most likely would get him arrested. When he did smile, any woman close enough to think he was smiling at her found him hard to resist.

By the time I left the snack bar that night, we'd talked, he'd smiled at me, and I was in love. It was an instant, almost chemical reaction that had occurred only one other time in my life, and, as on that occasion, I was not merely interested, I was one hundred percent committed.

Thereafter I dreamed about Eddie. I thought about Eddie. I

stared at Eddie (in the hospital snack bar, in the coffee shop, on the quad, at demonstrations, anywhere I could find him), trying to will him to call me, to talk to me, to do something with me. By the time of our first date, I had memorized him.

I was brought back to the present by a vicious contraction at the same time the car slowed to a stop at the hospital. The black policeman helped Eddie park the car, while I waited with his partner in the police car. He didn't talk much, spending those endless minutes unnecessarily brushing his thin mustache with his finger.

Eddie returned. He helped me out of the police car and then just stood there looking at me, smiling that smile. He seemed surprised at what he saw, and I felt a connection between us that had been missing for some time. I took his hand. Together we walked through the sliding-glass hospital doors into the fancy new building not fifty yards from the old hospital snack bar where we'd first met.

Will and Hank were born ten hours later, identical twins. Will weighed six pounds nine ounces, Hank six pounds five ounces.

The afternoon following the births, Eddie came to my hospital room carrying a grocery bag in the crook of his arm. I was sitting up in bed in a standard-issue blue and white hospital gown. He set the bag down at the foot of my bed, kissed me, then stood for a few moments with his back to me, watching his two sleeping sons in their clear plastic hospital bassinets, both swaddled in blue receiving blankets. They were turned on their left sides. Tiny white cotton caps covered their thin, fuzzy layers of light brown hair.

"I nursed them twice," I said proudly. "Once in the middle of the night. Once this morning. They've slept the rest of the time."

Eddie turned to look at me. "They're playing that trick Jessie played." He laughed. "Being real good, sleeping a lot in the hospital, waiting 'til they get home to stay up all night. How do you feel?"

"I feel great," I said. "I took a shower, ate a huge breakfast, and even slept some."

"Those are the good hormones. They just give those out in the hospital too, if I remember correctly," he said.

"I wasn't that bad last time, was I?"

"You were just exhausted. And this time will be three times as hard." He rubbed his hand across the stubble on his chin.

"Did you get any sleep?" I asked.

He pulled up a chair next to my bed and shook his head. "Instead I drove out to Six Flags this morning, thinking I might apply for that job I told you about."

"And I told you not to even think about that," I said. "You could never work there, Eddie. We'll figure something out."

"We don't have any choice," he said. "We need help. We need a bigger place to live. We need money. We have three children. So I went to Six Flags. I watched four people drawing these ridiculous pictures of tourists. Making a big nose bigger, a cowlick higher, and on and on, people paying half-assed artists to make them look stupider than they already look. For two hours I sat at a picnic table in the shadow of this huge roller coaster called the Cyclone, where people stand in line for hours just to scare themselves silly." He sighed. "You're right, LuAnn. I couldn't do it. I just couldn't work there. I'd be dead or crazy within a year. So I have a proposal. We'll go to Tallagumsa for that year instead and see how it goes." He held up one finger. "One year."

Suddenly my mind was made up too. "Oh, Eddie. Do you really mean it? You do! Tallagumsa will be wonderful. I promise. How can it not be better?"

"Lots of ways," he said. "Anyway, I stopped at the Piggly Wiggly and got boxes. They're in the car. And I got this." He opened the grocery bag and pulled out a pie, paper plates, and plastic ware. "Miss Reese's strawberry pie. I think we should buy one every week after we get there to remind us that we can leave; that if the time comes to leave, we go the way Liz Reese did—as fast as we can and we don't look back." He cut a piece of the pie and put it on a paper plate. "Pie, anyone?" he asked.

"Yes, please. I'm starving."

He handed me the piece.

I leaned over and kissed him. "I love you, Eddie Garrett."

"One year," he repeated. "I love you too, LuAnn Hagerdorn."

CHAPTER SIX

A s soon as Eddie left my hospital room, I called my father for the second time in less than twenty-four hours and gave him the latest good news: We'd be moving to Tallagumsa as soon as we could pack and say good-bye to everyone.

"I have no idea how long that will take," I warned him, "with the twins and Jessie and all."

"I'll have your brother-in-law bring Jolene to help you," Daddy said. "And I'll wire you a thousand dollars. That should make the move a little less painful."

Jolene Wilson had taken care of me since the day I was born— she was only sixteen at the time she started working for us—and I couldn't think of anyone I'd rather have sit for the twins and Jessie. She was steady, loving, not a critical bone in her body, and very physical, using hugs where most people used words. She had been at the apartment for two days when Eddie brought the twins and me home from the hospital. When we arrived Jolene and Jessie were sitting on the front steps waiting for us, Jessie's head resting on Jolene's shoulder.

Jessie ran down the steps to greet us. She was dressed up in a flowered purple and white spring dress Jane had sent while I was in the hospital and the patent-leather shoes she'd worn to the courthouse dedication. I thought the shoes had been ruined that day, but Jolene had worked some miracle on them and they looked good as new. A purple ribbon kept Jessie's hair out of her face. She looked like an angel.

Jolene was right behind Jessie, her worn-out work shoes—old loafers with the heels stomped in so they looked like bedroom slippers—slapping against each step and her washed-out barely still green uniform stretched taut across her chest and hips. Only four of the original six or seven buttons held the uniform closed, providing triangular glimpses of the blue jeans and madras blouse underneath. Except for her weight, which had increased steadily over the years, she always looked the same to me. Her chocolate-brown skin never seemed to age.

"Get away from there 'til it stops," Jolene warned Jessie as the car rolled in. Jolene held Jessie's hand and gently pulled her back a few feet. As soon as I opened the car door, Jolene released Jessie and she ran to hug me. Jolene was close behind her, obviously desperate to get her hands on Will and Hank. As far as she was concerned, babies made the world go round.

"LuAnn!" she screamed. "You're a sight, girl, a sight! Them babies! Look at them! Give 'em to me!"

Jolene opened the back door and took Will out of his car seat. He scrunched his face up and began to cry. She rested him on her chest and patted his back. He cried louder.

"He's a crier," Eddie said. He was busy unloading the trunk: my overnight bag, two potted plants, and a bag of all the stuff the hospital had given us for the babies—Pampers, formula, instruction manuals, certificates of birth bearing the babies' footprints, and presealed glucose-water bottles. "He eats and cries."

"Well, he ain't old enough to talk, bless his heart," Jolene said.

"Here," I said, taking Will from her. "Why don't you get Hank out."

Jolene removed Hank from his car seat. He didn't even open his eyes. She cradled him in her arms and stared.

"He's a sleeper," Eddie said over his shoulder from the front steps.

"They is something else," Jolene said. "Both of 'em looks like you, LuAnn. But Jessie, you was the best-looking and acting baby I ever saw."

Jessie grinned. I knew Jolene would one day tell each of the boys that they were the best too, but right now what they didn't know wouldn't hurt them.

I took off my flats, using my right foot to remove my left shoe and vice versa, and left the shoes next to the pile of stuff Eddie was to bring into the house. The grass under my feet and toes was cool and fine. With my free hand I picked one of the enormous lilac chinaberry blossoms from the front-yard tree.

"Our new house has two of these trees, Jessie." I handed her the fragrant flower. "Look, it goes with your dress."

She tucked the flower into her sash and smiled.

Over the front door a piece of posterboard hung from the trim. "Welcome Home" was written on it in red magic marker. Several figures—one large, two small—had been colored below the words. Eddie's head brushed against the bottom of the poster as he carried his load inside.

"Oooh! Who made that?" I stopped on the porch to admire the sign.

"Me!" Jessie said. "I drew you and Will and Hank. See, I even did Will's birth color." She pointed at a red dot on the child's thigh.

"It's his birthmark," I said. "You did a wonderful job, Jessie."

"Jolene helped," she said.

I bent over to kiss Jessie in thanks, lowering Will to the level of her face. He stopped crying and looked at her. "See? He likes you," I said.

"I know," Jessie insisted. "Jolene told me all about being a big sister."

I hugged Jolene and kissed her cheek. "You're wonderful!" I said. "Only two days here and you've worked miracles. As always. Thanks for coming to help. I don't think I would have been brave enough to leave the hospital if you weren't here."

"I always take care of my babies," she said.

"Will and Hank appreciate it."

"I mean you, girl," she said. "You is my baby. Get in that room and lay yourself down. You need your rest."

Inside the apartment, piles of newspapers and open boxes covered the living-room floor. Many of the boxes were already packed with books, records, tapes, and pictures. Despite the move in-progress, the room was clean and organized.

"Who did all this?" I was astonished to see how much work had been accomplished.

"All of us," Eddie said. He pushed a box aside and sat down on the living-room couch with a beer. "If we're going, we might as well go."

"Look in my room," Jessie said. "I packed all my toys."

"Then your mama gets in the bed," Jolene said.

"Okay," Jessie said without complaint.

I was relieved at how easy this transition was going to be. Jessie and Jolene had struck up a warm friendship in a matter of days. Much of the packing was finished. Eddie, although he seemed a bit distracted, was trying hard to get along. He hadn't said anything sarcastic about Tallagumsa or my family all day, which took some effort on his part.

The sense of anticipation surrounding the days leading up to our move reminded me of the summer before I left for college. Then, as now, there were high expectations and also a little sadness. Then, I was leaving my whole family behind, even Jane, who'd left for college her freshman year but come home and never returned after the summer semester. Then, I had not yet admitted it to Junior, but I'd known September would mark the end of our relationship as we headed off to different colleges.

Four seniors left town in 1969: Junior, Barbara Cox, Billy Vines, and I. With my move back home, that would make three out of four who'd returned. Barbara Cox had been lured away from a teaching job at Vanderbilt to become dean at the state college. Back in town a few months prior to Junior's return, she'd earned a reputation as an incredible fundraiser, a savvy recruiter of talented professors, and the main reason out-of-state applications at the college had tripled.

Because Barbara was very active in state politics, I had been surprised when I didn't see her at the courthouse dedication, but I was even more surprised when Barbara and Jane appeared at the apartment door in Atlanta six days after the twins and I got home from the hospital.

That afternoon I was lying in Jessie's bed, desperate for a nap, when the doorbell rang. Although I was exhausted after being up much of the night with Will, I quickly forced myself up and ran for the door. I would do anything to avoid the doorbell waking the twins.

Jane and Barbara stood on the front porch, both in suits and heels. Jane looked frumpy; Barbara looked like a poised and polished *Vogue* model. She had full pink lips, aqua-marine eyes, and light blond hair blunt cut in a straight line at her shoulders.

We all hugged and said hello.

"You look great, Barbara," I said. She'd always been attractive, but during high school when I'd last seen her she was still carrying a lot of baby fat on her large frame.

"You too," Barbara said.

"How kind of you," I said.

In fact, I looked dumpy, flabby, and exhausted. I had on my nursing nightgown, with Will's spit-up decorating one shoulder, wore no makeup, and hadn't washed my stringy, dirty hair since we got home from the hospital.

"Buck thinks Barbara's a dead ringer for Cybill Shepherd," Jane gushed.

Barbara waved her hand dismissively, but something that flickered in her eyes told me how much she enjoyed the compliment.

"Come on in," I said. "Careful where you step." I cleared a path through the boxes. "Y'all sit over there." I gestured toward the couch and a chair.

"Congratulations on the twins," Barbara said, sitting in a faded armchair.

I'd never noticed how ratty the chair and most of the other furniture in the apartment were until that moment.

"Thanks," I said. "They're asleep right now, so we have to be a little quiet. Would either of you like coffee or something?"

"No, no. Just relax," Barbara said.

I negotiated between a pile of books and another of records, removed a box of framed pictures from a comfortable chair, and sat down. I rested my feet on the embroidered footstool.

"I get congratulations too," Jane said coyly.

I looked at her, puzzled.

"I think I'm pregnant," she squealed.

"Oh Jane, that's terrific!" I said softly. "How long?"

"Just two weeks since I missed my period, so I shouldn't have said anything. Don't tell anyone," she said. She held a finger to her lips. "Mum's the word."

"You didn't tell Buck?" I asked.

"Oh, I couldn't keep it a secret from him. I know what you're thinking: If I have another miscarriage it'll upset him. But I won't have one. Besides, he'd figure it out. Every month we mourn my period, so he knows when I'm even a few days late. And guess what—I threw up this morning. Isn't that great?" She giggled and patted her tummy.

"It's wonderful, Jane. What's Buck up to today anyway?" I asked her.

"He's busy planning some big political thing for Daddy."

"It's a very exciting time in Tallagumsa, don't you think, LuAnn?" Barbara asked. She sat with her ankles crossed, her hands clasped in her lap. "If your father's elected governor, it would be a big boost both to the town and the college."

"If he runs," I said. "Last I heard, he hadn't decided."

"He's close—Buck said so last night," Jane said.

"I almost wish he wouldn't run," I said. "Eddie's not that thrilled about our moving back, and if we have to do a lot of campaigning he'll be even less happy."

"Well, maybe he'll feel a little better about moving after he and Barbara have their meeting," Jane said.

"What on earth are you talking about?" I asked.

"Is Eddie here?" Barbara asked. She pulled a leather notebook from her handbag.

I didn't answer, but I must have given her a funny look.

"Don't you know why I'm here?" Barbara asked.

"We're a few minutes early," Jane said, looking at her watch. "Didn't Eddie tell you we were coming?"

"I haven't seen him much since I got home from the hospital," I said. "Whenever I'm asleep he's awake, and vice versa."

Will began to cry. Upon hearing the sound, milk began leaking through my nursing bra, and two wet spots spread across my nightgown. "Excuse me."

I picked Will up from his bassinet in my bedroom and nursed him in my bed. Hank continued sleeping quietly in his tiny bed. After a few minutes Will quieted down, and I lay him down on the improvised changing table: my vanity with a piece of foam padding on top. When I took off his diaper, he peed all over my neck and chest before I had a chance to shield the general area with my hand. I laughed. I still had not gotten used to this basic difference in changing boys' and girls' diapers.

I put Will in the middle of the bed while I took off the nightgown, wiped my neck with it, then pulled on a pair of sweatpants and one of Eddie's T-shirts. I brushed my hair and put on some lip gloss, then looked in the mirror. Hopeless.

"Where's Jolene?" Jane asked when I returned to the living room with Will. Once again he started screaming his lungs out.

"The grocery with Jessie," I said. "So what's going on?"

I stood with Will resting on my shoulder, bouncing him gently in a futile attempt to relieve what I'd decided the night before at three A.M. must be colic.

"Barbara's a big fan of Eddie's work," Jane said. "And when she heard y'all were moving to Tallagumsa and that Eddie had taught journalism before, she called him. Was it yesterday?"

Barbara nodded. "We talked twice yesterday. I told him that

we have an immediate opening because, I'm embarrassed to say, my journalism professor ran off with one of his students. I also mentioned that I'm hoping he can teach a politics and the arts course this summer."

"What did Eddie say?" I asked.

"That he'd think about it and talk to me today. Since I spoke with him I found out from your father that Eddie's been trying to get his work into syndication, so I wondered if maybe we should do a show of his work at the college. I'm good friends with the head of the Tribune Press Syndicate, Willie Caldwell. I know he'd come." She raised her palm, as if to stop herself. "I should talk to Eddie before I go on about this. Maybe he wouldn't like the idea."

"I think he'd love it!" I said.

He did. That afternoon, while I bathed Hank in the plastic baby tub next to the kitchen sink, Barbara hired Eddie to teach two courses, one in journalism as soon as we moved, and one in politics and the arts that summer. A show of his best work would follow a few months later. Best of all, Eddie could continue to work for the *City Paper*.

Perfect, I thought. Everything was turning out just perfect.

On our last morning in Atlanta, Buck picked up Jolene early and drove her to our new house in Tallagumsa, where she could prepare things for our arrival. Before we left the apartment, we had our landladies, the Crawfords, and our neighbor, Adrienne, in for coffee and pie. Eddie bought two Miss Reese's pies for the event, one strawberry, one pear-apple. I'd attributed my initial favorable impression of the pie in the hospital to postlabor starvation, but in fact Miss Reese's pies were the best I'd ever tasted.

We all cried over our pie, especially Violet and Iris Ann, who weren't too happy that we were taking the "lights of their lives" away. They gave Jessie a pair of white gloves and a string of beautiful pearls. The boys received ornately monogrammed sterling-silver mint julep cups like the one the Crawfords had given Jessie when she was born. Adrienne presented each child with a personal astrological chart.

The twins were two weeks old the day we left Atlanta with a U-Haul full of everything worth taking with us attached to the car. Looking out the car window, I watched the chinaberry tree in the front yard recede from view.

We passed the Glad Bag Man on his park bench as we drove out of town.

I waved good-bye, relieved that we were leaving behind all the hassles and concerns of big city life.

CHAPTER SEVEN

Before the move, the Bledsoes and I had agreed on a leisurely turnover of the restaurant six weeks after my return to Tallagumsa. That would give me the time I needed to unpack, recover from too many sleepless nights, and get reacquainted with Steak House activities.

At the end of the six-week transition period, I would be on my own. I might have panicked if my friends Estelle and Roland hadn't been so knowledgeable about the restaurant, but both had run the place when the Bledsoes were out of town, and I figured I hadn't forgotten everything I'd learned during my years working there.

The Bledsoes, having spent their entire married lives running the Steak House, admitted they were ambivalent about retiring, and I suspected they would have resisted leaving at all if they hadn't been booked on a six-month round-the-world cruise. Although they expressed confidence in my abilities, it was clear that neither Mimi nor Howard believed the restaurant could survive for more than five days without them: they had never been off the premises longer than that.

Eddie didn't take any time off after the move. I'd hoped we could spend some time together, alone, but once the U-Haul was unpacked, he was either in his studio—the large open space on the third floor of the four-bedroom Tudor house I'd grown up in—or at the college.

All the years my parents, my sister, Jane, and I had lived in the house, what was now Eddie's studio had been used for Daddy's hunting equipment and his extensive gun collection. In place of the familiar gun racks, trophies, and cases, there was now a desk, where Eddie worked at his typewriter, a utility table, where he drafted cartoons, and floor-to-ceiling shelves across one long wall, where he put his work-related library and piles of papers.

Eddie nailed a six-by-six-foot bulletin board to the other long wall and stuck a strip of red duct tape straight down the middle. On the left side he tacked his recent and upcoming *City Paper* cartoons. On the right was the work he was considering for his show, the proposed contents of which changed regularly. There were cartoons about David Frost's interview of Richard Nixon, Billy Carter's endorsement of Billy Beer, Daniel Schorr's suspension from CBS, the federal antitrust suit against AT&T, and the many other events of the last ten years that had caught Eddie's attention and lit his imagination.

Eddie had always been happiest when he was busy and productive, and he seemed almost content in Tallagumsa, where for the first time in years he had the time, space, and opportunity to accomplish his goals. He turned out some wonderful political cartoons for the *City Paper* and took over the journalism course at the college without missing a beat. Barbara Cox told me that he had quickly become something of a hero with the kids at the college, in part because he spent so much of his time working individually with them, and in part because he had the kind of real-life experience often lacking in teachers. His show had been set for Wednesday, July 12, in the college social hall, and Barbara was working hard to include on the invitation list people who could help Eddie get syndicated.

Despite his seeming contentment, however, Eddie was true to his word and never missed a Friday night with a Miss Reese's pie, an unspoken but pointed reminder of the provisional nature of our stay in Tallagumsa.

One Saturday a few weeks after we'd moved in, I was in the den, a bright, cheerful room painted yellow and decorated in floral fabrics. I was unpacking books, dusting each one as it came out of the box, and arranging them in the built-in bookshelves. It was quiet. Jessie was with her grandparents at the lake, where she spent many weekend days, and Eddie was walking Will and Hank in their double stroller.

I had just dusted hardback copies of *Ragtime, All the President's Men,* and *Final Payments,* sliding them into place on the shelf, when I heard Eddie return and put the boys in their cribs. He stayed in the nursery for fifteen minutes, then came into the den.

"The boys asleep?" I asked.

"Yep," he said. "Even Will." He lit a cigarette and watched me. His look was mildly contemptuous.

"What?" I asked.

"Isn't it a little strange for you being the wife and mother in the house you grew up in? Sleeping in your parents' bedroom? Cooking in your mother's kitchen?"

I shook my head.

"Don't you feel any of the ghosts here?" he asked.

"You sound like Adrienne, Eddie," I said.

"I thought she just did astrology," he said.

"Same kind of thing. But no, I don't. All I feel is incredibly lucky that we have this house, great jobs, wonderful, healthy children, and Jolene."

"They're here, LuAnn," he said.

"Who?"

"The ghosts," he said. "You just won't allow yourself to see them."

I laughed. "Don't be silly, Eddie. You can't have ghosts without dead people. Here, help me with these books and stop looking at me like that."

He shrugged and sat down next to me.

I handed him a dust rag.

Once the unpacking was finished, I had more free time than I'd had in years, and more than I'd have after I took over the Steak

House. Jessie was in nursery school each morning, and Jolene watched the twins whenever I was out. Will and Hank could survive without me for increasingly longer periods of time as they began to get more of their daily nourishment from bottles. I took advantage of my freedom, taking long walks, riding my horse, and hanging out at the Steak House, reviewing with the Bledsoes the many details involved in running a restaurant.

My horse, Glorious Gloria—or Glory, for short—had been a gift from my father not long after Glory was born to a champion show mare at a Tennessee horse farm. She was an early college-graduation present, according to Daddy. A bribe to keep me in Tallagumsa, according to Eddie.

I'd trained Glory weekends before Jessie was born. After that I'd tried to ride and jump her at least once a month. Between my visits, a trainer worked with her, and a local teenage boy who lived nearby exercised her almost every day.

We kept Glory and my father's horse, Balzac, outside of town close to Clark Lake in one of Edwina Frickey's barns. Miss Edwina had lived outside Tallagumsa since the day she was born there, in 1885. Her grandchildren maintained her property and her horses. Because Daddy had done her some favor or other years before, her family took care of our horses for free. One of her two barns housed ten horses; in the other barn were her parakeets.

A light drizzle began to fall during my first trip out to Miss Edwina's after the move. There was just enough rain to warrant windshield wipers, but I didn't turn back. I'd been looking forward to riding Glory for too long.

I parked next to the horse barn. I could see the horses grazing in the east field at the top of a small rise a few hundred yards away. As I entered the barn to get a halter, I was overwhelmed by the smells of my childhood: an unforgettable mixture of hay, horse shit, and horse sweat. It was wonderful.

I grabbed the worn green halter from the stall marked "Glory" and walked across the soft ground toward the field. The rain had stopped.

Glory, a golden palomino with four white feet and a white mane and tail, stood out even from a distance. I fingered the sugar cubes in my jeans pocket and started to walk a little faster, anxious to touch her.

"Glory," I called when I was a few yards away from her. She and the two horses next to her turned and stared. One of them was Balzac, a black thoroughbred. He turned back to his eating, while Glory's dark hazel eyes looked me over. Then Glory walked up and pushed her nose against my pocket. Her nostrils flared a little.

"You're the smartest horse I ever knew," I said. I gave her the sugar and gently hooked the halter over her head. "Come on, Glory. Let's go."

In the barn, I put her in crossties and retrieved a tack box. Equipped with a hoof pick, I faced her and gently ran my right hand down the front of her right leg; she shifted her weight to her other three legs and lifted her front right leg. I bent over and dug in.

I was never one for mindless labor, unless it involved horses. Then, bring it on. As a girl I'd been happy to muck out stalls all day, as long as I got to ride when I was done. I figured it was only fair that I had to do a lot of dirty, boring work before I was able to do something as incredible as ride a horse. For me riding was the ultimate contradiction: It put you in your place and set you free at the same time.

During the six-week break between leaving Atlanta and taking over the Steak House, I often dropped by the restaurant and sat with the Bledsoes in their corner booth, where I could chat and learn, or I relaxed with my father and his friends, the members of the Coffee Club, along the wall booth.

The Coffee Club, as it had come to be known over the years,

numbered between five and fifteen men who met most week-day mornings and afternoons at the Steak House. They always sat at the same tables, along the wall booth, where they drank coffee, talked, laughed, and sometimes yelled as they tried to solve a multitude of problems ranging from the personal to the political.

Other members of the Coffee Club, besides Daddy and Junior, included Bev Carter, the sheriff who'd been deputy when my father was sheriff fifteen years ago, Skip Palmer, the druggist; Buddy Sheppard, the luggage-plant owner; Dr. Roy Stuart, our family doctor; Larry Potter, the garment-factory manager; Claude Vines, a retired state representative; and Cooper Bowe, who owned Bowe's Department Store; as well as several judges and deputy sheriffs. Most worked within walking distance of the Steak House. A few drove in for the company and the conversation.

On several occasions I encouraged Eddie to drop by and join them between classes or on his way back and forth to the college, but he wasn't interested.

My last weekday off before I started working full time, I packed a picnic lunch, put on shorts and a shirt over my bathing suit—which I could finally fit into again—and drove out to Clark Lake. Unfortunately, Eddie couldn't join me because of a college faculty meeting he had to attend.

I spent the morning on my parents' dock, swimming and soaking up the sun. Daddy was at work, and Mother was off with Jane on some Junior League project, so I had the place to myself. Except for a few houses in the distance, there was nothing but lake and pine trees, and a deep blue sky overhead.

After swimming for an hour, I slept. Almost two months old, Hank had started sleeping through the night, but Will seemed determined to be ornery and hadn't followed Hank's lead. Anticipating the demands of my job, I'd weaned the boys completely to daytime bottles but still breastfed them in the evening

71

and during the night. Over the last few weeks I'd had time to catch up on my sleep most days, but I was a little concerned about how I'd survive once I was at the Steak House full time.

After my nap and a quick swim, I tied my wet hair back with a hair band, pulled on my shorts over my bathing suit, and put on my tennis shoes.

I walked around my parents' lake property. Not far from the property line between their land and Connie Ream's vacation home was the chapel, the price my father had paid to get Mother to move out of town. He'd grudgingly gone along with her plan to build the chapel, but only if she put the small wooden building a good ways from the house, where he wouldn't have to see the large cross balanced atop the pointed roof every time he looked out the windows.

I'd only been in the chapel once, right after Mother and Daddy moved out to the lake a year ago. Inside there was room for two people. On the left was a bench with a purple velvet pillow and on the right a portable piano. Two stained-glass windows the size of record albums provided muted natural lighting. On the altar were candles and a two-foot-high brass crucifix that Mother had bought on a church trip to Mexico several years ago.

I didn't really understand my mother's religion—what motivated her, what she got out of it, or why the chapel meant so much to her. Jane and Buck were just as devoted to the church as she was. Daddy and I were the odd ones out. He went to church for political reasons, but had confided to me over the years that he didn't buy a lot of what organized religion had to offer. I'd quit attending services the first week of my freshman year at college.

I left the chapel and was about to head back to the dock when the sunlight glancing off the glass windows at Connie Ream's place caught my eye. I'd heard from the Coffee Club, a primary source of town gossip, that the *Washington Star* reporter Ben Gainey had rented the Ream house during his stay in Tallagumsa.

I walked through the woods up a steep incline toward the modern A-frame. A light blue boxy BMW with Washington, D.C., plates was parked in the driveway. I leaned my head to the side and squeezed the water from my dripping ponytail, then knocked. No one answered. I peered inside, saw no one, and began to walk away when I heard a man calling out, "Hello. Hello there."

Ben Gainey approached from the direction of the lake, wearing a navy-and-yellow swimsuit, a bath towel draped around his shoulders. Drops of water fell from his hair onto the towel.

"Hi," I said, walking toward him with my hand extended. "You probably don't remember me. I'm—"

"LuAnn Hagerdorn Garrett," he interrupted as we shook hands. "Newly returned to town, with husband and three children, to take over the Tallagumsa Steak House."

"I guess you do remember."

"Junior has talked a lot about you. He thinks I should interview you."

"Great. I've been enjoying one of my last days off before I take over the Steak House, and I thought I'd say hello. My parents' house is right over there." I pointed in that direction. "Past the chapel."

"I was wondering about that chapel." He looked toward the cross. "Your parents must be very religious."

"Mother is," I explained.

"Would you like to come in?" he asked. He briskly rubbed his hair with the towel and gave me a warm, friendly smile.

"Sure, for a minute. Thanks."

The main door of the Ream house opened into a large room with a cathedral ceiling. The kitchen was separated from the dining room–living room area only by a section of base cabinets. Several ceiling fans hung down from extended poles.

"Make yourself at home," Ben said. "I'll be right back." He walked down the hallway.

I sat at a round butcher-block table covered with piles of papers, a portable tape recorder, and at least fifteen steno pads.

On the floor next to the table was an open portable file drawer, with files and papers stuffed inside.

Ben returned with his hair combed and wearing Docksider shoes, a green polo shirt, and white shorts. He was very preppy looking, cute but not my type at all. I could imagine him as a boy on the family sloop, sailing into the bay as the sun set. Buck wasn't totally wrong: Something about Ben Gainey reminded me too of Robert Redford.

"What is all this?" I asked, gesturing toward his papers.

"A mess," he said. "Let me get you something to drink." He sneezed twice.

"Bless you," I said.

"Allergies," he explained. "Bad allergies. How's coffee sound? Is that all right?"

"Perfect," I said, yawning. "After swimming and then napping, I'm a little out of it."

Ben pulled a bag of coffee beans out of the freezer, ground them, and started the pot.

"All that mess on the table is my life now, actually," he said. "The book I'm writing—or trying to write. My future."

"Sounds serious," I said.

"I'm feeling a little overwhelmed right now. I'm behind where I thought I would be, and the whole project is harder than I ever imagined. Makes me wonder whether I should have just stayed home with my wife and the security of my reporter's job."

I smiled sympathetically. "It's scary taking chances, doing something new."

"And you? Aren't you nervous about taking over the Steak House?" he asked. He sat on the counter facing me across the room while he waited for the coffee to brew. "That's a tough job, I know. My parents were in the restaurant business, and the Steak House is a big operation."

"I worked at the Steak House all through high school and summers in college, and the Bledsoes have given me a crash course the last few weeks. I'm really lucky that one good friend is the hostess and another is the chef. Both of them have been at the restaurant a long time." I looked up at him. "If they weren't at the Steak House, I'd probably be more scared. As it is, I'm looking forward to my new life. Do you really wish you hadn't started your book?"

"No. I'm glad I'm writing it, but every now and then, I wonder if I made the right decision." He sneezed again.

"Bless you, again," I said. "I guess you know Junior says you're the best writer he's ever known, and that your book will change the way the country sees the South."

Ben looked down, embarrassed by what I'd said. "Junior's the charter member of a very small fan club. But I do hope to give readers a different view of this part of the country, show them what makes the South tick now, how life has changed for blacks and whites. Our new president is from the South. That was something people said could never happen."

"Only people in the North said that," I pointed out, laughing.

"True. There's a lot about the region that's not understood." He slowly swung his legs back and forth over the counter edge as we talked.

"I heard you're not including anything about the days of the civil rights movement in your book. I don't want to tell you what to write, but how can you possibly do a book about the South without something about that time period? And here in Tallagumsa, especially? How can you ignore the murders?" I tried to sound lighthearted, to disguise the powerful emotions I still felt about the murders of Jimmy Turnbow and Leon Johnson, but my voice was shaking.

I looked away from him, out the wall of glass. It was a quiet day on the lake, only a few fishermen and one water skier.

"Junior told me you worked hard on getting that memorial built for Johnson and Turnbow. Look, I can't leave the civil rights movement out completely, but that's not my focus. Books on the movement have been done and done well. What's interesting to me is what brings you back here, a woman who obviously feels very strongly about the murders and civil rights. You, Junior, Barbara Cox—all came back. Why? Your husband, Eddie, doesn't seem a likely candidate for Tallagumsa life either, from what I've heard and from looking at his cartoons. I think the South today is something worth writing about."

He turned around, hopped off the counter, and poured two cups of coffee. "Sugar or cream?"

"No, thanks. Do you mind if I turn on the fan?" I pointed to the nearest ceiling fan, the one above the living-room couch near where I sat.

"Be my guest. It gets hot over there next to the glass about this time of day. The switch is behind the floor lamp, on the wall."

I turned the fan knob. "I think it's morally wrong to ignore what happened," I said, trying a different tack.

Ben pushed some papers on the table out of the way and placed the cups of coffee there. He sat down and rummaged in his cardboard file drawer. "A few years ago I did some detective work on the murders and I got some unilluminating documents from the FBI." He pulled out a thin file and lay it across his knees. "During the seventy-six presidential campaign, I wrote a series of articles on the civil rights movement. I was shocked at how many unsolved murders there still were in the Deep South. That's when Junior was at the Department of Justice. We talked about what had happened in Tallagumsa, and I made a Freedom of Information Act request to the FBI to get whatever they had on the murders. Here's what I got on Jimmy Turnbow and Leon Johnson." He pointed at the file, then rubbed his red, watering eyes.

"So you are interested! Good!"

"I'm really not. I could spend my life pursuing unsolved murders."

"And why not?" I asked. "Seems a worthy enough occupation to me." I tried the coffee. Too hot.

"But it's old news. I think most people involved are dead, and I know the rest don't give a damn."

"That's not true. Fifteen years isn't that long a time. Whoever did it is probably still around here, living a normal life, pretending to be a regular person. And I give a damn."

"This is going to sound strange coming from a reporter, LuAnn, but I'm sick of digging up dirt on people. That was my life in D.C. At least for a little while, I'd like to look at the positive side, the good things people are capable of." He looked at me as he sipped his coffee. His dark brown eyes were flecked with gold. "If I can survive these allergies," he added, sniffing.

"See no evil, right?" I covered my eyes with my hands.

"Give a guy a break. That's not what I'm saying. I know the issue is there, but I don't have to write about every issue in the world."

"What did you get from that—what kind of information request did you make?"

"Freedom of Information Act. FOIA, people call the statute. Here, you want to see what we got?" He handed me the file.

I flipped through the papers inside. They were on FBI stationery. On each page words and in some cases full sentences had been blacked out. "What is all this?" I asked, pointing.

"That's called redacting. It's what the government does when it's unwilling to reveal information supposedly for some legitimate reason. Usually it's just to protect someone, typically the government, from embarrassment."

The whole file consisted of four short memoranda. Fascinated by this opportunity for a glimpse of the inside workings of the FBI, I read them.

MEMO

To: Carl Best, Chief, Atlanta Field Office
From: Special Agent Dorr
Re: Jimmy Turnbow and Leon Johnson
Date: August 28, 1963

I have confirmed that ████████████████████
████████████████) in the murders. Thus I expect a

speedy resolution of the matter. Hopefully, the State of Alabama will bring indictments here. Perhaps they will be able to get convictions with the ████████████████████ ████████████ If the State refuses to go forward, however, as often occurs in these cases, this would definitely be a good candidate for federal civil rights charges.

MEMO

To: Carl Best, Chief, Atlanta Field Office
From: Special Agent Dorr
Re: Jimmy Turnbow and Leon Johnson
Date: August 30, 1963

██
██
██████████████ Agent Moon and I will attempt to interview ██████████████ and other possible witnesses. As always in this kind of case, if we can secure even one cooperative witness ██████████████████ we will be lucky, particularly here where, according to ████████████████████████
██
████████████████ Tallagumsa, Alabama, the town outside of which the killings occurred.

For what it's worth, there is a rumor around town that

██
████████████████

MEMO

To: Carl Best, Chief, Atlanta Field Office
From: Special Agent Dorr
Re: Jimmy Turnbow and Leon Johnson
Date: September 5, 1963

As you know, it appears that the shells found at the scene of the crime came from the ██████████████████████
██

As I mentioned over the phone, ███████████ ███████████ After spending a few days in town, we've discovered that ███████████ ███████████ ███████████ This was not a complete surprise. We had some reason to believe that ███████████ ███████████ In a similar Mississippi case ███████████ ███████████ ███████████

MEMO (marked URGENT AND CONFIDENTIAL)

To: David Metzger, Assistant to the Director
From: Carl Best, Chief, Atlanta Field Office
Re: Jimmy Turnbow and Leon Johnson
Date: September 7, 1963

We recommend strongly that the Bureau ███████████ ███████████ ███████████ ███████████ Without our involvement, they will not bring a case. As you pointed out, ███████████ Not only is our best evidence gone, but any trial might ███████████ Department ███████████ civil rights cases in the Deep South. ███████████ ███████████

A few more interviews have been scheduled, just to tie up loose ends. One is with ███████████ ███████████ ███████████

"They can just delete anything they don't like?" I asked, shaking my head. "That's outrageous."

"Yep," Ben said. "You get used to seeing documents like this in my line of work. The paper appealed, as a matter of course, but we'll never see anything else, I bet. We rarely do."

"Who did you appeal to?"

"I think the first appeal is to someone in the Justice Department."

"Reading about the murders is strange," I said. "When it happened I was twelve. I didn't even know the FBI was in town. No one ever told me. You know, these aren't totally useless. You have something to work with here."

Ben put the documents back in the file. "This is my work now," he said, waving his arm across the papers on the table. "And I have a lot of it. In fact, I'm spending the rest of today and the weekend summarizing the interviews I did in Charleston and Nashville. Then I'll get to you and the rest of your town. Would you like a sandwich or yogurt or something? I'm getting hungry."

"Thanks, but I already ate." I looked at my watch. "I told Jolene, our babysitter, I'd give her a break after lunch, so I'd better get going."

"You seem pretty relaxed for someone who has three little children," he said.

"Jolene is better than Mary Poppins, that's why. Do you have children?" I asked.

"No," he said.

"I'd bore you with pictures, but I left my purse in the car over at my parents'." "Next week you should stop by the Steak House and visit. I'll show you a picture of the kids then. You should also come for the good food and to talk to people. Everyone who's anyone in town is there at least once most days," I bragged.

"So I've heard. In fact, I'm meeting your father there on Monday morning. See you then." He extended his hand and smiled. "And good luck, though it doesn't sound like you're

going to need it. In fact, maybe you could send a little my way."
He turned to go inside.

"My pleasure," I said, giggling like a school girl. I wondered why I suddenly felt so lighthearted.

At my parents' dock, I hurriedly took off my shorts and shoes and dove in, unable to resist one more dip in the lake's cool, calm water.

CHAPTER EIGHT

The twins were two months old the day I began my new career as owner and manager of the Tallagumsa Steak House. Will still wasn't sleeping through the night and had woken up the night before the big day for a three o'clock feeding. Unfortunately, I couldn't get back to sleep after that, tossing and turning, excited about work. At six in the morning I left home in the pouring rain. Eddie and the kids were still asleep. Jolene would come a little before nine, when Eddie and Jessie would leave, Jessie for morning summer camp and Eddie for the college.

At the Steak House, I parked my car in a space in front and unlocked the double glass doors into the foyer. Inside, I closed my umbrella and shook it out, then turned the bolt back to lock the door for the few minutes remaining until we opened.

I said good morning to the portraits of Mimi and Howard Bledsoe that hung above the stairway to the second-floor dining rooms. The pictures, dedicated on the Bledsoes' last official day at the restaurant, were their son's idea. I hadn't had the heart to say no, even though they were ghastly. The background for Howard's was a pale wispy blue, for Mimi's a pale green. The artist had given the Bledsoes a strangely angelic look, as if they were already dead, not just retired.

Two waitresses were setting up for the breakfast rush in the front dining room. Like all the waitresses, they were dressed in identical mustard-colored uniforms, and their first names were embroidered in black above their left breast pockets: "Cleo" and "Doris."

"Good morning," I said.

"Morning, hon," Cleo responded.

Cleo was over sixty and had worked at the Steak House since the year she turned thirty, when her husband had died in a tractor accident, leaving her with six children to support. Doris was in her thirties and had worked at the restaurant twelve years.

"Ready for your big debut, Sugar?" Cleo asked, approaching me and kissing my cheek.

The smell of the hair spray that permitted Cleo's hair to defy gravity made my stomach churn. Maybe I did have stage fright after all.

"I guess," I said. "I hope."

"You'll do fine," Doris said, popping her gum.

I knew I didn't have to ask her to get rid of the gum when we opened at six-thirty. I was lucky to have a full staff of qualified and committed waitresses.

"You think business will be slow with this downpour?" I asked.

"There's no tellin'," Cleo replied.

I went into the coat room halfway down the hallway and opened the small storage door next to the cigarette machine. I took out four black rubber mats and carried them two at a time to the foyer, where I covered the floor with them. With the heavy rain, the foyer would soon be home to a messy, dangerous puddle.

While Cleo, Doris, and two other waitresses prepared for the breakfast rush, I climbed the five stairs to the restaurant office, a small room with windows on all four sides built on a raised platform in the hallway between the front and back dining rooms. A customer once told Howard Bledsoe that the office looked like a glass elevator from a Hyatt hotel stuck between the first and second floors.

I liked being up in the office, particularly during the busy hours at the Steak House. Inside the office was quiet but not too removed, and from it I could see both dining rooms and the kitchen.

I sat down at the beat-up wooden desk. From my large

shoulder bag I pulled two pictures, one of Eddie and me on our wedding day, one of Jessie and her twin brothers on the side-porch swing at our new home. I placed the photos on the desk between the old Smith-Corona typewriter and the phone.

Gazing at the handwritten list of lunch specials Roland had left on the desk, I opened the typewriter and began to type. At the top of "Today's Specials" I typed the date, "June 5, 1978." For appetizers Roland had listed tomato juice, cabbage and carrots, fried oysters, and a quarter head of iceberg lettuce; the main dishes were chopped steak with onions, fried catfish, barbecued chicken, sirloin patty, and corned beef hash; the vegetables were mashed potatoes, mixed vegetables, onion rings, fried okra, and black-eyed peas; and the desserts were key lime pie, pudding parfait, pineapple upside down cake, rainbow sherbet, and Boston cream pie.

I had talked to Roland about introducing more interesting and healthy food—"city food," he called it—and he'd agreed to give it a try, slowly, maybe one new entree a month. At the end of this month he'd agreed to try a pasta with salmon and asparagus. I knew he could cook it. The question was whether anyone would eat it.

I was halfway through typing the list of specials when a busload of gospel singers arrived for breakfast. I saw the line of customers filing in at the same time Cleo appeared at my office door begging for help. This was a part of the job I definitely knew. I had a ball.

A few hours and nearly two hundred breakfasts later, the dining room was quiet, deserted except for a few late breakfast customers. The Coffee Club members would arrive soon. Everyone else was off to work and errands or back on the road. I turned the "Hostess Will Seat You" sign inside the front door around so that it read "Please Seat Yourself."

I glanced behind the beige plastic lattice barrier that separated the dining room from the waitresses' station to check the progress of lunch preparations. In the glass-fronted refrigerator were four chocolate meringue, three lemon meringue, two key lime, and three Boston cream pies. The coffee creamers were cleaned and refilled. Plenty of chocolate and regular milk cartons were neatly stacked inside.

Only six of the twelve brown plastic butter tubs had been filled. I peeked around the corner into the back dining room, an area that didn't open each day until lunchtime. Two waitresses sat at a table finishing that job with the remaining butter tubs, sheets of butter squares, and a pail of crushed ice.

In my office, I completed the list of daily specials and copied it, clipping each copy into the menu of items we served every day. The menu cover featured a drawing of the main block of Tallagumsa, including SP Drugs, Smith Hardware, the Steak House, and Bowe's Department Store. I was considering a new cover one day, maybe something with an art deco design. A black, gold, and red geometric pattern would be nice, but I didn't want to make too make many changes too fast.

Like Perrier water. I'd asked the Bledsoes what they thought of adding mineral water to the menu.

They laughed. "Nobody in his right mind would pay more for water with bubbles in it than they pay for a Coca-Cola."

"Good point," I said.

When I'd assured myself that I had time to relax for a few minutes, I sat down in the Bledsoes' booth—now *my booth*. With one leg tucked under me, I chatted with several customers who stopped by the booth, looked at the morning newspaper, and drank a cup of coffee.

Every table was set with table mats, flatware, and napkins, ready and waiting for the lunch customers. Only three tables were occupied. One of the busboys was mopping the foyer. Outside, the rain fell steadily.

I had always loved the morning lull. It was like the eye of a storm. We knew the peace and quiet was only temporary, usually lasting about an hour and a half, maybe two. Then, suddenly, a steady stream of people would rush in, eat, and leave. Just as suddenly calm would again prevail, and we'd all collapse. People seemed to magically appear and disappear.

I felt content in a way I had not in a long time. This was the ideal job. Was is it possible to know something so quickly, so surely? I did.

When my father came in early for his coffee break, I jumped up and greeted him at the door. "Thanks," I said, throwing my arms around his neck.

He kissed my cheek, grinned, and asked, "For what?"

"My job, the house, Jolene. Everything!" I gushed.

"It *was* my idea, wasn't it?" he said. "Damn, I'm smart. Now get me a cup of coffee and sit and talk to me for a while—if you have time."

"You're so modest, Daddy," I joked. "Coffee coming up."

The other Coffee Club members arrived within ten minutes. After a brief visit, I went back to my booth to eat something. Ben Gainey came in, waved hello to me, then sat down with the group of men for thirty minutes. He took notes in his steno pad and recorded some parts of their conversations on his tape recorder. The members of the Coffee Club obviously loved the attention. There was more than the usual laughing and loud talking from the wall booth that morning.

After the last of the Coffee Club members left, Ben walked over to my booth.

"Mind if I join you?" he asked. He set the tape recorder and steno pad on the corner of my table.

"Why, if it isn't Mr. See No Evil." I covered my eyes with my hands.

"Are you going to give me a hard time about that forever?"

"Maybe. You're an easy target. How are your allergies?"

"Much better, thanks. The pharmacist took pity on me Saturday and gave me a miracle drug."

"Is this an official or an unofficial visit?" I asked.

"Both: I need a good breakfast, and I'd like to start talking to you for the book."

"Have a seat then. I have a few minutes. It's pretty late to be eating breakfast, isn't it?"

"What's that you're eating?" he asked, referring to the slice of cinnamon toast I'd fixed after my visit with my father.

"Just a snack. I ate at five-thirty."

"I must admit I was sound asleep then—at six-thirty too."

"You didn't just get up, did you? What a cushy job." I smiled at him.

"I've been up—awhile, anyway. I swam in the lake, reviewed some notes, called the *Star,* and rushed over here to catch those guys before they left."

"The Coffee Club, you mean."

"Is that what they're called?"

"That's what most people call them."

"How long has there been a Coffee Club?" he asked.

"Forever, I guess. I know some of them were coming here when I was in high school. Different ones over the years, but there's always five or ten men sitting there, same time, same place, every day."

"They're helpful."

"Good, because from the looks of this morning they're going to make you talk to them again whether you want to or not." I laughed, then stood up. "You better tell me what you want for breakfast. It'll be too late to get it in a minute."

He gave me his order.

"Study this map while I'm in the kitchen. When I get back I'll answer questions about hot spots," I said, pushing the Steak House placemat toward him.

The placemat displayed a map of the state of Alabama outlined in black against a mustard background (the same mustard as the waitresses' uniforms) and included numerous points of interest, such as the capitol building in Montgomery, the Ave Maria Grotto, Vulcan, and the Boll Weevil Monument. Across the bottom border of the mat were the words THE HEART OF DIXIE in bold black letters. The same design had graced the placemats for over a decade. Mimi Bledsoe told me that one of the placemat salesmen had wanted to put the Steak House on the map, as if it were a state monument, but she'd thought that would be tacky.

When Estelle got to work at two that afternoon, I left the Steak House. As much as I wanted a nap, I wanted more to spend the time I had at home before the dinner rush with the children.

The rain had stopped during lunch, and the air was warm and muggy as we walked around the neighborhood. The twins were in their double stroller and Jessie was next to me. The neighbors we passed stopped and admired the children, receiving in return wide toothless grins from Will and Hank and a glowing smile from Jessie.

Not all the homes were Tudors, like ours. A few were colonials, and a few old southern Victorians. On each side of the block there were only three or four homes, each with spacious, beautifully maintained yards full of huge old azaleas and dogwoods, their blooms gone weeks ago and replaced by the flowering crape myrtles, hydrangeas, and delphiniums.

Darrell, Jolene's son, was doing our yard work when we returned to the house. He was bent over the lawn mower, pouring gas into the tank.

I fed Will and Hank bottles in the den, then put them in their cribs upstairs and watched for a few minutes as they tried to figure out what their hands were. The week before they'd discovered they had hands, Hank a day before Will. Since then, both of them were obsessed. They brought their hands together, spread them apart out of sight, brought them back again, and pulled on the fingers, repeating the process again and again until they grew sleepy.

I put Will's pacifier in his mouth. We'd finally gotten him to relax a bit with the pacifier. Of course, when he couldn't find it you could hear him all over the house, but sometimes the pacifier seemed to calm whatever was irritating him.

I left the boys to sleep and sat with Jessie in her room, surrounded by her collection of Barbie dolls. We played "Barbie moves away" over and over again until Caroline Cook, Jessie's new friend from next door arrived to play with her.

Jessie was adjusting to the move beautifully. She had her Granddaddy and Glady, her aunt Jane and uncle Buck, and Jolene, all heaping gobs of attention on her. She was only away from home three hours a day, compared to the eight or ten she'd spent in day care in Atlanta. Her camp and nursery school friends were also neighbors, and she'd quickly become part of the gang. She had everything to be happy about.

I went back to the restaurant at six, about the time Eddie was due home. When I left, Jolene was cooking dinner for the children and him. She'd leave when he arrived.

Driving to the Steak House, I felt as though I were deserting the children, leaving them at dinnertime without me or Eddie. I didn't plan on keeping this schedule forever, but had little choice for the time being. At that moment, I wished Eddie hadn't taken the teaching job, or that he could have waited until fall to begin. Then he could have been home while I put in all the hours at the restaurant.

I didn't allow this minor concern to dampen my enthusiasm, however, and when I walked into the Steak House for the dinner rush I paused briefly at the door to watch the scene inside. Waitresses were bustling around the front dining room, serving the forty or so diners. Two busboys were cleaning the remains from dinners already completed.

When a guest enters a busy, successful restaurant he is drawn in by the smell of good food, the sight of content diners and happy waitresses, and the sound of animated, interesting conversations. He sees a club he wants to join.

I shivered with delight. My restaurant. My hometown. I was back where I belonged.

CHAPTER NINE

W hy did the biggest, most important event in Tallagumsa history have to be in the upstairs dining rooms of the Steak House barely a month after I took over? I tried to convince my father and Buck that Daddy should announce he was running for governor in Birmingham, the closest big city, or in Montgomery, the capital, or anywhere else. I told them I wasn't ready after only a month, that the event might be a disaster. Neither listened to a word I said. I viewed their response as either a great vote of confidence or a sure sign of madness.

It was settled, though, and as the days of preparation passed, Buck nearly drove me mad too. He came by the Steak House daily, sometimes two or three times, with this or that screwball idea, order, or concern. This menu, that wine. This seating arrangement, that schedule. His demands never seemed to end.

Two days before the dinner party Buck rushed into the kitchen looking as if he might be on the verge of a sunstroke, his face beet-red, his shirt wet with sweat.

The dog days of summer in Alabama had begun. Every day was over ninety degrees, dead still and humid. The dog days were said to last forty straight days. If that was true, we had thirty-five to go, and Buck didn't look as if he'd last that long.

"We have to find a movie star to come to the dinner," he proclaimed.

"We don't know any," I pointed out.

"Everybody gets stars or country singers or somebody," he insisted.

"Wait here, Buck," I said. I went to my office and called

Daddy, asking him to come over and stop Buck before I killed him.

Daddy appeared within ten minutes, lectured Buck on the difference between a campaign manager and a Hollywood agent, and ordered him to leave me alone.

Buck finally calmed down a tiny bit after I talked Ben Gainey into writing an article on the election and my father for the *Washington Star*.

I didn't understand what Buck was so frantic about. My father had been elected mayor four times, with eighty percent of the vote each time. As a result of his generous work on behalf of most of the Democratic candidates in other parts of the state, he was well known outside Tallagumsa. There was no other credible candidate running for governor. The Democratic party was solidly behind him, and no Republican had been elected governor of the state in over one hundred years.

I wasn't worried at all about my father getting elected, but I was haunted by all the things that could go wrong at the dinner. The morning of the event I couldn't sit still, and I left Ben, who often joined me at my booth during the morning lull, sitting alone eating his late breakfast.

I rushed through the kitchen doors to check once again on preparations for the party.

Inside the kitchen, Estelle was removing large rectangular aluminum trays of dinner rolls and sweet rolls from the oven and dumping them, tray-by-tray, into the bread warmer. She looked a little silly wearing the oversized silver and red oven mitts on her small hands.

Behind the stainless-steel island that separated the waitresses from the ovens, the grills, and the cooks, I saw evidence of Roland's presence. Bacon and meat patties were frying on the grill, corn was cooking on the stove, and piles of French fries sat next to the grill, waiting to go into the deep fryer. But there was no Roland.

I walked up behind Estelle and gently tickled her back. "I don't think I'll survive until tonight," I said.

Estelle turned around. "It's going to be fine. No different than the Lions Club dinners."

"Except it's twice as big and four million times more important." I pretended to hyperventilate and patted my chest.

"I mean the food and the logistics," she said. "We've done this thousands of times. Don't worry."

"But you're working on lunch now, not the party," I said. "Shouldn't you do something about tonight? Just forget lunch! Maybe we should have closed for the day."

"It's not even eleven, LuAnn. Relax. Take a break. Go home."

Roland came out of the walk-in refrigerator, carrying a pack of chops. He walked to the grill and picked up a large spatula. As he flipped the meat patties over, grease splattered on his white apron. He moved the hamburger patties off the grill and snapped his fingers. "Shit!" he said. "I forgot to call that new fish distributor."

"Wonderful," I said sarcastically. "That'll be interesting. A dinner with no main course."

"All is well," Roland said, but I didn't believe him.

Estelle watched Roland walk out, appeared to think about something, then spoke. "Can I ask you something?" she asked softly, moving up close to me.

"Sure."

"What's going on with you and Ben Gainey?" Her mouth was set in a determined line.

"What do you mean?" I asked.

"He's here all the time, sitting with you at your booth, talking to you in your office. You go off with him all the time, and, well, it's starting to look funny."

"Are you saying I'm not working hard enough or that you think I'm fooling around with Ben Gainey? Or both?" I asked angrily. "Maybe I've cut back a little on the hours here, but not much. The restaurant's running smoothly and doesn't need my constant attention anymore. So what if I spend a few of those freed-up hours with Ben, helping him with his work?"

"I'm concerned, that's all, and I thought you should know," Estelle said. "Seems like when you aren't at your booth with him, you're off helping him meet people or showing him the town or riding horses with him or something. You do some of his typing. You make calls for him. You set up his appointments. You're always together, LuAnn."

"I can't believe you of all people would be worried about me."

"Look, I just felt like I had to bring it up, friend to friend." She removed her oven mitts and hung them on the wall hook.

"This conversation is helping me remember why I wanted out of Tallagumsa, Estelle," I said. "Remember when we were seniors? We talked about how you can't breathe around here without everyone knowing and then gossiping about it. First of all, he's a customer, and it's my job to be nice to my customers. I also think his work is fascinating. He needs my help, and I'm happy and flattered to give it. I enjoy listening to his interviews and hearing about his work. That's all. He's smart and he's fun and we're friends. Period."

"Fine, fine," Estelle said. "I just had to ask you, or I'd feel like I'd shirked my duties as your best friend. I don't want you to get yourself into something you can't get out of, LuAnn. You know—"

She stopped talking as the kitchen door swung open and Doris, who was working lunch and dinner that day, walked by us, popping her gum. She went behind the stainless-steel island, piled a plate high with food, grabbed two corn sticks from the bread warmer, and went into the back dining room to eat her own lunch before the lunch rush began.

"Estelle," I said, "I'm married, happily married."

"But you and Eddie haven't been spending any time together lately, none as far as I can see, and the way Ben looks at you, anyone can tell he's smitten. Don't you think it's possible that—"

"No, I don't," I interrupted. "Ben is my friend. That's all. Just like you are. Forget about it."

"You two ladies do not look happy," Roland said when he returned through the swinging door. "So what's going on? What are y'all so upset about?"

"Nothing!" I said.

"Doesn't sound like nothing," Roland said.

Estelle moved to one of the stainless-steel work areas, where she began to crack eggs, carefully separating the yolks from the whites for pie meringue. A small mountain of egg shells grew next to her right arm.

"Tell me," Roland begged.

"It's nothing!" I insisted. "Did you talk to the fish guy?"

"Yes," Roland said. "Dinner is under control, considering I have to cook city food."

"Leaf and romaine lettuce are not city food. Neither is tuna steak with bell peppers and mushrooms. They are just good, healthy food." I sighed. "Maybe I've made the menu too complicated. Do y'all really think tonight's going to work out?"

"We've told you a hundred times to stop worrying about tonight," Estelle said.

"I will if you stop worrying about me," I said. "Can you meet me upstairs in twenty minutes to start setting up, Estelle? First I'm going to clean the check-out counter. It's a mess up there, and it's the first thing all our guests will see."

"Sure, boss," Estelle said.

"Oh, and Buck is bringing by that gigantic picture of Daddy to hang behind the speaker's table, plus he has something for every place setting—a commemorative thing, a pen or something. He should be here soon. Do we have all the waitresses and busboys we need lined up?"

"Yes, yes, yes," Estelle said. "Believe it or not, I know what I'm doing here."

"Thanks," I said. I gave her a quick hug. "Sorry I got a little mad," I whispered in her ear.

"No whispering in my kitchen," Roland called out, "unless I'm included." He laughed.

Kneeling down behind the check-out counter, I moved cigars, Life Savers, and candy bars out, cleaned the glass shelves with Windex, refilled the boxes, and put them back. I was directly visible to anyone four feet tall or less.

Someone standing in front of the counter cleared their throat. "LuAnn," a familiar voice called, "could you get up and take my money please? I have a trial in five minutes."

"Just a sec, Junior," I said. I pushed myself up, holding on to the top of the cashier's stool for support. "Who are you putting in jail today?"

He handed me his check and a five. His top shirt button was open under his tie. It had always been difficult for him to find shirts that would close comfortably around his thick neck.

"Nobody," he said. "Taking a kid away from his crazy father and trying to find a place for a teenager who can't stop stealing. That's all I have on the docket for today."

He picked up a handful of thinly wrapped toothpicks from the fake gold bowl on the counter, each wrapper bearing the name of the Steak House, and stuck them in his jacket pocket.

I counted out his change. "One, two, three, four, and that makes five. You happy with your work here, Junior?"

"I sure am."

"Don't you miss D.C.? All the excitement, the big cases, politics, all that stuff?"

"Not really. I feel like I'm having an impact here. And it's nice and quiet, safe and predictable. You know me: I like life a little slower than some. I'm happy."

"I hear you may be using Tallagumsa as a stepping stone to something bigger," I said.

He shrugged and smiled. "We'll see." Then he folded one of the dollars I'd just given him several times over and pushed it through the narrow opening in the plastic container attached to the York mint-patty display. "I love these," Junior said, picking up a handful of mints. "How 'bout you, LuAnn? Restaurant life suit you?"

"I think so. Except for this to-do tonight. I hope I don't embarrass Daddy with bad food or lousy service on his big night. Are you coming?"

"Wouldn't miss it for the world. I'm sure it will be a success. You're doing a great job, LuAnn. Everybody says so."

"Thanks, Junior."

"See you tonight." He patted my hand gently, his large hand covering mine. Then he ambled away.

I knelt back down and finished restocking the top shelf of the cabinet with M&M's, Hershey Bars, Baby Ruths, and Butterfingers and tried to remember why I'd been so madly in love with Junior all through high school. Although I was fond of him now, I wasn't attracted to him in the least. Not for the first time I wondered: What made love come, what made love go?

That afternoon I hadn't been home from work even an hour when it was time to dress and go back to the Steak House. The party preparations and the heat had left me feeling very frazzled. I'd tried to leave earlier, in time to fit in a nap, but there'd been too many details to attend to.

Jolene bathed the children while I tried to choose an outfit. Usually I knew what to wear to a party, but that night, the more I stared at my clothes, the less I knew what would be right. Buck had instructed me carefully on what the children, Eddie, and I should wear for all the photo ops of the campaign, but I didn't own much that fit within his narrow range of approved clothes.

Five outfits lay across my bed. I had placed matching shoes at the ends of pants legs and a foot or so below the hems of skirts and dresses. It looked like a party was in progress. Only the bodies were missing.

After trying on every outfit, I was no closer to a final decision than when I started. Each seemed worse than the one before, and I felt bone tired, tired of lifting one arm after the other, picking up one leg, then the next, tired of buttoning buttons and zipping zippers. Dressed only in my underwear, I flopped down in the armchair by the bed, pushed the footstool away, and crossed my bare legs and feet Indian style. The next thing I knew, something brushed against my arm and woke me from a sound sleep.

Jessie held her "magic wand," a star made of a silver clothlike material that sparkled in the sunlight as though someone had covered it with glue and dipped it over and over again into a vat of sparkles until it seemed to explode with light. When she waved the wand, the purple ribbons attached to it had floated through the air and tickled me awake.

"Hey, honey," I said. "You look beautiful!" She had on a new dress from her aunt Jane, a sleeveless summer dress in a yellow, green, and lavender floral pattern with a giant yellow bow in back.

I looked at the clock. Five. Cocktails were at six, so I should already have been back at the restaurant. I'd slept for thirty minutes. "Where's Daddy, Jessie?" I asked.

She shrugged.

"Is he home from work?"

"No."

"He's working so hard, isn't he? You know why? His show is coming up soon. He'll hang all his best cartoons up at the college and people from all over can come and look at them," I said. What I was thinking, though, was that I'd never forgive him if he didn't get home soon. He knew I'd need help getting the kids to the Steak House. He knew it was important that we arrive together.

"Like the ones he draws for me?" Jessie asked, leaning against the bed. She had a scrapbook of cartoons Eddie had made just for her over the years, cartoons featuring Jessie and various members of our family.

"Exactly." I stood up and started to dress.

"Does he need mine?" she asked, a worried look on her face.

"No, sweetie, he has plenty of his own." The cartoons Eddie had finally chosen for the show had been framed the week

97

before and delivered to the college. The right side of Eddie's studio bulletin board was now empty.

"Jolene," I yelled as soon as I was dressed. After all that agonizing, I had chosen the outfit I'd started with. Buck would approve of the simple black linen dress, pearls, and black high heels.

"Yes?" she yelled back.

"Are the twins ready?"

"Just about."

"Great. We've got to get going. Will you come with me over to the Steak House and help with the kids until Eddie arrives? Please? I'm desperate."

I knew she'd say yes.

Jessie and I gathered the twins' diaper bags, bottles, a few plastic toys they liked to hold and suck, and the baskets they sometimes slept in. We put the things in the trunk of the car. I went back in for Will, stopping to grab a few extra pacifiers from his crib just in case, and Jolene picked up Hank.

Jolene and I walked out of the house with the boys. I grabbed the wrought-iron porch railing to steady myself—I wasn't used to walking in high heels. I never wore them to work. Hobbling a little, I reached the car, strapped the kids in, and drove us all to the Steak House.

My mother and father were seated in the middle of the head table as the guests of honor. Next to Daddy was Senator Harold Collins and his wife, Sally, then Buck and Jane. The present governor, Stu Gordon, and his wife, Didi, were on Mother's side, then Jessie and I. The oversized photograph of Daddy hung right behind us. Ben and Junior were at a table with a group of press people from around the state. A few photographers roamed the room, snapping pictures for different publications.

The cocktail hour had ended. The soup course had come and gone. Eddie still hadn't arrived.

He walked in just as the salad was being served, said hello to everyone at the head table, kissed me and Jessie, and sat down, no apology at all. He wore his usual jeans, a button-down shirt, and a tie.

"Go down and tell Jolene she can leave, then bring the twins' baskets up here," I hissed, furious at his timing.

"What's wrong with you?" he asked.

"What do you think?"

"I was busy at school, okay? I didn't realize how late it was. At least I'm here. There are a lot of other places I'd rather be."

"That's flattering," I said, smiling for the benefit of the people eating at the tables in front of the speakers' table.

He glared at me.

"Smile when you talk," I ordered Eddie.

"You know what I meant," he said. "I'd prefer anywhere to a bullshit political function. Why do I have to smile?"

"You're impossible," I said. "Just go tell Jolene."

I slipped my high heels off and walked around in my stocking feet, helping the waitresses clean up after the last guest left a little before ten. Jessie was coloring in a Raggedy Ann coloring book with her aunt Jane, who was still pregnant, thank goodness. My father and Buck were discussing the opening of the campaign: who'd come, who hadn't, what it all meant. Eddie sat at the far end of the room near the sleeping twins, smoking a Salem.

"Could I give you a hand?" Mother asked me as I piled silverware on a large round serving tray.

"Don't be silly," I said. "You just relax. I'm not going to work much longer."

Mother sat down near Buck and Daddy and placed her glasses on the table. She stared off into space, twisting her wedding band around her finger over and over.

When I was too tired to be of any further help, I approached Eddie. "I'm ready. You want to take Jessie home?" I asked. "I'll take the twins in the Toyota."

"I don't have my car," he said. "I left it at the shop this morning, remember?"

"I thought you got it. How'd you get here?"

"Barbara brought me. We came straight from the college."

"How sweet," I said.

"What are you sounding so nasty about? Jesus! All night you have been a total bitch."

"Can we just go?" I said.

As we walked out the Steak House doors, Ben's BMW pulled up to the curb. He rolled down his window and held out a large manila envelope to me. "I forgot to give you this tonight. The results of the appeal. There's more information from the FBI, but not much. I thought you'd be more interested than I am." he said.

I peeked inside. It was the FBI documents I'd seen at his house. "Thanks! I'll read them tonight."

"What's that?" Eddie asked as we strapped the children in my car.

"I'll tell you later," I said.

Eddie drove. I tried to read by the light of the overhead lamp. Far fewer words were blacked out in this set of memos:

MEMO

To: Carl Best, Chief, Atlanta Field Office
From: Special Agent Dorr
Re: Jimmy Turnbow and Leon Johnson
Date: August 28, 1963

I have confirmed that a Bureau informant, Dean Reese, was in the car involved in the murders. Thus I expect a speedy resolution of the matter. Hopefully, the State of Alabama will bring indictments here. Perhaps they will be able to get convictions with the help of Reese's eyewitness testimony. If the State refuses to go forward, however, as often occurs in these cases, this would definitely be a good candidate for federal civil rights charges.

Eddie switched off the car light. "The boys might wake up," he said.

I didn't argue.

After we got the children settled in bed, I took off my shoes and stockings, fixed a glass of iced tea, and sat down at the kitchen table to finish reading.

MEMO

To: Carl Best, Chief, Atlanta Field Office
From: Special Agent Dorr
Re: Jimmy Turnbow and Leon Johnson
Date: August 30, 1963

Dean Reese has provided me with the ▓▓▓▓▓▓▓▓
▓▓▓▓▓▓▓▓▓▓▓▓▓▓▓▓▓▓▓▓▓▓▓▓▓▓▓▓▓▓▓▓▓▓▓
▓▓▓▓▓▓▓▓▓▓ Agent Moon and I will attempt to interview each of them and other possible witnesses. As always in this kind of case, if we can secure even one cooperative witness (in addition to Reese) we will be lucky, particularly here where, according to Reese, ▓▓▓▓▓▓▓▓▓▓▓▓▓
▓▓▓▓▓▓▓▓▓▓▓▓▓▓▓▓▓▓▓▓▓▓▓▓▓▓▓▓▓▓▓▓▓▓▓
▓▓▓▓▓▓▓▓▓▓▓▓Tallagumsa, Alabama, the town outside of which the killings occurred.

For what it's worth, there is a rumor around town that they were shot by someone whose daughter was involved with one of them.

MEMO

To: Carl Best, Chief, Atlanta Field Office
From: Special Agent Dorr
Re: Jimmy Turnbow and Leon Johnson
Date: September 5, 1963

As you know, it appears that the shells found at the scene of the crime came from the ▓▓▓▓▓▓▓▓▓▓▓▓▓ which Reese turned over to us. ▓▓▓▓▓▓▓▓▓▓▓▓▓▓▓▓▓
▓▓▓▓▓▓▓▓▓▓▓▓▓▓▓▓▓▓▓▓▓▓▓▓▓▓▓▓▓▓▓▓▓▓▓

As I mentioned over the phone, we may have serious problems here. After spending a few days in town, we've discovered that Reese has a reputation for being an extremely unstable alcoholic, someone who is known for violent and unpredictable behavior. This was not a complete surprise. We had some reason to believe that there were problems with Reese. In a similar Mississippi case his evidence proved unreliable. We had kept him on the payroll though because we had no one else in the area. I have set up a meeting with him tonight.

MEMO (marked URGENT AND CONFIDENTIAL)
To: David Metzger, Assistant to the Director
From: Carl Best, Chief, Atlanta Field Office
Re: Jimmy Turnbow and Leon Johnson
Date: September 7, 1963

We recommend strongly that the Bureau ████████████ ██ ███████ and that we ███████████ any of the information gathered ████████████████████████████████. Without our involvement, they will not bring a case. As you pointed out, Reese's suicide ████████████████████████████. Not only is our best evidence gone, but any trial might ████ ████████████████████████ De- partment ████████████████████████████████████ ██████ civil rights cases in the Deep South. ███████████ █████████████

A few more interviews have been scheduled, just to tie up loose ends. One is with Liz Reese, the wife. It is unclear whether she'll cooperate. We understand that the Reeses' marriage was a very troubled one.

I couldn't remember exactly what was included in the documents this time that hadn't been in the documents I'd seen at Ben's, but I was sure Dean Reese and all the information relating to him hadn't been mentioned at all in the earlier version. Miss Reese's husband had been an FBI informant! I put the papers back in the envelope, picked up the phone, and called Ben.

"Did you read these?" I asked as soon as he answered.

"Yes," he answered.

"It's great stuff," I said.

"I told you that everyone involved was dead. Dean Reese is dead."

"Yes, but these memos are full of leads. You could talk to his wife, follow up on this Mississippi thing, play detective."

"You know his wife?"

"No. Daddy does, I think. Ever hear of Miss Reese's Pies? That's her. She moved away around the time Dean Reese killed himself. Reading these just now from beginning to end, you can see the FBI started out real optimistic about making a case and then they up and ran off. Something sounds fishy to me. Don't you think so?"

"No, I don't. I think it's pretty obvious why they left town: Their evidence killed himself," Ben said.

"But what about this Mississippi case they mention that Reese was involved in, and what about the possibility the murderer's daughter dated Leon or Jimmy?"

"LuAnn," Ben interrupted.

"Yes?"

"I am not going to get into all that. I have a book contract and my own plans, and I don't really want to learn anything else about some violent alcoholic who's dead."

"Who sent you these documents?" I asked.

"My editor."

"What does he think?"

"He thinks that the only reason the Justice Department gave

us this much is that Dean Reese is dead and there's nothing else there."

"If there's nothing else there, then why'd they leave so much of these blacked out?"

"I'm tired," Ben said. "We'll talk later. The *Star* is going to appeal the case again, just as a matter of course, but that's to the district court, and appeals there take years."

"Years? Can't we make the appeal go faster?"

"No. I'll tell you why when I come in for breakfast."

"See you tomorrow," I said reluctantly. "We'll talk more then."

"Your dad?" Eddie asked.

I was surprised to see Eddie standing in the kitchen doorway in his jeans; no shirt, shoes, or socks. He watched me as I hung up the phone.

"Reliving the high points of his speech?" he asked wryly.

I shook my head.

"Your mother?"

"No."

"Who was it?"

"Ben Gainey."

He looked at the clock on the kitchen wall. "At eleven at night? You already talked to him most of the evening at the Steak House. What's so important now?"

"There were some FBI documents in the envelope he gave me. Remember the ones I told you about that I saw right before I went back to work? You want to see them? They're pretty amazing." I picked up the envelope and offered it to him.

"Not really."

"But they're about the murders of Leon Johnson and Jimmy Turnbow, Eddie."

"Why do *you* have them?"

"Ben's not interested in it, but I am, so he gave them to me."

"Running a restaurant and raising three children doesn't keep you busy enough? You just have to stick your nose into everything."

"That's not it. I thought you'd be interested too. You always said it was important to bring their killers to justice. The memorial was your idea, as you insisted on reminding me the day of the courthouse dedication."

"Do you have a date with Ben tomorrow?" Eddie asked matter-of-factly.

"Of course not. Why would you say that?" Estelle's morning lecture replayed in my mind.

"Because you said 'see you tomorrow' to him."

"Oh, that. He comes by for breakfast most mornings, as do many people. I see him then. I work there, remember?"

"Maybe I should start coming in for breakfast."

"Fine with me," I said. "You've only eaten there three times since I took over. Be nice to see you for a change."

He turned and walked away.

I refilled my iced tea, pulled the documents out of the envelope, and reread them until I thought Eddie was probably asleep, then undressed, got in bed, and lay with my back to him. He began to stroke my back. I cringed, my stomach tightened, and I drew myself into a fetal position.

"Night," I said. "I'm really tired." I wasn't the least bit tired, but I was too angry with him to make love.

"How unusual," he said.

I didn't say anything when he got up, dressed, and left the house. I must have been asleep when he returned.

CHAPTER TEN

C all her Miss Edwina," I advised Ben. "Everybody does."

"Whatever you say, boss," Ben said.

"And you have to yell," I said. "She's pretty deaf. But her mind's all there. She is truly a grand old lady, with more stories than anyone I know."

Because Miss Edwina had lived here ninety-three years, Ben hoped she could provide a unique historical perspective on Tallagumsa.

I'd offered to ride out to her farm with him after she'd made it clear that she wouldn't talk to him without me there and because I enjoyed watching Ben work. In the back seat was a box lunch for her that I'd packed at the Steak House, where Estelle was covering for me until I returned.

It was another sweltering day, but in deference to my aversion to car air conditioners Ben had turned his off and rolled down all the windows. The thick hot air blowing through the car offered little relief from the heat.

"Are you going to go to Mississippi soon?" I asked.

"Wasn't planning on it," he said. "Why?"

"To check on the Dean Reese connection. The FBI document mentioned a similar Mississippi case. Remember?"

"Forget it."

"I can't. Yesterday Jessie and I returned some books she'd checked out to the library, and while we were there I did some quick research on unsolved Mississippi civil rights murders during the spring of 1963. There was Medgar Evers, shot in June, and a drive-by shooting into a black church in May that injured

106

several people. But nothing about Dean Reese in any newspaper. I also tried to call his wife when I got home. She's in Europe on business. I left my name and number."

"Why are you so set on solving this case, LuAnn?"

"I don't know. I guess there are a lot of reasons. It's hard to be white in the South and not feel guilty for all the horrible things that happened even if you weren't personally involved. But Daddy was sheriff when Jimmy and Leon were killed, and he was really, really upset over it. And I worked hard raising the money for the memorial, planning for it, and getting it built. Meeting Leon's and Jimmy's families and friends was what really hooked me, though. I spent a lot of time with them during the planning stages for the memorial and we became friends. Maybe it's everything. I just feel somehow personally responsible for helping solve the case and seeing that justice is done. That's why I bug you and why I'll continue to bug you, Mr. See No Evil."

Ben slowed down his BMW and looked at me. "You are one determined woman."

"I know," I said. "I'll get you into this one way or the other. You might as well give up now."

"We'll see," he said, laughing.

I directed him to make a left turn immediately after the turn I took when I came out to ride Glory.

In the distance, down the gravel road lined by weeping willow trees, was Miss Edwina's house.

The house, partially hidden by several large magnolias, was a one-story clapboard farmhouse onto which the family had added a bedroom here and a den there over the years. It was in pristine shape, maintained by her four living children, twelve grandchildren, and multitudes of great-grandchildren. Two of the grown grandchildren lived with her in the house. Others had built homes nearby.

The gravel driveway wound past the rose gardens and bird feeders and ended in a circular drive in front of the house.

Edwina hobbled to the front door to greet us. She was a large old woman. With each step she leaned to one side, took a shallow breath, then lifted the other foot, and with great effort moved forward. Her breasts formed the beginning of a large mound that continued uninterrupted down to her waist. Her hairline and hands were splattered with liver spots. She wore tennis shoes, carefully pressed blue jeans, and a sweat shirt. Her long gray hair was braided, and the braid was twisted neatly around the top of her head like a halo.

I presented the box lunch, hugged her, and introduced Ben.

"You look adorable," I said.

"Shoot," Edwina said, waving her hand as though swatting at a fly. "I look silly! My great-grandchildren want me to be 'in,' they said. 'In' what? I asked, but these clothes are comfortable. There's no denying that. I told them, 'At least you didn't give me hot pants!' " She laughed and turned toward Ben. "You didn't tell me he was such a handsome young man, LuAnn."

"Why Miss Edwina!"

"I may be old," Edwina responded, "but I'm not dead!"

All three of us laughed.

"Go get the iced tea, dear," she said to me. "Everything's all set out in the kitchen."

A few moments later, Ben and I were seated on the couch, Edwina on the matching love seat, each of us with an iced tea.

Ben explained to Edwina about the book he was writing and asked her to talk about what life was like here, anything she remembered, anything that stood out.

The tape recorder whirred and Ben jotted down some notes in his steno pad as Edwina spoke about the year electric lights came to town, the toilet her family had on the back porch, the Sears & Roebuck catalog pages that papered the inside walls of the house, and the red brick streets in town, torn up and paved in the late thirties. She related her baptism in a creek that was long gone and how their church met in a barn. She said she had every one of her babies without a doctor (an old black midwife named Early had helped), the first baby born when she was barely fifteen.

Ben was content for the most part to let her speak, asking a question occasionally when Edwina temporarily lost the flow of her story.

"How do you like these dog days?" Edwina asked Ben out of the blue.

"The heat, you mean?" he asked.

"Not just the heat. During the dog days mockingbirds don't sing, rattlesnakes strike anything that moves within their reach, cuts don't heal, and dogs go mad."

"Sounds serious," Ben said.

"We used to warn our children to stay away from strange dogs, in case they might be mad, and we locked up pets and hunting dogs so they wouldn't get in fights with rabid dogs. If you heard that there was a mad dog in town during the dog days, why that'd scare the living daylights out of everybody."

After a few hours Edwina began to wind down and Ben moved her gently into the present, asking whom she planned to vote for in the gubernatorial election. Edwina confided that she'd vote for my father. I could see that the interview was coming to an end. Edwina's eyelids were fluttering slightly and Ben was leafing through his notes. On a hunch, I asked her if she knew anything about the murders. I knew Ben wouldn't even mention it, and when I did he looked at me and rolled his eyes.

"Why would I know anything about that?" Edwina asked.

"It doesn't matter," Ben said quickly. "Of course you wouldn't."

"Well, son, I do know one thing about it, as a matter of fact," she said. She smiled at the surprised looks on our faces. "I don't guess it'll do any harm to tell you now, since he's dead. I think he's dead, anyway."

Was she talking about Dean Reese? I wondered.

She stopped for a moment to think. "I'm sure he is. Well, I'll tell you what it was. I heard that the FBI paid a visit on Floyd Waddy in Cullman and asked him some questions about it."

Floyd Waddy! "He's definitely dead," I said. He had been a good friend of my father's.

"I wasn't real sure because I didn't even know Floyd, but his wife's mother was best friends with my sister Haddie, bless her heart. That's how I came to hear of the FBI," Edwina explained. "Get me some more iced tea, LuAnn, hon."

As I stood up, I tried to suppress a grin. This was a real lead Ben couldn't possibly ignore. "I'll set out your lunch for you too," I said.

"I don't believe those nigger boys deserved what they got," Edwina was saying when I returned, "but they should have known something like that probably would happen."

"Why do you say that?" Ben asked.

"Well, they were trying to mix," Edwina explained. "It probably was one of those Yankee lawyers who got the niggers to sue, who got them thinking crazy. You know, they didn't need our university. They had their own schools. In my day they weren't allowed to drive or to try on clothes at our stores. We were all happier then. Them and us. Nobody says that anymore, but it's true. The Lord made us different, and we should keep ourselves separate. I've heard some even date whites now. The Devil's hand is in that sure as can be." Nothing in Edwina's countenance had changed. Her tone was as sweet as ever. She could have been discussing her great-grandchildren.

"Why don't you come get your lunch?" I suggested. "We'll talk more another day if you feel like it."

"Y'all stop and visit my parakeets on the way out, and the dogs too," Edwina said. She eased herself down into her kitchen chair for lunch.

I hugged her, but it didn't feel right after what I'd heard her say. When I turned to wave good-bye from the front door, her eyes were closed and her head was dropped in prayer.

I took off my sandals and carried them in my hand. Ben and I walked across the patio, toward the barns. Browning magnolia blossoms littered the yard.

I started laughing.

"What's so funny?" he asked.

"How could that sweet old lady say those horrible things?" I asked.

"Don't you ever hear people talk like that?" he asked. "Because that's sure not the first person I've heard say those things. You're in Alabama, LuAnn."

"I know where I am, thank you very much. I never heard *her* talk like that, that's all, and we've spent so much time together. My horses have been in her barn since I was little. Maybe her mind is going after all these years." I pulled open the door of the older of the two barns. Its wood was weathered a gray-blue shade. "You're not going to believe this, Ben." I laughed and held out my right arm as if making a presentation.

Inside the barn were hundreds of parakeets—at least three hundred yellow, blue, green, white, and lavender birds, imprisoned by the wire mesh that hung across each opening, a second skin inside the walls of wood, its openings too small for even a parakeet to slip through. The birds flew back and forth from one wire-mesh perch to another, congregating mainly at the windows and doors where light poured through. Fruit and seeds were scattered across the dirt floor, as were a few old hollow tree trunks.

"She sells them, most of them at Easter," I said.

"Only in the South," Ben said. He shook his head slowly back and forth. Then he pulled the lens cap off his camera and tried to capture the bizarre scene while I sat, thinking, on the seat of an orange tractor nearby.

"Why don't we try to talk to Floyd Waddy's widow, Berta, today?" I suggested as we drove out of Edwina's driveway.

"Where does she live?"

"Cullman, less than an hour away. Let's stop and I'll call her. We're not too far from my parents'. We could call from there."

"Do your parents know you're so into this?"

"Not yet. My mother would say it was silly. She's not particularly interested in controversy. And Daddy is so busy with the governor's race that I thought I should wait to tell him if and when I got more facts. I told you he was devastated when it happened. I know he'd be thrilled to have this solved while he's mayor. Of course, Buck would be happy with the good publicity."

"Is it okay if we call from my place?" Ben asked. "I need to pick up more tapes if we see Berta Waddy, and I could fix us a couple of sandwiches."

"I told you I'd get you to work on this," I said, grinning.

"I'll talk to her. That's all, though," he said.

At Ben's, he made the sandwiches while I called Berta Waddy from the kitchen phone. Making an effort to restrain myself, I avoided mentioning the real reason for my call. I explained that I was helping Ben locate people to interview for his book. He would like to see Berta, I said, because of her knowledge of fish farms, a booming business in the New South. Berta said she'd love to talk to Ben, but that it would have to wait until next week, when she returned from a church retreat for which she was about to leave.

I hung up and stood in front of the sink, looking out one of the windows at Mother's chapel. Ben walked up behind me and placed his hands on my shoulders. I turned around and saw in his eyes that he didn't want to talk about Berta Waddy.

For a while we just stood there, kissing and looking at each other. "Did you know you have golden flecks in your eyes?" I asked him.

He just smiled, took my hand, and led me slowly down the hall into the bedroom.

Only then did I admit to myself that this was exactly what I'd wanted for some time.

Hours later, we were still in bed. I'd called the restaurant to make sure everything was okay. I propped myself up on my right elbow and looked down at Ben. His eyes were just about half open. The thought of returning to work or going home was suddenly unbearable. I didn't want the afternoon to end. I didn't want the magic spell we were under to be broken.

"I know!" I said. "I'll take you to the Cow Palace. No book on the South would be complete without a paragraph on that famous landmark."

Ben pulled my hair back into a ponytail in his hand, drew me down toward him, and kissed me.

A little while later, in the shower, I thought briefly and guilt-ily about Eddie. It wasn't his fault that we rarely saw each other, that we were both too busy with work and the children to ever spend time alone. As I faced the falling water, Ben slipped into the shower and began to soap my back, massaging my shoulders, and then working his way down to the small of my back, where he lingered, his hands on my waist and his thumbs rubbing lightly. I arched my back with pleasure. My thoughts of Eddie vanished.

The sun had begun its descent in the afternoon sky when Ben and I left his house. He drove northwest from Clark Lake away from Tallagumsa. Within a few miles of the restaurant, we passed several Cow Palace billboards featuring huge cartoonish black and white cows.

"All these cows," I said, laughing. "And the best is yet to come. Slow down. There she is. Pull in here." I pointed to the giant plaster cow statue that dwarfed both the rectangular brick building—the Palace—and the nearby trailer, where the owners lived.

We went inside and ate barbecue sandwiches and cole slaw. Both of us were starving.

It was after seven by the time Ben dropped me off at the Steak House to get my car. I drove straight home.

The house was unusually quiet: no music, TV, or children talking and laughing. Eddie was sitting in a living-room chair. He wore a tan summer suit, a white shirt, and a burgundy and blue striped tie. I hadn't even known he'd bought a suit.

He had one beer in his hand. The six empties on the floor next to him were stacked in a pyramid. The room was thick with smoke. He was plainly furious and very drunk.

113

I walked past him into the kitchen. "Where's Jolene?" I asked when I didn't find her there.

"She's gone," he said very quietly. "When I got home from my show I let her go home."

The show. Oh, shit! I forgot his show. I chewed on my lip.

"Everyone was there. Your entire family, half the college, people from all over. But you weren't there. I was there. The best work I've ever done was there. Goddamnit, LuAnn," he said. "What is going on?" He knocked over the beer cans with a sweep of his arm.

"I forgot. I'm sorry." I was sorry—sorry that I was caught and that I didn't feel as horrible as I should have.

He jumped up, rushed toward me, and started yelling. "You forgot! You are too fucking much! Forgot!"

"Where's Jessie?" I asked, backing away from him.

"Next door at the Cooks'," he said. "The boys are asleep."

"I tried to find you," he continued. "I called all over. You weren't at work. Your car was, but you weren't. You weren't here. You weren't anywhere. But that's impossible—isn't it?—to be nowhere. I do know who you were with. There was one other person who was supposed to be at the show who wasn't. Your buddy, Ben. Where were you two?"

"Talking to Miss Edwina, Eddie," I said quietly. I stared down at the carpet, unable to meet his fierce look.

"Since this morning? It's after seven o'clock. Miss Edwina isn't that interesting."

"We were talking to her and then we were planning some of Ben's interviews for next week. Time got away from me. I'm sorry. I really am."

"I am too," he said. He turned away and walked toward the stairway, then stopped and looked at me. "I'm sorry about everything. I'm sorry you've changed so much. I'm sorry you won't let me touch you. Do you know how many times we've made love since we got here? Once. First I thought it was because you'd just delivered twins. Then I thought you were tired from moving, then from your new job. Now I don't know. You think you can do whatever you want here, that I and everyone else will just adore you no matter what. The Queen of the Steak House. Well, count me out. I'm leaving. I already told Jessie I had to go away for a few days. The twins won't even notice. They think Jolene is their only parent anyway."

"Don't dump it all on me," I said, meeting his intense gaze. "You haven't ever really been committed to Tallagumsa, Eddie. You didn't want to come and you've hated every minute of it, hiding at the college or in your studio. You ignore us most of the time. If I need a friend, it's you who are to blame."

"You don't know shit. I happen to like it here. I was surprised as hell, but I do like it. It's a better place for raising a family. My work is going great. I love teaching. Jolene is a gift from heaven. I think coming here was right. At least that's what I thought until tonight. But you don't notice anything I say or do anymore. Like I haven't bought a Miss Reese's pie in two weeks, and I hardly drink anymore. Tonight is a well-deserved exception. I have been here for you and the kids, LuAnn, but you are too self-absorbed, too self-important to see outside your little kingdom."

He walked upstairs to the bedroom and picked up his packed suitcases, then came down to the foyer and opened the front door. "You're reminding me more of your father every day. If I were you, I'd be real worried about that."

"Where are you going?" I asked.

"I don't know yet. By the way, I signed a syndication contract tonight. If you care."

I cared, just not enough to stop him.

CHAPTER ELEVEN

At my office desk five days later, I smiled and waved to Ben as he came through the front door of the Steak House. He sat down with the Coffee Club for their regularly scheduled morning discussion, and they greeted him like an old friend. I restrained my desire to rush out and talk to him, even though I wanted to know what Berta Waddy had said to him that morning.

When he saw me watching him, he smiled—an open, easy smile, the kind of smile you don't get from someone you've known a long time, the kind that isn't cluttered with everything that has happened to two people who've shared years of their lives.

Ben, cheerful and kind, was a welcome contrast to Eddie's bleak cynicism. I studied the picture on my desk of Eddie and me on our wedding day. Over the last five days I'd thought a lot about the way Eddie acted at the courthouse dedication: his sarcasm, his mood swings, his drinking. That was the Eddie I was glad to be rid of.

When I told Ben that Eddie had walked out, I assured him that he wasn't the cause, that Eddie's unhappiness about the move and his career had taken their toll on our relationship. Ben, it turned out, was less than thrilled with his marriage as well. During the first year of his two-year marriage, he'd realized that he had made a mistake, but it had been easier to hit the road than to deal with his mistake. Other than these thumbnail sketches of our other, married, lives, we hadn't focused on the specifics. Nor did we discuss what was going to happen when Ben's work was done and it was time for him to go back to

Washington. We didn't even think about it. Instead, we enjoyed our time together, glad to have found each other.

About half an hour passed before Ben left his seat with the Coffee Club, knocked on my office door, and came inside. He left the door open. "Berta Waddy was happy to talk to me until I got to the murders," he said. "Then she clammed up and refused to talk."

"Why?" I asked.

"I asked her that. She didn't really answer my question, though. She said she'd talk about anything but that."

"Why does she care? He's dead, after all. And even if he weren't, she wouldn't have anything to worry about. I'm sure Floyd didn't have anything to do with the murders, but he must have known something or heard something. You'd think she'd want the truth out now, wouldn't you?"

"Not necessarily," Ben said. "He was her husband, LuAnn, dead or not. Maybe he was implicated in some way. You can't expect her to be eager to tell me something that would make him look bad."

"I'm surprised. She usually loves to gossip about anything and everything. Do you want me to call her and try to get her to talk?"

"No, but thanks. It was just a lark anyway. I can't spend any more time here running down that story and alienating everybody. She was not happy to have it brought up. I've told you time and again that's how people feel."

"Why'd you bother to talk to her at all then?" I was irritated that he wasn't committed to the cause. "I thought you were finally going to pursue this."

"That's not what I said, and you know it. After what Edwina told us about the FBI, I thought, Why not check it out. But it's too distracting. At least Berta gave me some interesting information about catfish farming and its effect on the economy here."

"But it would be so great to get that story."

"Look, I talked to her for you. Now do something for me. Let it go, LuAnn. Most people want to move on past it."

Ben shut the office door with his foot. "I'd like to move on," he said. "On over to my house and bring you with me for an hour or so, if you know what I mean." He raised his eyebrows several times in a mockingly suggestive manner.

"I wish I could," I said. I tried but failed to suppress a grin. "Estelle's off all day. How's tonight for you?" I leaned forward and pinched him softly on the thigh.

"Fine with me, sweetie pie," he said, in a mock southern accent.

"By the way, I have big plans for you later this week," I said. "The Ave Maria Grotto."

"The what?"

"You were near it today in Cullman. The grotto is a shrine in an abbey of Benedictine monks. One of the monks there created a miniature Jerusalem, the whole city. He's buried there too, right near the gift shop. And we have to hit the Boll Weevil Monument in Enterprise soon."

Ben started laughing. "Only in the South."

"Yeah, don't you just love it?"

After Ben left, I rolled a blank sheet of paper into the typewriter and typed: "LuAnn and Ben." I hit the carriage return two times and typed: "Ben and LuAnn." Then I put my left elbow on the desk to support my chin and contemplated the couple I had created.

Staring at the names, I was reminded of how as a teenager the girls wrote their names coupled with their boyfriends' names anywhere they found a blank space. We wrote on schoolbooks (inside the covers, in the margins, and on the edges of the compressed pages of closed books), bathroom-stall walls and mirrors, school desks, the sides of shoe soles, wet cement, and even our hands.

After Estelle broke up with Johnny Bowe during our senior

year of high school, she had to buy extra-thick permanent black magic markers to blot out her prolific handiwork. The edges of her textbooks turned so black that an uninformed adult might have thought the books were manufactured with black pages. The bathroom walls were smeared with large blocks of magic marker, as though a mad censor were loose in the school. She bought rolls of paper towels to wipe out their names on lipstick-marked mirrors and a can of red spray paint to obliterate them on the walls of the underpass. Finally, she brought her daddy's pocket knife to school and scratched out the initials she had carved in her homeroom desk.

By the time Junior and I parted ways, we were out of Tallagumsa High School and I didn't have to go to such extremes to obliterate signs of him from my life.

Now, with Eddie, I had my wedding ring. Inside the band was engraved "Eddie and LuAnn, June 10th, 1973." I still wore the ring every day, just as I always had. I wasn't ready to take it off.

No one knew Eddie had moved out, and I was willing to go on that way indefinitely, keeping Eddie's departure a secret, telling anyone who asked that he was on *City Paper* business in Atlanta. It wasn't long though, only a week after Ben and I visited Miss Edwina and missed Eddie's show, before the inevitable occurred.

That day Jane and Mother came by the Steak House after one of my sister's OB visits. They joined me in my booth for lunch. As always, Jane began to reveal every detail of her exam.

Mother listened attentively, even though she'd been there with Jane during the exam.

"What about your weight?" I asked when Jane completed her account. She wasn't even four months pregnant and already had gained thirty pounds. That day she wore a large and loose green muumuu decorated with pictures of watermelon slices.

"He said I should be a little more careful," she admitted as she finished the last of her French fries and milk shake.

"This heat will be hard to take if you're too heavy," I warned. "And the weight's not easy to lose."

"You always did," Jane said. "The twins were only two months old when you were back in great shape."

"But it took a lot of starvation," I said. I didn't bother to remind her that I was four inches taller, six years younger, and had never gained as much as she would.

"This is so special for me that I can't worry about weight," Jane said, dismissing my concerns. "I feel like it must be good for the baby, that if I don't eat when I'm hungry I could hurt him." She shrugged and smiled, then reached for another sweet roll and eagerly peeled off its crinkled paper cup.

"It's hard," I acknowledged. "Especially with the first. With Jessie I worried about every twitch, ache, and pain. I also worried when there were no twitches, aches, or pains. You can't win."

I looked at my watch and stood up. "I have to go upstairs to help set up for the Lions Club, and the twins have their four-month checkup this afternoon, so I'm on a tight schedule today."

"We need to talk!" Mother said dramatically. She grabbed my wrist and there was a brief, uncomfortable silence, during which she and Jane exchanged meaningful looks.

"What?" I asked, sitting back down. "What's wrong?"

"I think you need to know that we saw Eddie and Barbara Cox in her car this morning," Mother said in a conspiratorial whisper. "They didn't see us."

"We didn't want to tell you, but how could we not?" Jane asked. Her tone was anguished. "We were on our way to the doctor's, and there they were at the light, just ahead of us. We couldn't miss them."

"Maybe it wasn't them," Mother said hopefully.

"You know better, Mother," Jane said. "We're sorry, LuAnn." She reached over and took my hand.

Only then did I realize that because Mother and Jane believed that Eddie was out of town (as I'd told them he was), they assumed that *he* was running around with Barbara behind *my* back. I almost laughed. "He's not in Atlanta—I know that; he never was. We had a fight last week and he moved out," I explained. "I didn't want to make a big deal out of it, though. I'm sure everything will be fine."

"Well, I don't know which situation is worse," Mother said, folding her paper napkin carefully and dabbing at the corners of her eyes.

"I told you running the restaurant wouldn't work out," Jane said. "Remember? The day of the courthouse dedication. Daddy's always got to have his way, though. He never listens to me. Now look at the mess you're in."

"Oh, Jane, it's not the restaurant. It's a lot of stuff we have to deal with. We have our share of problems, that's all."

"Such as?" Mother asked.

"Do we have to go into it now?" I asked. "I really need to go upstairs." I stood up again.

"I'll pray for you," Mother said.

"Just don't put us in the bulletin, Mother," I said. "Please." In her church's bulletin each Sunday was a list of people in need of group prayers: cancer victims, widows, alcoholics, and the like. I'd be humiliated if either Eddie's or my name appeared in the list.

"And why not? It couldn't hurt," Mother said. "More good has come from that bulletin. You wouldn't believe."

"It helped me get pregnant," Jane said.

"I'd give the credit to the fertility drugs you took," I said.

"Don't you ever miss the church?" Mother asked.

"Not really," I said. "I'm sorry. I just don't."

"You and your father," Mother said. "I blame him for your views, LuAnn. You two were out gazing at stars, thinking you could get whatever you wanted in life without the Lord's help, when you should have been studying the Bible."

"Different people need different things, Mother," I said, leaning over to kiss her cheek. "Don't worry about me. I'm fine. I'm happy. Really."

I wasn't happy the only other time Eddie left me. I was a mess.

One night right after Thanksgiving my senior year of college, he called our apartment an hour after he was due to go with me to a movie. He said he was in Tennessee and told me that he'd needed to get away, not to worry, he'd be back soon.

"When?" I asked.

Soon.

Two weeks passed. I was walking across the quad, fighting a strong, chilling wind, when he appeared out of nowhere, looking as though he'd never left, carrying a notebook and a textbook under his arm.

"You're back," I said dryly, looking past him.

"I had to get here for my poetry seminar this morning. It was my turn to make a presentation," he said.

"That's the only reason you came back?"

"Of course not."

I sighed and frowned.

"What's wrong?" he asked.

"What do you think? You took off. I had no idea where you were or what you were doing, if you were dead or alive, if you would ever come back."

"I was riding my motorcycle around, very much alive."

"For two weeks?"

"Yes."

"Where?"

"Alabama, Mississippi, Tennessee."

"With?"

"Nobody."

I looked at him skeptically. The wind picked up, driving the small piles of autumn leaves into a frenetic airborne dance.

"I have never lied to you," he said. "And I swear I never will."

Starting to cry, I snapped my down jacket closed and began to walk away.

Eddie grabbed my arm and guided me to a stone bench next to the sidewalk marking the quad's perimeter. We sat down.

"Why would you do that, right after we talked about . . ." I asked, crying.

"To think about what we talked about. Getting married was not something I'd planned on doing any time soon—until I met you. I needed time to be alone, that's all."

Tears ran down my cheeks, onto my jacket and jeans. My head was bent down and my long straight hair fell across the sides of my face.

"You know what my seminar talk was on this morning?" he asked.

I shook my head.

"You."

I eyed him suspiciously.

"No, really. About how special we are. What I feel for you is not like anything I've ever known. LuAnn, how many other people do you think have what we do?" He opened his textbook to a paper-clipped page and pointed to a Yeats poem.

WHEN YOU ARE OLD

When you are old and grey and full of sleep,
And nodding by the fire, take down this book,
And slowly read, and dream of the soft look
Your eyes had once, and of their shadows deep;

How many loved your moments of glad grace,
And loved your beauty with love false or true,
But one man loved the pilgrim soul in you,
And loved the sorrows of your changing face;

And bending down beside the glowing bars,
Murmur, a little sadly, how Love fled
And paced upon the mountains overhead
And hid his face amid a crowd of stars.

"Especially these lines," he said, underlining with his finger the words "But one man loved the pilgrim soul in you, And loved the sorrows of your changing face."

"What about these?" I asked, pointing to the last verse. "You fled. You ran away from me."

"I didn't, LuAnn. I went looking for you." Then he moved my hair out of my face with his hand, turned my head, and looked at me to see if I understood what he meant.

I did. "Here I am," I said.

Eddie was the only person I'd ever known who could talk to me about my soul and not sound silly.

But that was a long time ago.

CHAPTER TWELVE

A group of Tallagumsa High cheerleaders celebrating their number-one rating at the national cheerleader camp in Mississippi filled the usually quiet time during the afternoon lull with giggles and high-pitched squeals.

I managed to relax with a cup of Sanka in my corner booth anyway, where I read a *Birmingham News* story about the first test-tube baby, Louise Brown.

Ben finished a brief interview session with the Coffee Club. After they left, he stayed in his seat and opened the mail he'd picked up at the post office. From the corner of my eye, I could see him glance over at me. I looked over; he turned away and then stared down at his mail. We played this cat-and-mouse game for several minutes. What's he up to? I wondered. The first thing that came to mind—the very worst thing I could think of—was that his wife had written to announce that she was pregnant. (He'd only been home to D.C. once since he got to town and had never said a word about the visit upon his return.) Or maybe she'd decided to come down for a visit. I couldn't imagine having her in my restaurant or watching her walk down First Avenue with him.

Finally, he came over to my booth and sat down across from me.

"Want some more coffee?" I asked.

"No," he said. He set his pile of mail on the table. An assortment of letters and bills was on the top. A large manila envelope was on the bottom. He kept one hand on the mail, as though we were outside on a windy day. He looked odd to me, not quite the Ben I knew, as though his features had shifted slightly out of place. He cleared his throat, swallowed, and looked around the room. "I need a cigarette," he said.

"You don't smoke," I said.

"I used to." He got up, walked around behind the booth to the cigarette machine in the coat room, and bought a burgundy-and-white pack of Carltons. He returned, lit up, and started coughing.

"What is going on?" I demanded.

"I just got some information that I, um . . ." His voice trailed off. He seemed mesmerized by the smoke curling up from his cigarette.

"What, Ben? What's the big mystery? Would you look at me, please."

He took a deep breath and met my eyes. "This manila envelope has the FBI documents, all unredacted. Someone from the Justice Department leaked them to my boss."

"That's great! Can I see?" I reached for the envelope.

"Just a second," he said sharply. He clamped his hand over mine.

"All right! I won't touch it. What's the matter with you? You are acting very strange."

He sat quietly for a moment, then sighed loudly and released my hand. "Jesus! I don't know what to do," he said. "Here, you might as well read them too." He removed the papers from the envelope and gently pushed them toward me. He took another drag on his cigarette and coughed again.

Clipped on top of the papers was a note handwritten on a piece of *Washington Star* stationery. It read:

Ben,
   A good friend at Justice gave these to me after he read the article you wrote about Newell Hagerdorn and the Alabama governor's race. Looks like your book might have to wait.

—Frank

The FBI documents were attached to the note. This time nothing was blacked out.

MEMO

To: Carl Best, Chief, Atlanta Field Office
From: Special Agent Dorr
Re: Jimmy Turnbow and Leon Johnson
Date: August 28, 1963

I have confirmed that a Bureau informant, Dean Reese, was in the car involved in the murders. Thus I expect a speedy resolution of the matter. Hopefully, the State of Alabama will bring indictments here. Perhaps they will be able to get convictions with the help of Reese's eyewitness testimony. If the State refuses to go forward, however, as often occurs in these cases, this would definitely be a candidate for federal civil rights charges.

MEMO

To: Carl Best, Chief, Atlanta Field Office
From: Special Agent Dorr
Re: Jimmy Turnbow and Leon Johnson
Date: August 30, 1963

Dean Reese has provided me with the names and addresses of the men in the car with him: Newell Hagerdorn and Floyd Waddy. Agent Moon and I will attempt to interview each of them and other possible witnesses. As always in this kind of case, if we can secure even one cooperative witness (in addition to Reese) we will be lucky, particularly here where, according to Reese, one of the men who was with him that night and the one responsible for pulling the trigger is the Sheriff of Tallagumsa, Alabama, the town outside of which the killings occurred.

For what it's worth, there is a rumor around town that they were shot by someone whose daughter was involved with one of them.

MEMO

To: Carl Best, Chief, Atlanta Field Office
From: Special Agent Dorr
Re: Jimmy Turnbow and Leon Johnson
Date: September 5, 1963

As you know, it appears that the shells found at the scene
of the crime came from the Sheriff's personal gun which
Reese turned over to us. The fingerprints on the gun
haven't been checked yet. We spoke with Hagerdorn and
Waddy, the two men named by Reese. Floyd Waddy was
indignant; he has a strong alibi. Sheriff Newell Hagerdorn
laughed at us.

As I mentioned over the phone, we may have serious
problems here. After spending a few days in town, we've
discovered that Reese has a reputation for being an extremely unstable alcoholic known for violent and unpredictable behavior. This was not a complete surprise. We
had some reason to believe that there were problems with
Reese. In a similar Mississippi case his evidence proved unreliable. We had kept him on the payroll though because
we had no one else in the area. I have set up a meeting with
him tonight.

MEMO (marked URGENT AND CONFIDENTIAL)

To: David Metzger, Assistant to the Director
From: Carl Best, Chief, Atlanta Field Office
Re: Jimmy Turnbow and Leon Johnson
Date: September 7, 1963

We recommend strongly that the Bureau cease all involvement in the investigation of the above-mentioned
deaths and that we not reveal any of the information gathered to anyone, including State authorities. Without our
involvement, they will not bring a case. As you pointed
out, Reese's suicide has thrown the case into a tailspin. Not

only is our best evidence gone, but any trial might result in serious embarrassment to the Bureau and the Justice Department and damage our chances of successfully pursuing other civil rights cases in the Deep South. In short, it would do far more harm than good.

A few more interviews have been scheduled, just to tie up loose ends. One is with Liz Reese, the wife. It is unclear whether she'll cooperate. We understand that the Reeses' marriage was a very troubled one.

I put the FBI documents down on the table. I felt my face flush hot and red and heard my heart beating loudly in my ears. Instantly the din from the cheerleaders receded, and it seemed that Ben and I were growing larger and larger, turning into giants who towered over all the irrelevant specks of people around us, people too tiny to see or hear or care about.

"What could that mean?" I asked, trying to make some sense of what I'd just read.

Ben took my hand in his. "Are you okay?"

"No, I'm not. Who wrote this? It's not real, of course. It's some sort of hoax or a very bad joke," I said.

"How can you be sure?" he asked.

I jerked my hand free and put it in my lap, then glared at him. "Of course I'm sure. You don't believe this, do you?"

"I just opened that envelope a few minutes ago and thought I had to show the documents to you," he said. "Beyond that, I haven't thought about what they mean. I know as much about them as you do."

Cleo walked up and interrupted us. "You have a phone call, LuAnn."

"I'll call them back," I snapped. I didn't bother to look up at her.

"But it's the Alabama Best Milk accountant you've been calling for two days," she said.

"I said I'll call him back!" I insisted, turning toward her.

Cleo shook her head as she walked away.

"It's ridiculous, Ben," I continued. "You should write them back and make them do something about it."

"Write who? The Justice Department? The FBI?"

"Whoever you need to write to see that these lies are fixed. It's obviously a political dirty trick by someone who doesn't want Daddy to win the election. That Republican who just entered the race—Ollie Beckwith, maybe him. Your newspaper should know better than to send out this kind of trash." I tore my paper napkin into little pieces as I talked.

"Look," Ben said. "My editor sent me these, not some kook. I've worked for Frank for five years, and he is the most honest man I know. He wouldn't have sent them if he didn't believe they were honest-to-God FBI documents. His source had to be unimpeachable or I wouldn't have them."

"Could we sue the FBI, then, to correct them?"

"Don't you want to ask your father about this before you start filing lawsuits?"

"No, thank you."

"I'm sure there's an easy explanation for all of this. Just ask your father. He can probably clear it up in a second."

"Of course he could if he knew anything about it, but he doesn't, Ben. Don't you see that I would know all about this if there were a shred of truth to it? I'm not a stranger here like you are. I would know. There's no way something this big could be kept a secret."

"Still, LuAnn, it won't hurt to ask him. Just see what he has to say."

"Fine, if you want me to I will, but I can tell you already what he'll say."

"Is he still at work?"

"Probably. This is so weird," I said. "I feel like it's a 'Candid Camera' routine or something. Next thing you know you'll pull the microphone out from under your sweater."

"Do I look like Alan Funt?" he joked.

I ignored him. "Okay." I stood up. The pieces of napkin in my lap fluttered to the floor like confetti. "This is stupid," I said.

"Just get it over with," Ben said.

I didn't want to call my father, but I had to do something. "I'll call from my office," I said.

"I have the most bizarre thing to tell you about," I said to my father after his secretary, Franny, got him to answer the call. I giggled nervously. "You won't believe this, Daddy, but Ben just showed me some documents he got from some nut in Washington about the Turnbow-Johnson murders, and, well, you'll die, but they say that Dean Reese told the FBI that you and Mr. Waddy were involved in the murders." After a few seconds of silence, I said, "Daddy, are you there?"

"Yes, I'm here, honey."

"Well, I know it's a dirty trick or something, but Ben insisted I call you, that you might have heard something back then about this nutcase Dean Reese talking about you and all. You know how reporters are. I shouldn't have bothered you at all, right? That's what I told Ben."

"Ben has these papers, you say?"

"Yes."

"How lucky. I've noticed y'all seem to be pretty chummy lately. The best thing is for you to tell Ben to give them to you and then both of you forget all about them."

"What?" I asked. I probably sounded surprised. This was not what I had expected to hear from him at all.

"Look, sweetie, this town has been through enough over those poor boys. It was a long time ago, and it's done with. I don't wan't to go into it, but if Ben doesn't drop the whole thing innocent people will be hurt. I promise you that. Good people who had nothing to do with anybody dying. And who would help Ben with his book if he drags all this out again? You just do what I said now."

"What if he won't ignore them, Daddy?" I was pretty sure Ben wouldn't simply give me the documents and forget he ever saw them.

"You can do it. I know you," Daddy said.

"But what should I tell him?"

"Tell him justice was done. It's true, and the rest is nobody's business. You trust me, LuAnn, don't you?"

"Of course."

"And you love me?"

"Daddy, yes."

"Then just listen to me. It would be a big waste of his time and ours too. Tallagumsa deserves not to be dragged into that hornets' nest again. Don't worry. Just do what I ask."

"Okay, but—"

"No *buts*. Go on now."

"Maybe you could talk to Ben for a minute yourself, Daddy. He's right in the front dining room."

"No, hon. Now you're giving me a headache."

"I'm sorry. Forget I ever called."

"I'll be fine if you do what I say."

"We have to talk, Ben," I announced. I had grabbed my purse from my office file drawer and told Estelle to cover for me so we could leave the restaurant immediately. "Let's go for a ride."

"What about the dinner rush?" he asked, surprised that I would miss it.

"They can manage without me. I told Estelle you needed help with an important interview," I said.

We climbed into Ben's BMW.

"I have a favor to ask," I said as he pulled away from the Steak House.

"First, what did he say?" Ben asked. "And, second, where are we going?"

"He said forget about it. Why don't we go to your house?"

"He what?" Ben asked incredulously.

"Really, he did. Don't act so shocked. It's not because he did anything wrong."

"Oh?"

"*Oh?* What's that mean? *Oh?* Daddy made some very good points. This town has suffered enough over the murders, and if you get started on this wild rumor you've got here it'll stir up all those bad feelings again. He said nothing would be accomplished either—nothing good, anyway. And—listen to this and stop looking so amazed—he said some innocent people would be hurt. *And* he reminded me that no one would look kindly on you anymore, on your work or your book."

"Doesn't he want to talk to me about it?" Ben asked. He sounded shocked.

"Not really."

"That seems a little cavalier, don't you think?"

"I can see your point, but I know he wouldn't lie to me. I trust him. You have to trust him too."

"I don't really know what to say, LuAnn. I certainly didn't expect this response from him." He looked troubled.

We reached Ben's house. In the living room we talked and argued until he agreed to think about what my father had asked. I kissed him, anxious to make up and hopeful that this would be the end of the matter. My kiss exploded into fierce lovemaking, a mixture of anger, passion, and fear. Afterward we lay on the living-room rug and watched the sun descend toward the lake, turning the wisps of white clouds in the sky pink. It was a peaceful scene that made me all the more agitated.

I got up and carried my clothes into Ben's bedroom. He followed. As I straightened my skirt in Ben's bedroom mirror, I talked to his reflection. "Just throw the documents away and forget they ever existed," I said lightly.

I walked across the room and sat on the bed next to him. "Come on," I said, trying to maintain a gentle, flirtatious tone. "Please." I so wanted this to be a problem I could conquer with charm.

"What if the documents are telling the truth?" he asked.

"How can you say that about my father!" I jumped up and walked to the mirror, where I began to brush my hair.

"Well, what if they are the truth?" he insisted. "Couldn't

that be why he's asked me to throw the papers away? Think about that."

"No, I won't think about anything so ridiculous. This is a stupid conversation. And you're behaving like an ass." I brushed harder and faster. "I can't believe you'd even suggest that. Don't ever say anything like that again."

Ben got up and walked to the dresser. He took hold of my shoulders, turned me around, and looked at me, his hands coming to rest on my waist. "You must know that the matter wouldn't be resolved even if I destroyed the papers. I don't have the only copy. Apart from me, the FBI, the Justice Department, and my paper have copies. Someone at Justice obviously wants the world to know about what's in them. We need to learn the truth."

"But I know the truth!" I said.

I swatted his arm with my brush and moved his hands off my waist. Then I sat down in the chair across from the bed.

"You have to believe Daddy! Sometimes it takes a long time to *prove* the truth, and sometimes you can never prove the truth about something that happened fifteen long years ago. All you're going to accomplish is to ruin my father's reputation."

"It's not up to me. I'm surprised my paper hasn't called yet," he said.

"Why?"

Ben lay down on the bed and rested his forearm across his eyes. He took a deep breath. "This story isn't going to go away no matter what I do. Something pretty screwy happened at the FBI, something that involved the present front runner for governor of Alabama—and my paper knows it. If I don't look into it, someone else will."

He looked over at me. "If I could do what you want me to do, I would. But it's not in me to do something like that, and I don't think it's in you, either. I suspect you'd hate me for that at some point. And I'd be miserable. I've never fabricated a story or destroyed evidence, and I hope I never will."

"Come on, Ben, please, for *me*? Just forget them."

"This isn't about you."

"It most certainly is. He is my daddy and that's what he wants. I know: You could tell your paper and they could tell whoever sent this that you talked to everybody in town and there's absolutely no truth to those documents. That's that. Over and done with." I tried to calm down. A more reasonable tone might convince Ben that I was right.

"But that's not true."

"What if you got a call and some crazed stranger said that your father had killed someone fifteen years ago and you were certain that it wasn't true and that following up on it would cause only pain and misery?"

"That's not a fair comparison, LuAnn!" He stood up and paced around his room, hitting his hands together, trying to contain his anger. "But the answer is that I would pursue that, and I will pursue this. That's the only way to find out what really happened."

"But it could take so long. What will everybody think about you if you start asking questions about the murders and Daddy and Mr. Waddy, even though it will turn out all right someday? And what about us? You couldn't even come in the Steak House if you start on this."

Ben stopped walking and stood in front of me. "You want to play this game? Okay. Let me ask you something then: What if you were Leon Johnson's mother, or Jimmy Turnbow's? How would you feel? Wouldn't you want someone to pursue every lead possible? No matter what anyone said? This is exactly what you've wanted ever since we met. You're the one who pushed me to pursue this. You asked me to do it for their families. I told my editor to move the appeal on the redacted documents along quickly, that there were people here who cared, and I was talking about you. You know damn well that if the documents hadn't named your father you'd still be pushing me full steam ahead."

I knew he was right, but I didn't want to think about those lies I'd read another minute. I ran from the house. Ben followed, calling after me. I kept running toward my parents' house. Ben yelled again, but as my distance from him increased his voice faded.

I slowed to a walk along the lakefront and started picking up flat stones almost the size of my palm—a habit from my childhood, when we'd spent summer days skimming stones across the lake. Standing at the bottom of the trail, I stared through the trees at my parents' modern glass-and-wood house. Each fist gripped a handful of smooth, damp stones.

I walked up the path to the house, slowly opening my fists and dropping the stones one by one onto the ground. Neither of their cars was parked in the driveway. I peered through the picture window across the back of the house and tried the door. It was locked. I knocked. No answer. I went around to the front of the house. No answer there. I turned and walked away.

Taking the trail just to the right of the house, I walked toward Mother's chapel. I was surprised to find that once inside the chapel I was comforted, whether by the chapel as a sacred place or by the physical refuge it offered me at this particular moment when I had nowhere to go, I didn't know.

I sat on the bench and tried to catch my breath. Suddenly I was on my knees in front of the altar, hands clasped together, head bowed. I was so bewildered by what Dean Reese had said fifteen years ago, by my father's reaction to it, by Ben's refusal to accommodate him, and by unarticulated fears about what it all might come to that I would do almost anything, even pray.

CHAPTER THIRTEEN

I went to work the next day, hoping that I could lose myself in the restaurant's demands. Wishful thinking. Every time the Steak House door opened, I looked up. Every time the phone rang, I flinched, my anxiety exacerbated because I didn't know who or what I was waiting for.

For the first time in weeks, Ben didn't call or come by the Steak House for breakfast or coffee. I hoped that he was meeting with my father and faring better with him than I had, but I had the feeling this was not going to be resolved so easily. Otherwise wouldn't Daddy have dealt differently with the accusations when I called him? Wouldn't he have set the matter straight then and there?

In the late morning, my mother phoned me at the restaurant. Annoyed that she would interrupt my vigil, I trudged up the stairs to my office to take the call anyway.

"Your friend Ben was just here," she said.

"What?" Since seeing the FBI memos, I had imagined any number of different scenarios, from good (the author of the documents revealed they were a hoax) to bad (my father was accused publicly of murder), but I had not considered the possibility that Ben might involve Mother.

"He asked me some questions about your father."

"You're kidding!" I said, annoyed. "What did he want to know?"

"Whether your father had been a suspect in the murders. He told me you saw the FBI memos that he showed me."

"It's a mistake, Mother. Some horrible mistake. I begged Ben to ignore it and get on with his book, but he won't."

"He also talked to Berta Waddy this morning."

"He told you that?" I swiveled back and forth in my desk chair as feelings of helplessness and dread mushroomed inside me.

"No, Berta called me."

"Why would *she* call *you*?"

"Because your father's name came up when Ben talked to her. She called here to speak with Newell, but he's at the club playing golf, so she told me. And—"

"Wait! What did you tell Ben?" I interrupted.

"I told him I thought I should talk to you first."

"Why? I don't know anything about any of this!" I must have yelled, because I saw Estelle, who was in the front dining room, look up at me, curious. I closed my office door.

"Maybe you should come over here," Mother said. "You sound upset."

"And you sound fine for some reason. Does Daddy know Ben's talking to half the world about this, spreading lies everywhere?"

"I don't think so. Not yet, anyway. It won't be long now; you know Berta."

"Can you stop a reporter from investigating? There must be something we can do. We can't allow him to—"

"LuAnn, your father was questioned by the FBI," Mother interrupted me, in an urgent burst of words. "He was a suspect."

"You have finally gone too far, Mother. Are you crazy?" I turned my chair around until I faced the empty back dining room so that the customers in the front dining room couldn't see my undoubtedly distraught face. "Why would you say such a horrible thing?" I asked, then I hung up the phone.

I dialed Ben's number. He was the one causing all this pain. He was to blame. His line was busy. I tried again. Busy again. Every time I heard a busy signal, I dialed again. My breath accelerated with each attempt, as if the physical action of turning the dial was more than I could bear. Finally, his phone rang.

"How dare you talk to my mother!" I demanded when he said hello. My voice was shaking.

"What's the matter, LuAnn?" he asked.

"You have to stop this, now, before it spreads any further. Talking to Berta Waddy, you might as well be talking to Channel Six."

"I won't be able to see you again, you know."

"I think you could if you wanted to. I haven't done anything unreasonable. You, however, are not behaving rationally."

"Everything you're doing is unreasonable!"

"I tried to reach your father, but I haven't been able to, so I talked to two other people, LuAnn. Only two. It's not exactly on the television news."

"Yet! Do you even care about what I say, Ben? Do you care at all? Or have I been just a distraction for you, someone to fill up your time while you were away from home?"

"You know that's not true. I care very much about you, too much probably, but I have to go ahead with this. The paper just called. They've assigned someone in Washington to pursue the leads on that end. If your dad would just cooperate, I'm sure we could resolve this right away."

"Since you believe that, why not stop the whole thing right now?"

"Don't be so mad at me, LuAnn. This is not something I have any control over. You know this has nothing to do with you and me."

"No, I don't."

"I miss you already," he said, gently.

"Get used to it," I said, and I slammed down the phone.

Without thinking, I picked up the Tallagumsa phone book. On the front was a photograph of a large sailboat gliding across Clark Lake. I turned to C and ran my finger down the page to "Cox, Barbara."

After Mother and Jane saw Eddie and Barbara in her car together, raising the possibility of a relationship between them, the

139

idea had slowly worried its way into my consciousness. Although I didn't want to admit I was interested, I suddenly needed to know whether Eddie was staying there. I didn't think ahead to what I would do if he were. I didn't think at all. I simply needed to know that minute. I dialed Barbara Cox's number from my office.

The phone rang four times, then it was answered.

"Hello," Eddie said.

I hung up, crying.

Less than twenty-four hours earlier, I had been on top of the world. Now my world was spinning out of control at an unbelievable rate of speed, leaving me confused and shaken. I fumbled around and got my things together. The only place where I might be able to find some respite was at home. There I could rock the twins, hold them tight, and try to lose myself in their warmth and sweetness. Or I could cry my heart out with them and they'd never have a clue. Although I would have to pretend all was well with Jessie, who was having enough problems adjusting to her father's absence without seeing me fall apart, taking a walk or playing with her and seeing her original child's response to the world couldn't help but jolt me out of my misery.

I was on my way down my office steps when Jane came marching through the front doors of the Steak House and up the hall toward me. Even before she spoke I knew something was wrong. Jane never came into town in pants, but here she was wearing orange cotton pants, a maternity top smudged with dirt, and loafers without stockings. We met at the bottom of the steps.

"Mother's at home crying her heart out because of the way you talked to her, LuAnn," Jane said sternly. "You treat her like a distant cousin. She's your mother!"

"She shouldn't say those things about Daddy," I said.

"Would you just listen to me for one minute, LuAnn? Daddy was questioned by the FBI. Don't look at me like that! Someone told the FBI he was involved, and two FBI agents came to our house and questioned him. I was at home. I saw them." She made her accusations quietly, almost in a whisper.

I looked at her in amazement. Why would *she* lie about this? "Let's go upstairs," I said.

I led Jane up the stairs, then down the hall to the last dining room. Nothing was scheduled for the upstairs dining rooms all afternoon or evening, so they were dark and empty. I flicked on one of the light switches but left the other three switches off. Jane sat in a chair while I paced.

"But why didn't I know?" I demanded. "Why didn't I know anything about any of this?" I was frantic. Although the Steak House wasn't cold, a chill gripped me, and I wrapped my arms tightly around my chest.

"You were twelve years old, a child," Jane said. "There was no reason to upset you if the investigation didn't go any further. That was a very unhappy time in our lives. Lucky for you, you had no idea what all was going on. Then the excitement died down and it was like nothing ever happened."

"But something horrible did happen. Two people were killed and Daddy was questioned. I can't believe this. Didn't people think it was a little strange when I organized the memorial for Jimmy and Leon? I'm surprised someone in town didn't point out that the daughter of a suspect had some nerve raising money for a memorial," I said.

"No one else knew about any of it, LuAnn," Jane said.

"How could no one know?" I asked.

Jane scowled, sat on the floor, pushed her loafers off, and leaned against the wall. "I can't get comfortable," she said, shifting her weight, trying different positions. "I don't see how you could ever sit down, pregnant with twins."

"Lie down on your left side," I suggested.

She did, resting her head on her left hand.

I sat down on the floor a few feet in front of her. "It's impossible to keep a secret in this town," I said.

"Everyone has secrets, even here," she said. "No one ever knew the FBI was in town except a few people. It was all very hush-hush."

"What did Daddy tell the FBI?"

"I wasn't in the room when they talked, but he told me afterward that he'd said he wasn't involved."

"That's it?"

"That's it. Oh, and I heard him laugh when they came to the door. They said something, and then he laughed, sort of a nervous laugh."

"Why? Why would he laugh?"

"He didn't ever explain it to me."

"And you never found out? Didn't you ask him? You must have wanted to know," I insisted.

"Yes, I asked him."

"And what did he say?"

"That there was nothing to worry about." Sitting up, she reached her left hand behind her neck and massaged the area.

"That's all?"

"Yes."

"Did you ask him what the FBI said to him? And what he said? What it was all about?"

"Yes, yes, yes. He acted exasperated, you know how he does, and he said, 'I told you. Everything's fine. Don't worry.' "

"You should have made him explain everything to you."

"That's real easy for you to say, LuAnn. You've never had to ask him to do anything he didn't already want to do. He's a very stubborn, selfish man. It's not worth it, making demands on him, believe me."

"I don't agree with you, but . . . you don't think he was involved, do you?"

"We weren't ever close the way the two of you are, but no, I don't think he killed anyone. Back then, though, I hated him enough to hope he was the murderer, to wish they'd lock him up forever and throw away the key."

"Jane! How can you talk like that?"

"I was very angry at him."

"But why?"

"My life hasn't been the fairy tale yours has been, LuAnn, especially when I was a teenager. You always had everything you wanted: You were blessed with beauty and brains, you were head cheerleader and homecoming queen, you had Junior. And Daddy adored you. He still adores you. I didn't have any of that. We had a lot of problems; you can't even imagine some of them." Jane's eyes teared up.

"Like what?" I asked.

"That's all over and done with." She sighed and looked past me into the dark end of the dining room. "It's Buck I'm worried about now, not me. If all this gets out it's going to kill him. He's devoted his career, his life, to Daddy. He worships him."

"You haven't told Buck yet?"

"I'm hoping Ben will stop his investigation, that the whole thing will disappear," Jane said. "It did once."

"Me too," I said. "God, I hope it does."

That afternoon, after a brief visit home and a few much needed hugs from the kids, I watched from my office as my father came in and joined his friends for coffee. His shirtsleeves were rolled up and his tie was loosened a bit, concessions to the heat. I was relieved to see him, happy to hear his voice. There was just no way I could connect what the FBI documents said about him with the man I and so many others knew and loved.

When he stood up to leave the Steak House after twenty-five minutes with the Coffee Club, I rushed down out of my office and met him at the table. "Are you okay, Daddy?" I asked.

"Never felt better," he said.

"Where are you going?"

"I've got to run a few errands," he said. "Then get back to the office."

"Can I tag along with you? I need a break."

"Sure, but don't you have work to do?" He took one last

swig of his coffee and set some change on the table.

"Not much." I linked my arm through his. We left the Steak House and began walking down the street. "Where to?" I asked.

"Harold's Gun Shop and Jerry's Barber Shop."

"What do you need at Harold's?" I asked.

"Some shells. I'm going to kill me a reporter."

"Daddy!"

"A little joke," he said. But he didn't laugh.

"Maybe you shouldn't go in the gun shop."

"And just why not?"

"It might make things look worse."

"Things! You call what your harebrained friend is running around saying 'things'! Your choice in men sure leaves a lot to be desired."

He gave me a withering look. I had seen the look before, but never directed toward me. All the kindness I was used to seeing had been snatched out of his eyes, and I turned away, feeling as though he'd hit me.

"I'm sorry," I said.

"It's not your fault," he said, softening a little, "even though I know you'd be the first to point the finger if it weren't your old dad we were talking about. Right?"

"But it is you."

"Did you even try to stop Ben, like I told you?" he asked. "Did you, LuAnn?"

"Yes, I did. I swear. He just can't."

"You mean he won't. Nosy bastard."

"He's not. It's his job, Daddy."

"He gets paid to be a nosy bastard then."

A few blocks from the Steak House he stopped in front of the portable plastic sign outside Harold's Gun Shop. Christmas colored bulbs decorated the perimeter of the sign, which advertised "Handguns, Rifles, Shotguns, Black Powder, Hunting Apparel, and Knives."

"Are you coming inside with me?" he asked.

"I've never been in there," I said. "Maybe you shouldn't go in either. What if Ben sees?"

He shook his head, disgusted. "Don't start telling me what to do, LuAnn!"

He walked in. I followed.

Harold was behind a glass-counter case full of handguns. Behind him, rifles lined the wall. "Afternoon, Mayor, LuAnn," he said.

I wanted to tell Daddy not to smile at Harold, not to shake his hand, that it might look like there was something suspicious between them. Just being in the gun shop made me feel dirty. Why wasn't my father more sensitive? I stood off to the side, by the camouflage clothes.

"We've got snakes all over at the lake, Harold. Two boxes of number-five shot shells should do the trick," my father said. "I need a new hunting hat too. Mine's falling apart."

"They're right over there, near where LuAnn's standing," Harold said.

Daddy picked out a hat and put it on the counter.

Harold handed my father a bag with the boxes of shells inside and put the camouflaged hunting hat on Daddy's head.

Daddy paid and we left.

"You look like a goof ball," I said. "Wearing a hunting hat downtown." We both laughed.

We walked around the corner to Jerry's Barber Shop and sat down on the wooden bench to wait while Jerry cut two other customers' hair.

Finally, since my father obviously wasn't going to make it any easier, I got up my nerve and asked, "Don't you want to talk about it, Daddy?"

"No."

"Come on. You'll feel better."

"I don't feel bad, I told you." That look again.

"Are you mad at me?" I asked.

"No, LuAnn, I am not mad at you, but I will be if you don't stop annoying me."

"Please," I begged. "I need to know what happened. I *know* you didn't do anything wrong. I just want to hear what happened. Why they talked to you of all people, why you're named in those documents. What does Dean Reese have to do with you?"

He took one of the boxes out of the bag and poured the shells into his new hat. He examined them, ignoring my pleas.

"I don't think that's too much to ask of you, Daddy!" I continued. "This is tearing me up, and you can stop it. I can't stand not knowing. I'm a wreck. Just tell me the truth, please." Tears I'd fought all afternoon found their release now.

He took on a pained expression, as if I were a dog that had misbehaved. "You remind me of your mother, the way she used to carry on like I don't know what, bothering me endlessly. For the last time, LuAnn, I'm not going to discuss this with you, or your mother, or Ben, or anybody! It's not anybody's business." He turned slightly toward me.

I fought to suppress a sob.

"I'll say three things, all true," he said, counting them off on his fingers. "One, this is all a bunch of old bullshit that somebody was bound to get around to eventually. Two, I had nothing to do with those boys dying. Three, Dean Reese was a mean, vindictive son of a bitch. Take it or leave it."

I took it.

Jerry, the barber, pointed toward the empty chair.

Daddy unrolled his shirtsleeves and buttoned the cuffs. As he walked toward the barber chair, he turned around to look at me. "At least you don't look like her, kiddo," he said. He popped one of his suspenders and grinned.

After his haircut, my father returned to his office. I didn't know where to turn, who to turn to, or what to do. I couldn't bear to see anyone, so I walked past the Steak House, got in my oven of a car, and headed east out of Tallagumsa, out Old Highway 49 toward the memorial, the tree.

That July afternoon was no different from every other dog day that month. It was miserably hot. As I drove, the road shimmered in front of me and a thin haze turned the sky bright white. Sweat trickled down my chest, between my breasts.

At the tree, I pulled off the road, parked my car, and got out, kicking two beer cans out of the way. Behind the fence, the field was crowded with cornstalks towering about ten feet high.

I sat down cross-legged on the ground under the pine tree and pulled up a few blades of grass. I was tempted to talk to Leon and Jimmy and try to get their story when I heard a car coming to a stop a few feet away. I raised my head. It was Ben.

"I thought I might find you here," he said as he climbed out of his car. We had come to visit the tree and the memorial twice since Ben arrived in town.

"Have you been driving by here all day hoping to see me?" I asked.

"No. But I've been by your parents' place, your house, and the Steak House. So I figured you had to be riding your horse or else you were here. I tried here first. May I sit down?"

"It's not against the law," I said.

He sat down facing me. "How are you doing?"

"Not so great."

"You look beautiful," he said.

"Wonderful."

"I've been trying to reach your dad," Ben said. "He refuses to return my calls. I don't know what to make of it."

"Just don't act suspicious," I warned. "He's a busy man, that's all."

"I'd really like to talk with him. I need to talk to him. I can't help but think he's avoiding me."

"He barely talked to me about this whole mess, so don't feel left out."

"He talked to you?"

"Yeah, sort of. He said he had nothing to do with the murders, and that Dean Reese was a son of a bitch."

"So why did Dean Reese say—"

I interrupted him. "I don't know why! Goddamnit! I don't know! You find out, Ben. You're the reporter." I threw the blades of grass onto the ground and wiped the sweat from my forehead with the back of my hand.

"You're still mad at me, I guess."

"I'm mad that this has happened. I'm mad that we can't see each other."

"But we *could* see each other, LuAnn. We should. You and I just started something. We shouldn't throw it away before we know what we've got. I need you, LuAnn."

"That's easy to say."

"It's true. I'll be miserable without you."

"Then stop this before it's too late."

Ben grimaced. "Haven't you heard a word I've said? It's already too late."

"I don't want to believe that."

"You have to," he insisted. "Can I still call you?" he asked in a gentler tone.

"I guess so."

"But we can't see each other? That's crazy."

"No, we can't! I can't go to bed with someone who thinks my father may have killed someone. I *should* hate you. I'm surprised I don't."

"You shouldn't hate me."

"What would my daddy think if he saw me hanging out with you now, if he even saw us talking? I wish I didn't care, but I do. This isn't New York City, after all. I have to live here with all these people for the rest of my life."

We sat quietly for a few minutes.

Ben sighed. "I wanted to tell you: A retired FBI agent in Baltimore who worked on the case has agreed to an interview with one of our reporters. That's all my news. I'll let you know when I know anything else. Mostly people are avoiding me and refusing to talk."

"I told you that would happen," I said. "Nobody will help you. They love my father too much."

"I don't care about them. I just wish you would come with me right now," Ben said. He touched my knee.

I looked at his hand there, and for a second I wished that I could do just that.

"Please," he said.

But I shook my head, got up, and drove away.

CHAPTER FOURTEEN

I spent the following days in a numb and teary haze, going through the motions of my life: work, the children, sleeping, eating, and more work. Buck and my father thought I was overreacting. After all, the FBI had investigated the matter once fifteen years ago and nothing had come of it. They therefore saw no reason to postpone or cancel the upcoming major fundraising event planned at the farm of Birmingham millionaire M. Aaron Bullock.

Anxious for any distraction, I volunteered to oversee the setup of the party at the Bullock farm. Buck was shocked and elated that I was finally getting on board the election bandwagon. He didn't realize that I would have accepted almost any offer to escape from the Steak House where so many people were talking about the documents, Ben, and my father—mostly negative talk about "the Yankee traitor." Within days of Ben's receiving the documents, it was hard to find anyone in Tallagumsa who hadn't heard about Dean Reese's accusations against my father. The farther away from town I could get, the better.

Buck loved M. Aaron Bullock because Mr. Bullock had been an early supporter of my father's bid for governor, because (Buck claimed) he was the spitting image of Lyndon Johnson, and because he was famous all over the Southeast for his Christmas decorations.

Every Christmas, Bullock had his farm—including the seven barns, the mansion, the greenhouse, the tennis and pool fences, the pool house, and hundreds of the larger trees—hung with miles and miles of green, blue, orange, yellow, and red Christmas lights. Each year he invited the world to take a look, and the world came. Voters and the children of voters cherished Bullock's Christmas extravaganza, and they'd love my father too, according to Buck, once they knew Newell Hagerdorn and M. Aaron Bullock were buddies.

After working at the Bullock farm the morning of the fundraiser, I returned home to rest and to get Jessie, Will, and Hank. Roland, worried about my mental health, drove back down with me and the kids. By this time every summer, Roland's hair was streaked with varying shades of red, and his freckles were so dense that his skin took on their red-orange coloring.

Will and Hank, almost five months old now, were dressed in matching green and white seersucker short overalls and white shirts, compliments of Jane and Buck. During the air-conditioned car ride, the boys were all sweet smiles and "aahs," "oohs," and "baahs," but the day was another hot, still, gnatty dog day, and within minutes of leaving the car, their golden hair was matted to their heads with sweat and an ugly red heat rash appeared on their necks. They were miserable. Will threw his red and blue plastic ring toy on the ground every few minutes, then howled in misery until it was retrieved. Hank fidgeted, his face puckered in discomfort.

Jessie wasn't too happy either, but not because of the weather. Her father had been gone three weeks, and his absence was wearing on her. Although he came by the house each day while I was at the Steak House, she needed him home all the time. On the drive down to the Bullock farm I could hear her playing with her Barbies, convincing them and herself that Eddie would be at the party, even though I told her that wasn't likely. Once the festivities began, Jessie walked from one group to the next, searching for her father.

We and the other early arrivals at the Bullock farm sought relief from the overpowering sun under the large yellow and white striped tent that covered the tables of food and drinks. At Buck's behest, Bullock had strung Christmas lights from every available strut and pole. The lights would be turned on at sunset following Daddy's speech.

Around seven o'clock, just as dusk and a hint of a breeze brought some relief, one of the waiters found me and told me I had a phone call. I followed him into the house and picked up the kitchen phone. It was Ben.

"How did you find me here?" I asked.

"Your father's campaign schedule isn't a state secret," he said. "Buck gives any reporter who asks a detailed daily schedule. Hopes we'll write something."

"I'd hoped you wouldn't be writing about Daddy ever again," I said.

"I'm afraid I am. The *Star* is breaking the story this afternoon," he said.

"What?" I asked, shocked. "But it's too soon, Ben."

"I can't put it off. I wish I could," he said. "I've postponed it as long as possible."

"But maybe Daddy would cooperate more now," I said. "If he knew the story was coming out."

"I've tried to talk to him every day for a week, including today, LuAnn, and you know as well as I do he won't budge. He told me so. No question about where your stubborn streak comes from."

"What's the story going to say?"

"That Dean Reese, an FBI informant, told the FBI that your father and Mr. Waddy were with him in the car and that your father killed Turnbow and Johnson. It'll say the FBI covered it up because of its own problems with Dean Reese—to save their own asses, in other words. So your father won't look like the only bad guy."

"That really makes me feel a lot better," I said. An ugly image formed in my mind of my father, Floyd Waddy, and Dean Reese together in a car out Old Highway 49 near the tree. I couldn't bear the thought of that image being conveyed to the world outside Tallagumsa.

"A little something for everyone: murder, politics, coverup. You can't help but have a hit, Ben." Waiters from a Birmingham restaurant bustled past me, leaving the kitchen with trays of food, returning with empty trays. None of them noticed my distress.

"That's not my goal, LuAnn," Ben said.

"When will it be in the news here?"

"Probably tonight on television, tomorrow in the papers."

"Everywhere else?"

"The same."

"Who wrote the story?" I asked.

"Me," Ben said.

"Your wife must be very proud."

"She doesn't know yet, LuAnn. Jesus Christ, don't you think *you'd* be the first to know?"

I didn't respond.

"Do you want to know anything else about it?" he asked.

"What else should I know?" I asked.

"Just that reporters will be desperate to interview you, and photographers will be after you for your picture. Maybe even your kids. You need to talk to Jessie and explain it to her."

"You're so full of cheery news, Ben."

"I'm not happy about this either," he said. "I'm lonely without you. Can I come by later, keep you company?"

"No, but thanks for calling. I mean it. Bye."

I hung up the phone and stood stock still until I realized that I was holding my breath. Lightheaded, I grabbed the edge of the kitchen counter for support and tried to breathe. Then I walked slowly down the hall to the guest bathroom, locked the door, shut the toilet cover, and sat down. I took one deep breath, then another. As I threw my head back, for one last deep breath, I noticed the wallpaper: little covered wagons, each pulled by two horses, guided by a pioneer man with a pioneer woman at his side. I imagined the man taking care of the woman through Indian attacks, tornadoes, floods, childbirth, and the other traumas of pioneer life. Who could help me through this? Who could make everything better, as my father had always assured me he could when I was a child?

I came outside at the far end of the mansion and looked around. The rolling farmland was dotted with cows and horses. The party was behind me. Halfway up the driveway to the house, close to the barns, four Hereford cows blocked the way of an approaching car. The driver flashed his headlights on and off twice, and the cow facing the car moved on across the road. The others followed. I thought of the Cow Palace Restaurant and tried to recall the fun Ben and I had had that day, but I couldn't find even the memory of those feelings.

Should I divulge the news now or wait until the fundraiser was over? I decided to wait and let Daddy have at least these few hours.

My sense of isolation and anxiety grew as I stood with most of my family and fifty or so guests under the party tent. Jessie had given up trying to find Eddie. Instead she was hitting everyone she knew, a little too hard to be cute. I'd never seen her act so wild. During a break from the hitting, I heard her sternly lecturing Will and Hank.

I walked to within earshot.

"If you hadn't been born," Jessie said, "I would still have a daddy."

I didn't have the energy to try to explain to Jessie that Eddie's leaving had nothing to do with the twins. Obviously, although I'd tried, I hadn't done a very good job of protecting her from the effects of the events of the last three weeks: my affair with Ben, Eddie leaving, the FBI documents. All were taking a terrible toll on my family.

My appetite was gone, but I tried a few bites of food in hopes that my misery would go unnoticed. It was useless. The very thought of food was nauseating.

"Don't you feel well?" my mother asked as I picked at my food. "You're eating like a bird." Mother's curls were drooping in the heat, but otherwise she looked collected and comfortable in a lightweight white percale suit. Her American flag pin was on the right lapel.

"I'm okay, Mother," I said, more sharply than I'd intended. I put down my plate and hid my shaking hands in the pockets of my sleeveless cotton dress.

"I saw something interesting the other day while I was eating at the Holiday Inn," Buck said.

"Traitor," Roland said. "Their food's horrible."

"It's not as good as yours, Roland, but I was nearby and I was hungry. Anyway, I was looking out the window at nothing in particular when a bus pulled up. The destination on the bus was 'HEAVEN.' It was from the New Hope Baptist Church."

Roland laughed. "Where can I catch that bus? Because I'm going to need it one day if I'm going to get there."

Buck and Jane joined the laughter. Then, looking toward the podium, Buck exclaimed, "Newell's about ready to give his speech. Everybody up there with him," he suggested.

Mother, Buck, and Jane walked toward Daddy.

Suddenly I couldn't stand another second of this. "Jessie, I'll be right back," I said. "Roland, will you keep an eye on the kids for a minute?" I walked away from the speech and past the house toward one of the more isolated fields. Two of Bullock's huge black and tan German shepherds appeared at my side and licked my hands.

"Let's go for a walk," I said, happy to have them for company. I clucked my tongue and started down the steep hill.

The dogs and I walked across the field for a few minutes, stopping at a new barn I hadn't noticed during the two days I'd spent here preparing for the event. Inside it smelled like pine and looked like a carnival. Strings of Christmas lights hung from the rafters straight down to the ground and formed a canopy across the ceiling. I flipped a light switch. All the hanging lights came on. I smiled despite myself. I ran to the other end of the barn and flipped another switch. The ceiling was awash with red, yellow, blue, orange, and green.

The dogs barked, then left my side and trotted between the

rows of lights to the entrance I'd just come through. Roland ran in the door, panting.

"I saw you come down here. Is something wrong, LuAnn?"

"Who's with the children?" I asked.

"Your sister. What's the matter?"

"I guess you'll know soon enough. The story about the murders is coming out today and it blames Daddy. Ben called here to tell me." I walked around the barn, up and down the narrow aisles created by the strings of lights. I unscrewed three of the burned-out bulbs, looked at them in the palm of my hand, then threw them as hard as I could against the wall. They exploded, one after the other. The German shepherds ran back and forth between me and Roland, barking wildly.

"It's not the end of the world," Roland said.

"Maybe it is," I said. "For me." I walked to the door and tried to pass through.

Roland grabbed my arm. "Do you believe what Dean Reese said?" he asked.

"No," I said. "Do you?"

"No," he answered.

"That makes two of us."

"Come on, nobody in town believes that crap," he said.

"But most of the world will believe whatever they hear on the news. I would if I weren't his daughter."

I shook loose from Roland's grip and pushed aside several strings of lights so that I could get by them and lean against the barn wall. Then I slid down to the ground and called the dogs to me by snapping my thumb and finger together and patting my thigh. One of the German shepherds passed through the curtain of hanging lights in front of me and lay down beside me with his head in my lap. I put my head on the dog's back.

"I am at a loss," I said in a whisper. "A complete and total loss." I smoothed away the tears as they fell faster and faster onto the dog's back. "And I'm so damn tired of crying. That's all I do anymore, and I don't see life getting any easier any time soon."

"It will," Roland said. "I promise. When my mother died

two years ago I didn't think I could stand it. Every day for months I woke up with an awful sadness in me. And your father isn't dead. He's in some trouble, but that comes with the territory. He can take it."

"*I* can't! I can't!" I cried. "Oh Roland, I need to go home," I said quietly. "Could you get the children and my stuff and bring the car, please? I'll wait here. I just can't go back over there. Tell Mother I'm sick or something. If Jessie wants to stay with Mother or Jane I guess that's okay. I know—you could give everyone the news."

"No thanks," he said. He tightened his ponytail and left without a fight. I suppose he didn't have the heart to argue with me.

I didn't want to watch the ten o'clock news, but I had to.

"New information reveals an FBI coverup of an informant's involvement in the Tallagumsa 1963 civil rights murders," the anchorman reported. "Three local men have been identified as suspects in the two unsolved murders. The *Washington Star* has reported that Dean Reese, a former Tallagumsa resident and an FBI informant, was involved in the murders of Jimmy Turnbow and Leon Johnson when the young men were on their way to integrate the university in August 1963. Before Reese's suicide, he informed the FBI that Newell Hagerdorn, then the sheriff of Tallagumsa, and Floyd Waddy were in the car with him when the shots were fired." The anchorman recapped the FBI documents I'd read that day at the Steak House and explained that the FBI had purposely failed to share that information, as well as other evidence, with state authorities. In closing, he detailed my father's political history and mentioned that a reporter from Washington who was living in Tallagumsa had reopened the case.

The phone rang. I didn't answer. When the ringing stopped, I took the headset and stuffed it in my pajama drawer. I took one of the Valium tablets Dr. Stuart had given me a week earlier to help me sleep. Around three in the morning I got up, drank some soda water, and checked on the children. They were sleeping soundly, exhausted from the day at the Bullock farm. I took another Valium and fell asleep again.

I awoke neither upset nor calm. I felt as though someone was pushing a pause button between each thought and action, leaving me curiously unconnected—not only to my surroundings but also to myself. It wasn't great, but it was a lot better than the alternative.

I got Jessie to school without falling apart. In the car I told her that some of the people who didn't want her grandfather to be elected governor were saying some bad things about him and that it was normal in an election and not to worry about it.

"Like what?" she asked.

"Like he's a bad guy, stuff like that," I said.

"Oh!" she exclaimed. "Can Julie come over today?"

I didn't take my usual parking space in front of the Steak House. A news truck from Channel Six in Birmingham was parked there, and inside the restaurant foyer I could see six men waiting. At least one of them held a video camera. Another had a still camera slung around his neck. What to do? Go home, wait in the car until they left, go to the beauty parlor and get a wig? There were no easy outs. This was what I had to look forward to for the indefinite future. I drove around the block again and decided I had no choice. I had to face them. I parked half a block away. At the sight of me walking up the sidewalk, the crowd of newsmen dashed out of the foyer and surged around me.

"Good morning," I said when they blocked my path. Three microphones were thrust in my face.

"Mrs. Garrett, any comment on your father's role in the deaths of Leon Johnson and Jimmy Turnbow?" one asked. At the same time another asked, "Is your father resigning from his office as mayor?"

The video camera was on me; a still camera clicked various views of me. My heart beat faster and faster. Thankfully, I had on sunglasses. Hopefully, it would be difficult to tell how upset I was.

"All I can tell you now is that my father was not in any way involved in their deaths," I said. "He is innocent. He will not resign. You should direct any further questions to his office. If you'll excuse me, I have to go to work."

Two of the reporters tried to ask another question at the same time. "Will he drop out of the gubernatorial race?" one asked. "How does it feel to have this happen after you raised the money for the Turnbow-Johnson memorial?" another yelled.

I pretended I didn't hear the questions, pulled open one of the double-glass doors to the Steak House, and went inside.

Estelle was at the cash register, checking out a short line of breakfast customers. In the front dining room, there were two tables of strangers whom I assumed were reporters. Everyone in the room stared at me. I walked through the dining room toward the kitchen, nodding at people, saying hello, acting as if this were any old morning. I heard Estelle ask Doris to take over the register. She followed me back.

"Poor baby," she said, hugging me after we'd both passed through the kitchen doors.

Roland was cooking at the grill. He blew me a kiss. "Feel better?" he asked.

"Better than I thought I would, I guess. I got Jessie to school. I'm here. I'm alive. I'm not hysterical. Are those reporters out there, Estelle?"

She nodded.

"If they eat or order coffee or something, they can stay. If they come in and bother people, or just sit and sit, you can ask them to leave. Be polite. I don't want or need to read about anyone here getting in a fight with any reporters. Call the sheriff's office if you have any problems. Everybody back to work."

I went up to my little office and sat at my desk. It was past time to type the list of today's specials, but the surge of adrenaline I'd received when confronted by the reporters outside had ebbed, and I was suddenly both emotionally and physically drained. I rested my head on my typewriter and then, remembering all the nosy reporters who could see me through my glass-walled office, sat up.

While typing the first few lines of the specials of the day, something caught my eye, and I looked up. Eddie was walking up the hallway toward me. He hadn't set foot in the restaurant since he left home. I pretended I didn't see him, walked quickly and quietly down the steps from my office, and tried to hide by scrunching down in a booth in the back dining room. He wasn't far behind me. A moment later he stood looking down at me.

"Here to gloat?" I asked, sitting up.

"No, LuAnn, I'm not," he said. "I'm here to see if you're all right, if there's anything I can do. I tried to call after I saw the news."

"It's a little late for your concern," I said. "You left me. You're living with another woman. You probably think it's funny that Daddy's being crucified by Ben." I glared at him, stood up, and walked away toward the rear kitchen doors.

"LuAnn," he called after me. "Would you give me a—"

I ran into the kitchen, where I couldn't hear what else he had to say.

That night I dreamed I was lying in the back seat of my father's 1969 gold Chevy Impala. The car swerved back and forth over the double yellow line on the steep, narrow, two-lane road to my parents' house at Clark Lake. My father turned his head 180 degrees around to smile or look at me as he talked. When I tried to move, I couldn't; when I tried to speak, he couldn't hear me. Still I screamed, "Stop, stop, please Daddy, stop!"

In my dream, I could hear a car coming from the other direction, its horn honking at us. My father got back in his lane momentarily, just long enough to avoid crashing into the other car. As the car passed, I could see that the driver was Eddie.

"That boy tried to run us over," my father said. He talked, smiled, and drove faster and faster.

"Remember how when you were little, LuAnn, I used to drive with no hands?" he said. "You're not too old to get a kick out of that, are you, sweetie? Watch. Watch Daddy. But don't tell your mother." He took his hands off the steering wheel and held them up, turned around, and smiled again. The car went completely out of control.

I awoke right before we crashed. The clock showed it was six o'clock, too close to my seven o'clock wake-up time to get back to sleep. I sat up in bed and pulled my legs toward me, covering them with the front of my over-sized T-shirt. Tight as a cocoon, the white cotton shirt held my knees close to the skin of my stomach and chest as I rocked slowly back and forth.

CHAPTER FIFTEEN

hip Tuckahoe, a former charter member of the Coffee Club and a family friend, held the job of county attorney for twenty-five years before stepping down to spend more time at home in nearby Cullman with his ailing wife Betty. Ironically, it was Chip's decision to leave the prosecutor's position that gave Junior Fuller the opportunity to take the job when he moved back to Tallagumsa. On August 22, 1978, a grand jury, at Junior's urging, indicted my father for murder. On August 25, Daddy hired Chip to represent him.

Buck had wanted my father to choose one of the more flamboyant, well-known Birmingham lawyers, but when Daddy interviewed one of them and gave him the same run around he'd given me and everyone else, the lawyer refused to represent him.

Chip Tuckahoe, on the other hand, like me, accepted my father's position. Chip wanted the case. I was Newell Hagerdorn's daughter. What choice did we have but to trust him?

A week after the indictment was handed down, Chip, a short, pugnacious man with thick, wavy brown hair, arrived at Daddy's office for their second meeting, the purpose of which was to assess the legal avenues available for avoiding or substantially delaying the trial.

Unable to function very effectively for the past week, I had decided to skip work and join them. For the meeting I wore cut-off jeans, a T-shirt, and flip-flops. They didn't care what I wore, and the idea of dressing up, or doing anything requiring thought or effort, depressed me.

My father, on the other hand, looked fit and relaxed as he took his seat behind his large mahogany desk. Chip and I pulled up two red leather chairs across from the desk and sat down facing my father. Two walls of the spacious corner office were taken up by windows; the other two were covered with photographs of my father with various state and federal politicians, shaking hands, eating, fishing, hunting, and partying, and a large collection of family photos. Through the windows I could see the Newell Hagerdorn County Courthouse where the grand jury had charged Daddy with two counts of murder. There, tomorrow's arraignment and any future trial would be held.

"Our best bet," Chip explained once the meeting began, "and I really believe we have a good chance at this, is to get the charges dismissed based on the fact that it's been so long since the crime occurred. It's practically unheard of to try someone fifteen years after a crime was committed."

"I thought Junior said there was no statute of limitations on murder. I remember he said so at his press conference after he got the indictments," I said.

"That's absolutely true," Chip said. "Our arguments here are based on your rights to a speedy trial, a fair trial, and to due process, Newell. The State totally fucked up the case—excuse my French, LuAnn—but they didn't even try to pursue the matter when they should have. And the feds covered up all the evidence they had, purposefully concealing it from the State and everyone else. You didn't do anything to obstruct the case. Jesus Christ, you gave evidence to the FBI agents who were in town. And where's the physical evidence now, the guns, the shells? Are the witnesses alive? I can't believe everything and everyone is intact after fifteen years. And I doubt they can prove that whatever evidence they do have was handled properly from the time of the crime until the date of the trial. I've had plenty of cases dismissed in instances where the trial came just a few months after the crime and the police couldn't establish chain of custody. Fifteen years is unheard of.

"Usually the court won't stop a case to hear these arguments," Chip continued, "but this is so unusual, and the legal arguments so complex, that I think we could postpone the whole trial for arguments and briefs and appeals, maybe take a whole year just for that."

"What about the claim made in several editorials that the trial has to go forward to prove the system works, to provide justice where justice was denied?" my father asked. "That would suggest there wouldn't be the kind of delay you're talking about." He picked a cigar from the gilded box on his desk, removed the cellophane wrapper, and reached for his lighter.

"There is way in hell a court will have this trial and cause a lot of hysteria and pain if there's even one chance in a thousand that a court will later rule there didn't need to be a trial. Besides, it's not 1963. The law now is pretty favorable toward minorities; the community is too. That era is behind us, a question for the history books, not the courts."

"I suppose you'd remind the court that this case is eating up the soul of our town," my father said, puffing on his cigar until it lit. "It's not healing old wounds but ripping them open again." He offered a cigar to Chip.

"Thanks," Chip said, taking a cigar out of the box and lighting it. "I like that, Newell," he said, scribbling on his yellow pad with one of the fifteen or twenty perfectly sharpened number-two pencils he kept in his briefcase. "The soul of our town," Chip repeated approvingly.

"I've been a politician so long I can come up with something that pulls on the heartstrings on just about any subject," my father said dryly. "Now, what else is there?"

"We can try to fashion something like what worked two years ago after the State got indictments for the murder of Willie Edwards. That murder was in 1957, after the Montgomery bus boycott. The defendants were charged with holding a gun on Willie Edwards until he jumped off the Tyler Goodwyn Bridge. There was overwhelming evidence that the defendants had killed him because they mistook him for a black fellow who they'd heard was dating a white woman."

"That reminds me," I said. "One of Ben Gainey's FBI documents said maybe the daughter of whoever killed Turnbow and Johnson was dating one of them. Have you looked into that?"

"I will," Chip said, writing again.

"That's a big fat waste of time," my father said. "Don't bother."

There was a knock at the office door. "Yes?" my father called.

Sheriff Bev Carter, dressed in his official blue uniform and hat, took a step inside. "Afternoon, y'all," he said. "Chip asked me to come by and talk some about my grand jury appearance."

"Can't we do that after the arraignment?" my father asked. "We've got a lot to cover today, and I've got town business to attend to as well."

"Fine with me," Chip said.

"Just let me know when you need me," Bev said. He closed the door behind him.

Daddy pushed a button on his intercom. "Franny," he said, "get me a cup of coffee. Any for you, Chip? LuAnn, honey?"

We both shook our heads.

"Just one," he said into the intercom.

"So what happened in the case you were telling us about?" my father asked. "The one at the Tyler Goodwyn Bridge." He leaned way back in his chair and listened.

"Old Judge Embry down there is an ornery geezer who never even got to the questions of delay we've been discussing. He just quashed the indictments twice, ruling that the state hadn't specified a cause of death. Believe it or not, he held that merely forcing a person to jump from a bridge does not naturally and probably lead to the death of such person. So no crime."

My father leaned forward. He looked surprised.

"That's pretty revolting," I said, "but I guess we have to use whatever we can to get Daddy out of this. Could you fashion some kind of argument like that, Chip?"

"I'm working on it," Chip said. "We can move for a change of venue too—that's the place the trial occurs—arguing you couldn't get a fair trial here."

"Why would you do that?" I asked. "Daddy's more popular here than anywhere else in the state. Why move it?"

"Good point," Chip said. "Maybe you should consider law school, LuAnn. Frankly, the only reason to try to move the trial would be to add to the delay."

There was a quick knock. The door opened before anyone could answer. Franny came in, nodded at us, and put down the coffee on Daddy's desk pad. She stirred it once, took the spoon, and left.

"Go ahead, Chip," Daddy said.

"We can also delay the trial some by moving to suppress any physical evidence they have. We don't know what that is yet, but even if they have the gun or the shells, we'd make the same chain-of-custody arguments we would use to argue you can't get a fair trial," he said.

Chip pulled a book of Alabama statutes from his briefcase and opened it to a page marked with a slip of paper. "We could even challenge the grand jury. Maybe one of them was unqualified to serve under the Alabama code or maybe one of them is related to you within the fifth degree. I've never tried that argument, but if you want time, motions can give it to you. Probably a year, even two."

"What if none of that works and he has to go to trial?" I asked.

"We can drag out the jury selection. Finding a panel we can accept could take months. Some people nowadays are even hiring jury consultants to help pick a favorable jury, though I doubt that's necessary here. Then there's trial preparation and the like—takes months. One problem with delay, one real big problem, is you are not supposed to get out on bail after your arraignment. These are capital offenses."

The hair stood up on my arms. *Capital offenses.*

"Bobby Lee wouldn't keep me in jail and you know it," my father said. "Ricky wouldn't either." Bobby Lee and Ricky were two county judges.

"Are they the only possible judges for tomorrow?" I asked.

"They sure are," Chip said. "I went by this morning to check. You're probably right, Newell, and since nobody tried to arrest you after the indictment I doubt they'll try to lock you up now."

"Doubt?" I repeated, worried that Chip wasn't absolutely sure.

"I just don't know what Junior wants to do," Chip said. "I'm surprised he brought this damn case in the first place. I wouldn't have, not in a million years."

"I'm not surprised," I said. "He wants to make a big name for himself and run for office or get a federal judgeship. Just indicting Daddy has gotten him more publicity than he could have hoped for otherwise."

"The boys' families will be breathing down Junior's neck, urging him to have you put in jail immediately. And I saw that the NAACP has a few people in town," Chip said. "I'm sure they'd like you in jail as of yesterday. One of them was outside the courthouse this morning with a petition to have the name changed."

"Any signatures?" My father smirked. "I'm sure as hell not going to sit in jail for something I didn't do for some cause. What else do we have to cover today, Chip?"

"Not much," Chip said.

"If Daddy ever has a trial, what are the chances of conviction?" I asked.

"Zero to none," Chip said, smiling. "First, as far as anyone can tell, they've got a real circumstantial case. Juries don't like that. And around here, as you just pointed out, your father is a very popular man. It shouldn't be hard to get an acquittal unless there are blacks on the jury. Even then we'd get a hung jury, not a conviction, and I don't think Junior would try you twice."

"Why wouldn't there be any blacks on the jury?" I asked.

"Not many live in the county, and of those less than forty percent are registered to vote—that's where we get our jury list. I can probably strike the few who get summonses. It's a rare day when an Alabama jury convicts a white man for killing a black man. In fact, I read last week that four thousand racially motivated murders occurred in the South between 1886 and 1966. How many whites got in trouble? I can't name more than a few."

"As horrible as those numbers are—I mean, what they stand for—they make me feel better about your odds, Daddy," I said.

My father rolled back his chair, stood up, and put on his suit jacket. We were dismissed. "I want to think about all this and we'll talk again in the morning, Chip," he said.

"The arraignment is in the morning," Chip said.

"I know when it is," my father said harshly. "Meet me here at eight o'clock."

"I'm telling everybody to stay away from the arraignment," he said to me. "I don't want a big to-do. No need for it."

"Mother's not coming?" I asked, surprised.

"She's happy to stay home. Your sister is supposed to be in bed anyway, so she's not coming. And Buck wants to pretend this isn't happening."

"Well, I want to come," I insisted. "I really do. Please."

"I don't know why, but I guess I can't stop you," he said. "As they used to say in the good old days, you're free, white, and twenty-one."

The arraignment was in Courtroom B on the first floor of the new courthouse. When the building was dedicated in April, I'd felt that the grandeur of the marble floors, the carved oak doors, and the high ceilings imparted a sense of justice. Now I saw the same space as cold and heartless, a reminder of just how powerless I was to help my father.

I arrived at court early to avoid the press and the demonstrators I assumed would be on the courthouse steps. After the news stories broke, three fully outfitted Klansmen had stood outside my restaurant a few hours each day for a week in support of their hero, my father. I had done my best to ignore the Klan, and I was just as anxious to avoid the placards and glares of the Birmingham NAACP members who were in town.

The courtroom filled up quickly between eight-forty-five and nine o'clock, primarily with reporters (Ben was in the first row), the extended families of Jimmy Turnbow and Leon Johnson, and a few members of the Coffee Club. The rest of our family had stayed away, as my father had requested.

At five before nine, my father and Chip came in following their morning meeting. Chip didn't look happy. He walked quickly, his squat frame bobbing up and down with each step. My father, looking relaxed, winked at me when he passed. I wondered what was going on.

Bobby Lee McNabb, the senior judge in Tallagumsa County, entered Courtroom B at exactly nine. Judge McNabb was a small olive-skinned man, with thin black hair and a large beak nose.

The bailiff stood up and ordered us to stand as well.

Bobby Lee McNabb called the court to order and told us to sit down again. "Good morning, everyone, Newell, Chip, Junior. Welcome to you out-of-town folks. Sorry to see y'all under these circumstances, but here we are and we might as well proceed with *The State of Alabama v. Newell Hagerdorn*.

"I'll read the indictment," he continued. He read: "The grand jury of Tallagumsa County charges that on or about August 27, 1963, Newell Hagerdorn did: (1) unlawfully and with malice aforethought kill Jimmy Turnbow by shooting him with a shotgun; (2) unlawfully and with malice aforethought kill Leon Johnson by shooting him with a shotgun; against the peace and dignity of the State of Alabama."

As Judge McNabb talked, a peroxided-blond woman in a skin-tight knit dress typed every word he said on a little machine that looked more like an adding machine than a typewriter.

"How do you plead, Newell?" the judge asked.

My father stood up. "Not guilty to both charges," he said. Then he sat down.

"We should talk about our schedule," Judge McNabb said,

balancing a large desk calendar upright in front of him.

Chip and Junior stood up. They made an odd couple: Chip was five foot two inches tall, Junior six foot five inches.

"Today is August the twenty-ninth," Judge McNabb said. "Junior, you'll be prosecuting, right?"

"Yes, Judge," Junior said.

"Let's hear what you're thinking about for a trial date," Judge McNabb said.

"I hoped we could get the trial done in between Thanksgiving and Christmas," Junior said.

"And motions?"

"One month from today," Junior said. "If that's enough time for the defense."

"Chip, what does the defense say to those proposals?" Judge McNabb asked.

"We'd like to go to trial no later than October second," Chip said.

A buzz of conversation began among the spectators. Junior looked confused. Judge Bobby Lee McNabb, obviously surprised, pounded his gavel.

"We have only two motions, and we can make them today—right now, in fact," Chip said. "First, we move to waive a jury trial; and second, we move for discovery of all material we're entitled to under Rule 16. That's it. The mayor wants this resolved as quickly as possible so he can get on with his life and the election."

"The State have any objections, Junior?" Judge McNabb asked. "The court and the prosecutor have to agree before there can be a jury waiver."

"I haven't thought much about trying this without a jury," Junior said slowly. "I just don't know. The trial date too, that's awful early. We may have difficulty getting all the evidence together in time for an October trial."

"Your Honor, if I may, the State shouldn't bring an indictment if the State's not ready to proceed with a case immediately," Chip said.

"Could we take a break?" Junior asked.

Court was adjourned. The buzz that had begun when Chip dropped his bombshell erupted into a cacophony of voices. Several reporters, including Ben, rushed out of the room. I assumed they were placing calls to their legal experts to see what this could mean. I wished I knew. The day before we'd talked in Daddy's office about delay and more delay, and now he was asking for a trial date in just over a month. What about all the motions Chip could make? What about a jury that would surely acquit? What was going on? The families of Jimmy and Leon looked suspiciously in my father's direction, no doubt wondering what sort of trickery he was up to.

In the hallway outside the courtroom, I grabbed my father's arm and pulled him down the hall, away from the reporters. "You come too, Chip," I ordered. I yanked open the door to Courtroom D. It was empty. The three of us went inside. The door swung slowly shut behind us.

"What was all that about?" I asked. "What are you doing, Daddy?"

"I told you not to come, remember? Last night, after looking at the whole thing, I realized that what I want is as quick and quiet a trial as possible," he said. "If we use all the means of delay Chip says are available, I'll delay myself right out of the gubernatorial election."

"Not if you get the case dismissed," I said. I could hear how whiny I sounded, but I couldn't help it. The situation seemed to grow more ludicrous by the day.

"But then everyone will say I won by playing technical legal games," he said. "A dismissal would just give the press and my opponents too much ammunition and increase the chances that the FBI and the Justice Department will look into the murders again, dragging everything out even longer. The whole affair will be never ending. I need—I want—a speedy resolution and a final one."

"But why not take the jury, then, and be sure of getting off?" I asked. "If a jury acquits, how can anyone complain?"

"My political opponents would argue they let me off because I was white, the way all southern juries let off all white defendants. And if the jury is hung we might have to start all over. Jury selection and a jury trial would be a media circus. Everybody respects Bobby Lee; he's no Judge Embry. He'll make a fair decision based on the evidence, and Ben Gainey and all those other reporters will tell the world how I won fair and square."

"But you're charged with two capital crimes, Daddy. You can't take this chance."

"You don't think I did it, do you, LuAnn? That's not why you're so upset, is it?"

"No! But I would feel a lot better if you had a defense *or* if I understood why any of this nightmare was happening. Just tell us the truth."

He smiled at me as if I were a foolish child. "There is nothing to worry about," he said. "The State cannot prove its case. Plain and simple. Right, Chip?"

"Maybe, maybe not. I'm not happy with your father's decision, LuAnn," Chip said.

"Don't let him do it then," I said. I flopped down on the next-to-last courtroom bench.

Chip patted my shoulder. "I think we're taking a big risk," he said. "But your father has the final say. I've advised him of the risks and benefits of every approach. That's all I can do."

"This is the stupidest idea you've ever had," I said.

"No, the smartest," my father said. "Listen, the government can't prove I killed anyone because I didn't; the people will see there's no truth to the charges. I'm going to win the case, end this bullshit once and for all, and win the election too."

"Do you think I should admire you for avoiding the easy way out, for holding the government to its burden of proof? I might agree with your approach if you were going to testify, if you'd finally explain all this. Will you?" I asked. I didn't bother to look at him as I spoke. I figured I knew what his answer would be.

"No," he said.

I wanted to hit him. "Chip! This is ridiculous!" I said. "Make him listen."

Chip shrugged. "Once Newell Hagerdorn makes up his mind, I don't know any way to change it. If you do, LuAnn, let me in on the secret."

"I give up," I said quietly.

I got up and walked to the doors, where I caught sight of several reporters who'd been watching us through the small glass windows in the doors. When they saw me, they moved quickly out of sight, trying to hide their prying eyes.

CHAPTER SIXTEEN

M y family traditionally had a Labor Day cookout at Clark Lake with Jolene and her family. Since the arraignment had been less than a week before Labor Day, I'd assumed we'd just skip it this year. I was wrong.

The day was pleasant, with the temperature in the high eighties and low humidity. My father was in a great mood—happy, he said, that the trial would be over soon and everything would be back to normal.

Before Jolene and her family arrived at my parents', I helped Mother carry out bowls of salads and trays of hot dogs and hamburgers to the picnic table. She didn't seem at all concerned about the events of the last month or the upcoming trial. All her energy was focused on making the picnic a success, taking care of my sister, and planning for the church bazaar.

On my last trip to the kitchen for mustard and ketchup, I caught sight of Ben walking up the path from the direction of his rental house. He carried his steno pad in one hand and wore his camera around his neck. My father smiled and shook Ben's hand. Ben looked around, saw me, and waved. I stared at him, then ran inside the house to find out what was going on.

Buck sat at the dining-room table stamping fundraising envelopes for Daddy's gubernatorial race. Buck's enthusiasm for the election had waned briefly after the newscast accused Daddy of being involved in the murders and then again after the indictment, but he was still the campaign manager. If he felt any anxiety, he never let on publicly.

"Buck! Why is Ben Gainey here?" I demanded.

174

Buck stopped writing, but didn't put down his pen or look at me. "Your father wanted him," he said.

"I thought he hated him," I said. "I thought he couldn't stand to be near him. I thought he wanted to shoot him, for God's sake."

"Newell doesn't like or dislike Ben particularly, but he's decided that Ben should be with him regularly from now through the trial. His view is that Ben broke the story, and Ben should write the happy ending as well. Besides, Ben will be fairer than any of the other Yankees covering the case. As for why he's here today, the publicity will be great. You know, with Jolene's family here. We need some good press." He counted the number of envelopes in the pile he'd just made.

"I don't want him here!" I said.

"Go tell your father," Buck said, smiling. He stood up and patted me on the back, well aware that I wouldn't say a word to Daddy.

"Fine, but I'm not going to be nice to Ben."

"You sound just like a four-year-old," Buck said.

While we were arguing in the house, I heard cars pulling up. I looked out. Jolene, her husband, two daughters, and seven grandchildren (ages one month to fifteen) arrived in the two old cars my father had given them over the years. Only Jolene's son, Darrell, was missing.

I went out and greeted our guests. Jolene had on shorts and a T-shirt commemorating the family reunion she and her family had attended in the hills of Tennessee the year before, where they'd met hundreds of other members of the Wilson clan.

"Hi. Where's Darrell?" I asked Jolene.

She frowned. "He couldn't come," she said, looking past me toward the shoreline.

"He couldn't or wouldn't?" I said.

She didn't answer.

"Come on," I urged her. "Just tell me."

"Don't you tell your daddy, but Darrell called us Uncle Toms for coming, say we betrayed our race and all this like that.

175

'Mr. Newell didn't do nothing,' I told him. But he wouldn't listen. Lordy, I never seen him like that."

"Don't worry, Jolene," I said. "I understand."

"Don't say nothing," she said.

"I won't. I swear."

Jolene hugged me. "I wish it'd all be over with."

"You and me both," I said.

I had told Jolene about the allegations against my father a few days after I first saw the FBI documents.

I had been in the carport, about to get in my car and return to the restaurant after my afternoon break, when she'd come out carrying Will and Hank.

"I needs to tell you something," she said.

I shut the car door and leaned on it. "I'm all ears."

Jolene put Hank and Will in the double stroller and as she strapped them in, said, "I be calling Eddie today, tell him you miserable and that he best come back home now."

"You will not!" I said.

"Watch," she said. "You been crying for days now, I know it's bad for you, girl. You try to hide, but I know."

"It's not just Eddie, Jolene. I wish it were so simple."

"What is it? Somebody dying?"

"It's Daddy."

"He sick?"

"No. But some people are saying he was involved in something real bad a long time ago." I paused. Might as well tell her. She'd hear about it from someone sooner or later. "They say he killed Jimmy Turnbow and Leon Johnson."

"Pooh! Why you take that serious?" Will began to fuss in the stroller, anxious to get on with his walk. Jolene stuck his pacifier in his mouth.

"I can't help it. It is serious."

"Bless your heart. You should be worrying more 'bout Eddie than about something like that. People say anything. Don't matter. Mr. Newell will be just fine. You got your life, your own family now. Take care of what's yours, baby girl. If you don't, Jolene'll take care of it for you."

"I was worried you'd be mad with Daddy or me when you heard."

"You know me better than that."

During the Labor Day cookout, I sat on a blanket in a clearing inside a circle of pine trees. I picked at my hamburger, cole slaw, and potato salad, watched the children, and tried to ignore Ben. Will was sitting up next to me with a pillow wedged behind him. Occasionally he fell over without warning, but it didn't seem to faze him. Hank was inching across the blanket, first by putting his head down and his bottom up, then putting his bottom down and his head up, like a see-saw.

Will toppled over. I reached down to prop him back up and stopped short when our eyes met. Both of the boys' eyes, blue at birth, had only recently settled into a gray that was clearly Eddie's. It was spooky. Even when I managed to forget about Eddie for a few minutes, one look at either twin's eyes brought his image back to mind. I missed Eddie terribly, more as every day passed, yet I refused his calls and made sure I missed his visits out of a combination of guilt, embarrassment, and anger.

Jessie played tag with some of Jolene's grandchildren in the yard and the nearby woods. I was surprised and happy to see that she was enjoying herself so much. That morning she'd had a horrible temper tantrum, threatening never to go anywhere with me again. She wanted her daddy, she cried. I'd held her tight and rocked her in my rocking chair, fighting my own tears, until she calmed down, a scene we'd repeated several times since Eddie left.

If only Jessie's magic wand could turn back the clock to April, I would refuse Daddy's Steak House offer on the spot and stop the chain of events that had brought us to this point.

* * *

"How are you?" Ben asked, looming over me and the boys.

I ignored him.

He sat down.

"Why are you here?" I asked in a tired voice.

"I was invited," he said.

"But you knew I'd be here. You shouldn't have come. It's not fair to me."

"Of course I knew you'd be here. That's one reason I came. Look at your father. He's having a great time cooking with Jolene's husband and playing with the kids. You, on the other hand, are the most anxious person I've seen in a long time. You need to stop this one-woman crusade for your own good."

"Any other criticism you'd like to make about me?"

"I'd hoped you'd stopped blaming me by now," he said. He sneezed twice and I handed him a Kleenex from the diaper bag.

"You've been working hard on ruining my father's reputation and my life and I should thank you?" I asked.

"I've been working on a story, that's all."

"Same thing."

He stood up. "I give up, LuAnn. If you decide you're going to act like an adult, let me know." He turned to walk away, then stopped. "Did you hear about your memorial?" he asked.

"What about it?"

"Someone painted it red. I'm afraid it's a mess." He sneezed again and walked toward the lake.

After lunch, Jessie and the older kids waited on the dock for their turns riding around the lake in Daddy's motor boat while the rest of us cleaned up.

"What do you think of Daddy's trial plan?" I asked Mother when we met at the trashcan, where we scraped food off the plastic picnic dishes.

"I guess it's a reasonable approach, under the circumstances," she said. "We'll have to see."

"Is Jane going to testify at the trial?" I asked.

"I don't know."

"Oh, Mother, you must know. Y'all talk every day. Has Junior said anything about her testifying?"

"I don't want to get into it today," Mother said. "It's been such a fine day so far. Can we just take a break from the soap opera of Newell's trial?" She walked away and began to pick up more dirty dishes.

I followed. "I'm worried, Mother."

"Don't be. Your father always takes care of himself. You should be more attentive to yourself, and to your husband and children, and stop worrying about him."

"You sound like Jolene," I said.

"Maybe you'll listen to one of us. Have you seen Eddie lately?" she asked.

"No."

"He says he's tried to talk to you several times. He's very concerned about you. He'd like to talk."

"I didn't know the two of you were so close," I said. "When do you talk about me behind my back?" I asked.

"That's not fair," Mother said, frowning. "I'm worried about my grandchildren and my daughter. I have a right and a duty to help. You seem to be consumed with your father's trial, about which you can do nothing, while your life and your family are falling apart."

"Eddie and I have nothing to talk about. Is Jane going to testify or not?" I persisted.

"If she has to, she will, yes."

"What's she got to say that's so important that Junior has to put a daughter on the stand to testify against her own father? The FBI can testify about everything she knows."

"Not all of it," Mother said.

"What do you mean? What else is there?" I asked, not so sure that I wanted to know the answer to my question.

"Can we please talk after our guests leave?"

"Just tell me now, for God's sake, Mother. Or I'll go get Jane to tell me."

"I wish you wouldn't take the Lord's name in vain. Your sister just went home to lie down and she doesn't need you bothering her. Her blood pressure's off the charts," Mother said grimly. She put down the stack of plates she'd just collected. "Let's go inside."

We entered through the back door and sat down in the living room. She took off her glasses and rubbed her eyes. "I want you to stay calm while I tell you this, please," she said. "The night of the murders Newell woke Jane up from a nap and asked her to keep an eye on you. I was away. He told her he was going to patrol the road Jimmy and Leon were scheduled to use, to make sure they'd be safe because there had been some threats against them. He came home in the middle of the night. The next day he told her he'd been detoured by a bar brawl, that he'd been too late, and when he got there they were dead."

"What's wrong with that?"

"None of it's true, that's what. Bev Carter was at the bar brawl. Your father wasn't." She reached for the cross she wore on a gold chain around her neck and rubbed it with her thumb.

"Jane doesn't have to testify! She could refuse. I would."

"And go to jail?"

"Yes, I would."

"Then you're a bigger fool than I thought. You know, dear, you could support your father without giving up everything else. It's not a war."

"It is a war, and Jane's a traitor and a liar."

"Oh, LuAnn. Why don't you believe Jane? She has no reason to lie."

"She hated Daddy then, she told me. I think she still does. She wants to hurt him. Does he know? Does he know what his own child is going to testify to?"

Mother shrugged. She put her glasses back on and looked at me curiously.

I jumped up, hurried out of the house, and ran down the hill to the dock. When Daddy docked the boat and several of Jolene's grandchildren got off, I rushed on.

"It's our turn, Mom," Jessie whined on behalf of herself and the other children waiting their turn.

"I need to talk to your grandfather, Jes. We'll be right back." I pushed the boat away from the dock with my foot, then restarted the motor. I was shaking my head in dismay as I approached my father.

"You look a little upset," he said.

"Do you know what Jane says happened, what she said to the grand jury?" I yelled over the sound of the motor.

"What did you hear?"

I told him. He just smiled.

"Daddy! You have to tell her not to testify."

"That wouldn't be a real smart thing to do. If anyone found out I'd have another scandal on my hands. She'll change her mind, though," he said. "She'll never testify at trial against me. Never." He smiled confidently.

I wished I could share in his faith.

CHAPTER SEVENTEEN

By the first day of my father's trial, I'd managed to alienate just about everyone I loved. I had trouble believing that Jane wouldn't testify, and in my self-appointed job as Daddy's protector had rushed to her house after the Labor Day picnic and accused her of lying to the grand jury. I'd tried to convince Jane not to testify, sure that anything she had to say was not true, only to upset her so much that Buck ushered me out the door.

Mother, furious when she heard I'd argued with Jane, who was under doctor's orders to control her blood pressure, told me she'd given up on me. "I hope," Mother said, "that we'll be able to make amends after the trial. But I must admit it won't be easy. You're making this so much harder than it needs to be, LuAnn."

So the first day of the trial, I wasn't surprised to find Mother, Buck, Jane, Eddie, and Barbara Cox all seated on the prosecutor's side of the courtroom. Maybe I was reading too much into the seating arrangement, but I didn't think so.

The trial began on a Thursday. Because there would be no jury to pick, no jury to posture and argue to, Chip and Junior thought the proceeding would last only three days.

"Will Bobby Lee decide the case Monday afternoon as soon as the trial is over?" I had asked Chip one day over coffee at the Steak House with him and my father.

"Unlikely," Chip said. "Judge McNabb will avoid issuing an opinion while the courtroom is full of so many fanatics, and he may need to do some research of his own and write something up. Unless he dismisses the charges after Junior's case."

"That's my plan," Daddy said.

"Don't count on it," Chip said. "After the government's case, I'll make a motion for judgment of acquittal—an MJOA it's called. That's a hard motion to win, though."

"If the judge doesn't dismiss the indictment and your client still stubbornly refuses to testify, what can you do for the defense part of the case?" I asked.

"We've got character witnesses. That's about it. But who knows?" Chip said. "Maybe you'll change your mind, Newell. Maybe when the time comes you'll take the stand and let us all in on whatever it is you aren't telling."

"Don't count on it," my father said.

Not long after I took my seat in Courtroom G that first day, Bobby Lee McNabb entered through a door in the back of the courtroom wearing his judge's robe.

The bailiff, John Barrett, called the courtroom to order: "All rise for the Honorable Judge McNabb."

Because I'd known Bobby Lee McNabb all my life, I had trouble thinking of him as "The Honorable" anything. I knew him when he was bald. I watched his slow transformation when he got hair transplants. I knew his daughter, Miriam, the class slut when we were in junior high school; she was plagued by an even larger beak nose than her father's. I knew Bobby Lee went to AA meetings in Cullman. I knew his olive skin was darker than usual on the day the trial began because he had been to a conference in Bermuda a week earlier. I knew all that, and more, but the information didn't give me a clue as to what Bobby Lee McNabb's verdict would be.

In contrast to his style at the arraignment, Judge McNabb called Junior "Mr. Fuller" and Chip "Mr. Tuckahoe" once the trial began. After several negative press comments about the familiarity of all the parties at that first court session, Judge McNabb met in his chambers with Junior and Chip and told them that he would conduct the trial with a little more formality. There would be no first names used—and, he added as they were leaving, he didn't want to hear any lawyer or witness using the word "nigger."

After a few preliminaries, Judge McNabb asked that Junior call the prosecution witnesses together to be sworn.

The witnesses for the State came forward. My sister, Jane, six months pregnant, pale, puffy, and at least fifty pounds heavier than her prepregnancy weight, stood and joined six men in front of Judge McNabb.

The group took the oath to tell the truth and nothing but the truth.

"You must wait in the witness room until the bailiff comes to get you," Judge McNabb explained to the seven prosecution witnesses. "You may not communicate with each other or anyone other than the attorneys in the case regarding your testimony until all witnesses are released. Follow Mr. Barrett, the bailiff, to the witness room," he directed.

The seven witnesses turned and followed John Barrett out of the courtroom.

Junior's first witness was the coroner, Phil Vogel. Phil was close to retirement age, almost sixty-five. He and my father were not friends. They weren't really enemies either, but they'd never gotten along. Phil was a deacon in the Southern Baptist Church who on more than one occasion had lectured my father about committing his life to Christ. Phil wore a large cross tie tack, and his white hair was slicked back with Vitalis. His hands and head shook from the Parkinson's disease he'd had for a few years.

"Please state your full name," Junior said. Junior had never been able to keep still, and he walked back and forth in front of Phil as he questioned him, his hands clasped behind his back most of the time. Junior's deep voice resonated throughout the room.

"Philip Cable Vogel."

"Your address?"

"Box 67, Route 9, Tallagumsa."

"What is your line of work?"

"I'm the county coroner," Vogel said.

"How long have you held that position?"

"Sixteen years," Vogel answered. "Before that I was the deputy coroner for twenty years."

"What are your responsibilities as county coroner?"

"I am required to ascertain the cause of death for anyone who dies in this county." As he talked he rubbed his thumb and forefinger together over and over. I had trouble taking my eyes off his hands.

"How do you determine cause of death?" Junior asked.

"Depends on the circumstances."

"Well, Mr. Vogel, let's say I was walking down the road and I came upon a dead body somewhere in the county. After I let you know, what would you do in such a case? What would be your routine?"

"I would go to the scene and try to figure out the cause of death, like I said. I'd look at the bodies, take pictures, study the area. If I can't tell by just looking, then Dr. Stuart would do an external exam or if necessary an autopsy and report his findings in writing to me."

"What would happen next?"

"I'd take statements from any witnesses, and if it looks like the cause of death was some unlawful means or other I'd summon a panel of six jurors and they'd look into the cause of death."

"And that's called?"

"An inquest."

"How does the jury proceed with an inquest?"

"They subpoena witnesses, take testimony, and decide whether or not the victim died naturally. If not, they render a verdict on who they think killed him and how. Then I can issue an arrest warrant for that person."

"Were you coroner on August 27, 1963?" Junior asked.

"Yes."

"Did you have occasion to investigate two deaths that night?"

"Yes."

"How did you learn of the deaths?"

"The sheriff."

"Who was the sheriff then?"

"Mayor Hagerdorn."

"The defendant?" Junior asked.

"Yes," Vogel answered. "He called me at home and told me I better get out there, about six miles after the turn-off onto Old Highway 49, and take a look."

"Did you go?"

"Yes. I drove over there. A car was all smashed up against a pine tree. One of the dead boys was in the car, slumped over the steering wheel. The other was on the ground, about twenty yards away, sprawled on his stomach."

"What were the names of the dead men?"

"Jimmy Turnbow and Leon Johnson."

"Could you ascertain from looking at them what the causes of death were?"

"Yep. From looking and because the sheriff showed me some of the shells he'd found around the car. Shotgun. Blew off Leon Johnson's face. Jimmy Turnbow left the car alive. He got shot and died right where I found him." Vogel shook his hand very hard, as if it had fallen asleep. The finger rubbing abated.

"How do you know that Jimmy Turnbow wasn't shot in the car and *then* died where you found him?" Junior asked.

"No blood in the car other than Johnson's, the one driving, and none trailing from the car to where Mr. Turnbow was found lying on the ground. There would have been some if he'd got shot in the car, there would have been some on the ground too. There was plenty where we found him."

A soft moan, then crying came from the other side of the courtroom.

"Who else was at the scene, Mr. Vogel?" Junior asked.

"The sheriff, three deputies, an ambulance," Phil Vogel answered.

"What were the names of the deputies?"

"Bev Carter, the sheriff now, he was one of them. I don't remember who the other two were."

"What were they doing?"

"The deputies and the sheriff were walking around, looking all over the ground and in the car for evidence, and the ambulance was waiting for me to take a look so they could take the bodies away."

"Did you form an opinion as to whether Mr. Turnbow and Mr. Johnson met their deaths as a result of unlawful means?"

"Yes. They did."

"Did you take any statements in connection with your investigation?"

"No."

"Did you issue a report?"

"No."

"Did you ever convene a jury?"

"No."

"Did you arrest anyone for the crime?"

"No."

"Didn't you say those were things you would normally do in the course of your duties as county coroner if you believed a death was by unlawful means?"

"Yes."

"Why weren't they done in this case, Mr. Vogel?"

"The sheriff told me not to worry with it."

"Sheriff Hagerdorn?"

"Yes."

"Did he say why?"

"No, just said I shouldn't bother with it."

"What did you do?"

"Just what he said."

"Which was?"

"Nothing. I didn't pursue it."

"No further questions."

Junior sat down, and Chip Tuckahoe stood up to cross-examine for the defense.

"Just a few questions, Mr. Vogel," Chip said. He stood next to the attorney's table, occasionally glancing down at a yellow pad on which he'd made some notes.

"When did Mayor Hagerdorn, then sheriff, tell you not to pursue an inquiry into the deaths of Turnbow and Johnson?" Chip asked.

"A few days after they died—maybe a week," Vogel answered.

"Where were you when he talked with you about it?"

"At the home of Dean Reese."

"Why were you there?"

"Reese was dead. I was doing my job."

"Busy week," someone snickered behind me.

"Could you tell us the circumstances of that death?"

"Objection, Your Honor," Junior said. "Newell Hagerdorn isn't being tried for the death of Dean Reese."

"But Dean Reese's life and death are a critical part of this case, Your Honor," Chip argued. "Mr. Fuller can't introduce bits and pieces of evidence concerning Mr. Reese and restrict my development of those same areas."

"I don't believe I've mentioned Mr. Reese," Junior said.

"Fine," Chip said, slapping his palm with one of his sharp yellow pencils. "If the State will agree not to mention Mr. Reese during the remainder of this trial, I'll be glad to end this cross-examination now."

"I withdraw my objection," Junior said.

"Mr. Vogel," Chip continued, "you were saying that Mayor Hagerdorn told you that you needn't worry about the case anymore while you and he were at Dean Reese's home after Reese died. Is that correct?"

"Yes."

"What was the date of Reese's death?"

"It was September 6, 1963."

"Did the sheriff call you to come to the Reese home?"

"No, I called him. The deputy, Bev Carter, had called me up, and after I got there I called the sheriff and reported Reese's death to him."

"What did you tell him?"

"That it looked like Dean Reese had stuck a gun in his mouth and shot out the back of his head. The gun was right next to him. We checked it out. His gun, his prints. Fortunately, he did it in the garage, not the house."

"Fortunately for his wife," someone behind me whispered.

"When the sheriff got there, what did he do?" Chip asked.

"He looked at the body, went in the house for a while, came out, and told me not to worry about the Johnson-Turnbow case anymore."

"What had you done up to that time on the Johnson-Turnbow case?"

"Not much."

"What exactly had you done at the time of Dean Reese's death?"

"Nothing, exactly." Vogel began rubbing his thumb with his forefinger again.

"You must have had plans for an investigation?"

"Yeah, I did."

"What were they?"

"I can't remember. That was a long time ago."

"At the time of Reese's death, did the sheriff know you hadn't begun work on the Turnbow-Johnson case?"

"I never told him, so I guess not. Only a week or so had passed; there was no big rush."

"When were you going to start your investigation of the Turnbow-Johnson case?"

"I don't know. A few days."

"Didn't you think it would have been a waste of time? Isn't that why nothing had been done?" Chip asked. "Didn't you say on more than one occasion that you weren't going to have an inquest?"

"Well, it's true. Nobody was going to get in trouble for shooting two Negroes. Why bother with an inquest?"

From across the aisle came a loud hissing.

Judge McNabb banged his gavel twice. "Next time I hear that or anything like it from the spectators, the perpetrator will be escorted out of my courtroom."

"They don't know what 'perpetrator' means on the other side of the aisle," someone near me said.

Judge McNabb hit his gavel again.

Mr. Vogel looked out toward the commotion. His head shook slightly. "It's a fact," he continued. "Those were different times. Nobody got in trouble for killing niggers—excuse me, Negroes—especially in a situation like that, where they were aiming to integrate the university. That's just how it was."

"Before the day you went to Dean Reese's house, that day he shot himself, hadn't Sheriff Hagerdorn talked to you about the importance of your investigation on at least two occasions?" Chip asked Vogel.

"Yeah, I guess."

"Please answer 'yes' or 'no.'"

"Yes."

"Didn't he urge you to get going, to move on it, to act?"

"Yes, he did."

"But you ignored what he said, didn't you?"

"Yes."

"No further questions," Chip said.

"Redirect?" Judge McNabb asked Junior.

"No, Your Honor," Junior said.

I was proud of Chip. What I'd thought during Junior's direct exam of Phil Vogel would be devastating for my father turned out to be not so bad after all.

Maybe our luck was finally changing.

CHAPTER EIGHTEEN

"Call your next witness," Judge McNabb directed Junior as soon as the coroner had completed his testimony.

"The State calls George Dorr," Junior said.

The bailiff left and a few minutes later returned, followed by a dour man around seventy years old who had a large beige hearing aid in his right ear. Of average height and weight, he wore a gray cardigan sweater, a white shirt, and black pants.

Chip had explained to me that those FBI memos I'd seen, several of which were from Dorr, weren't admissible as evidence. Nor would Dorr be allowed to testify about any of the things Dean Reese had told him.

After his name and address were given, Junior asked Dorr, "Are you employed?"

"No," Dorr answered. "I'm retired."

"What did you do before you retired?"

"I worked for the FBI," Dorr said.

"The Federal Bureau of Investigation?"

"That's right."

"When did you begin working for the FBI?"

"In 1930."

After several questions about his training and experience, Junior asked Dorr, "Were you employed by the FBI in 1963?"

"Yes."

"What was your job description?"

"I was a special agent."

"Where was your office?"

"The Atlanta field office."

"Did you work on one type of case or many?"

"During the late fifties and early sixties I worked primarily on civil rights cases that arose in the South."

"Who was your supervisor in 1963?"

"Carl Best, the chief of the Atlanta field office."

"Did you ever come to Tallagumsa, Alabama, in the course of your work?"

"Yes, I did."

"Could you describe why you came to Tallagumsa?"

"Because Jimmy Turnbow and Leon Johnson were killed outside Tallagumsa and we were investigating their murders."

"Did you know anyone in Tallagumsa prior to your visit?"

"Yes. Dean Reese."

"In what context did you know Dean Reese?"

"He had given us information on several occasions."

"Was he an employee?"

"Sort of. We paid him for information on a case-by-case basis."

"Did you have similar relationships with other individuals?"

"Yes."

"Why?"

"We had informants all over the South. We needed them for information on the Klan, demonstrations, assaults, harassment, killings, and the like. We used the information to save lives. We also used it to prod state authorities to get them to move on some of the worst cases. If they wouldn't, and we had a strong enough case, the Justice Department sometimes filed a federal case, which we helped prepare."

"Did you talk to Reese before you visited Tallagumsa?"

"Yes, I called him to see if he had any information on the murders."

"What did Reese tell you when you called him?"

"Objection," Chip said. "Hearsay."

"Sustained," Judge McNabb said.

"Did you talk to Dean Reese on the phone?"

"Yes, I did."

"What did you tell him?"

"That I wanted to know if he knew anything about the murders."

"Did he give you any information?"

"Objection," Chip said. "Hearsay."

"I believe Mr. Dorr can testify as to whether Mr. Reese gave him any information without repeating what Mr. Reese may have said," Junior argued.

"You may answer the question," Judge McNabb said.

"Yes, he did," Mr. Dorr said.

"As a result of that information, did you come to Tallagumsa in August of 1963?"

"Yes."

"On what day did you arrive?"

"I arrived on August 30, left again that afternoon, and returned to Tallagumsa on September 4. I left town for good on September 8."

"Did anyone accompany you to Tallagumsa?"

"Yes. Another special agent, Frank Moon."

"Is Mr. Moon still an agent?"

"He was until he died two years ago. He was shot in the line of duty."

"What happened after you and Agent Moon got to Tallagumsa on August 30?"

"We talked to Dean Reese and the sheriff."

"Who was the sheriff?"

"Newell Hagerdorn, the defendant."

"Could you describe your August 30, 1963, conversation with the defendant?"

"It was before lunchtime. Agent Moon and I dropped by and told him generally why we were in town. The sheriff was very cooperative. He told us how the young men died, showed us the location on the map, gave us some shells and wadding he and his deputies found at the scene of the crime, as well as the shot removed from the bodies during the autopsy."

"What did you do with the items?"

"Sealed them in FBI evidence bags, marked the bags with the date and my initials, and turned them over to Ray Bartozzi, one of our firearms identification men in Atlanta."

"You also testified you saw Dean Reese that same day, the thirtieth of August. Is that correct?"

"Yes."

"Where was that meeting?"

"At his home."

"Did Dean Reese give you anything at that meeting?"

"Yes. A gun."

"What kind?"

"A shotgun."

"Can you recall the manufacturer?"

"It was a Winchester Model 21 Custom, with a walnut stock and fancy checkering on the forearm."

"Do you know what gauge it was?"

"Twelve."

"What did you do with the gun?"

"I marked it with a tag with my initials and the date and took it by the sheriff's office to see if the sheriff could identify it. Dean Reese had told us it belonged to—"

"Objection, Your Honor," Chip said.

"Sustained," Judge McNabb said.

"What happened at the sheriff's office?"

"Sheriff Hagerdorn wasn't there. The deputy, Bev Carter, was, and he identified the gun."

"What did you do with the gun?"

"Drove it back to Atlanta with the shells and shot and gave them all to Ray Bartozzi."

"Why?"

"We wanted to know if it was the gun that killed Jimmy Turnbow and Leon Johnson and whose fingerprints were on it."

"Did you ever talk to the defendant, then-sheriff Hagerdorn, again?"

"Objection," Chip interrupted. "May we approach the bench, Your Honor?"

Judge McNabb nodded. Junior and Chip approached the judge, their vast height difference accentuated by their proximity to one another. I stared at their backs, unable to hear what they were saying. They left the bench.

"Answer the question, Mr. Dorr," Judge McNabb said.

"What was the question?" Dorr asked. "I'm afraid I've forgotten."

The court stenographer read it back.

"Yes," Dorr said. "On September 4, Agent Moon and I went to the defendant's home to talk to him."

"Why?"

"He was a suspect in the murders."

"Was he home alone?"

"No. The door was answered by a young lady, I think a daughter. She called him to come to the door. I don't know if anyone else was there."

"What happened then?" Junior asked.

"The defendant came to the door but didn't invite us in. We all stood on the front porch. I told him we were sorry to be there but that we had reason to believe that he was involved in the murders of Leon Johnson and Jimmy Turnbow."

"What did he say?"

"He laughed."

"When you say 'He laughed,' was it a nervous giggle or a hearty laugh?"

"Your Honor," Chip interceded, "I don't believe the witness is qualified as an expert in laughing."

"I'll let it in," Judge McNabb said. "Go ahead."

"Not so much nervous, but shock and disbelief."

"What did he say?"

"That it was the most ridiculous damn thing he'd heard in a long time. He said he was not involved, that he'd never killed anyone in his life. That he could guess who'd told us and he was surprised we didn't have better judgment."

"What happened next?"

"I told him we thought his shotgun was the murder weapon and asked if he could explain that."

"Did he say anything?" Junior asked.

"No, he seemed truly taken aback," Dorr said. "He appeared to be thinking about something but didn't say anything."

"Did you talk with him further?"

"Only a little. We asked if his daughter had ever dated a Negro."

"Why?"

"Our investigation had uncovered this as a possible motive for the crime."

"What did the defendant say?"

"He said that this was getting way out of hand, why didn't we go do our job, something like that."

"And then you left?"

"He walked in the house and shut the door."

"Did you talk to anyone else that evening?"

"Yes. We visited Floyd Waddy at his home. We asked him what he was doing on the night of August 27, 1963, and we told him he was a suspect."

"What did he say?"

"He was furious. He called his wife to the door and repeated what we'd said. According to her he was with ten other people at some kind of party that night. We got some of the names. He slammed the door in our faces. Later we checked it out. His alibi seemed airtight."

"When was the last time you saw Dean Reese?"

"The night of September 5."

"Where did you meet him?"

"In a deserted barn."

"Do you remember where the barn was?"

"No, I wouldn't be able to get there now. I just remember the barn was off Route 23 and was not far from town."

"Where was Agent Moon?"

"At the hotel; he had a stomach bug or food poisoning. We didn't know which, but he was pretty sick."

"Can you describe Dean Reese as he appeared to you that evening?"

"He was in his twenties—midtwenties I'd guess—tall, kind of a big stomach. He had a tattoo on his upper arm: a heart, and inside the heart the name 'Liz.' He smoked constantly, looked real tired, had dark circles under his eyes. But he was relaxed. Other times I'd seen him he'd been real hyper."

"Tell us about what happened at the meeting with Reese."

"As I said, I met him in this abandoned barn. There were two chairs and a small table in the middle, and on the table was a tape recorder. We sat down, talked a few minutes, then he told me—"

"Objection," Chip said. "Hearsay."

"Sustained."

"What happened next?" Junior asked in an exasperated tone that conveyed his frustration with the defense for impeding his search for the truth with technicalities.

"He made a statement into the tape recorder."

"What happened to the tape?"

"I took the tape back to my motel room and marked it with an evidence sticker, initialed and dated the sticker, packed the tape in a brown envelope, which I also marked, and then took the package back to my office in Atlanta when we returned."

"Do you know where the tape is today?"

"Yes, I do."

"Where?"

"It's in that box there, under your table in a tape player."

Chip jumped up quickly. Several pencils flew across the defense table. "Objection, Your Honor! This is the first we've heard that this tape existed. The witness told the grand jury he didn't know where the tape was, that the tape was lost. The prosecution can't bring it up now, mid-trial. That tape should not be admitted under these circumstances."

"We aren't trying to sneak anything by anyone here, Your

Honor," Junior said. "We didn't get the tape until yesterday. This was the best we could do."

"No, it wasn't. You could have told us yesterday," Chip asserted.

"The State had to listen to the tape," Junior answered. "The witness had to listen to it as well. And if the defendant hadn't insisted on starting this trial absurdly early, we'd have had the tape to the defense well before any reasonably scheduled trial began. We have done everything we could. I apologize for the timing. Now the tape is here, and we submit it is admissible."

"Being sorry doesn't make it admissible," Chip said.

"You're right. If Mr. Dorr can authenticate the tape, that makes it admissible," Junior said. "The only basis for excluding the tape would be if it isn't what it purports to be—that is, if the tape has been altered or if the tape isn't really a recording of Dean Reese making a statement on the night of September 5, 1963. Mr. Dorr will testify that the statements on the tape are those he heard Mr. Reese make on the night of September 5, and that the tape has not been changed in any way since the day the tape was made. Therefore, it's clearly admissible."

"If the tape can be authenticated, I will admit it subject to the defense having the opportunity to inspect the recording, assure themselves that it is authentic," Judge McNabb said. "Go ahead with your examination."

Junior pulled a brown cardboard box out from under the attorney's table and removed an old-fashioned reel-to-reel tape player. A tape was already in the player. He lugged the machine over to the witness stand. "Let the record reflect that we have marked a reel-to-reel tape as State's Exhibit One for Identification."

"Mr. Dorr, have you ever seen Exhibit One for Identification?" Junior asked.

"Yes."

"When?"

"The night of September 5, this tape was used to record a statement made by Dean Reese." Dorr stood up slightly and bent down over the reel. "Those are my initials and the date in ink on one of our evidence stickers, right there."

"Was anyone else present when this tape was made, other than you and Mr. Reese?"

"No."

"When did you last see the tape, prior to yesterday?"

"It was in my file cabinet in my office until I retired. When I retired I sent it to archives. Then when I got the subpoena to appear before the grand jury here I asked archives to find the tape. It took awhile, but finally they did, yesterday. An agent drove it over from Atlanta immediately."

"Who brought the tape and the tape player to the barn on September 5?"

"Reese did."

"Who turned it on and off that night?"

"He did."

"What happened the first time it was turned on?"

"I spoke. I said that he and I were at a barn off Route 23, that Reese was going to make a statement about the murders of Jimmy Turnbow and Leon Johnson."

"May I play the first minute or so of the tape marked as Exhibit One for Identification now, Your Honor?"

"Go ahead," Judge McNabb said.

Chip sighed audibly as Junior carried the tape player back to his table and put it down there.

Junior turned on the machine. A voice exploded out of the speaker.

Dorr, who appeared to be in pain, reached for his ear and adjusted his hearing aid.

"Sorry," Junior said, turning the machine down. He rewound the tape and started over. The beginning of the tape was exactly as Dorr had described it. Junior turned off the machine.

"Is that an accurate recording of what you said at the beginning of the taping with Dean Reese on the evening of September 5?" Junior resumed his pacing again.

"Yes, it is."

"What happened next?" Junior asked.

"Dean Reese just talked. I listened. The tape recorded him."

"May I play a bit more?" Junior asked Judge McNabb.

"Yes."

Junior then played another few seconds of the tape. A man's voice said, "My name is Dean Gilbert Reese and this is my statement to Agent Dorr."

"Is that Dean Reese speaking, Mr. Dorr?"

"Yes, it is."

"You're absolutely sure?"

"Yes."

"Is that an accurate recording of the first words he spoke into the tape recorder on the night of September 5?"

"Yes."

"I move that State Exhibit One for Identification be admitted into evidence," Junior said.

Chip stood again. "I must object again, Your Honor, to anything on that recording that Mr. Reese may or may not have said being admitted into evidence," he argued, his face growing bright red as he became genuinely incensed. "It is preposterous and patently unfair. Reese is not here for me to cross-examine, and for the many reasons hearsay is inadmissible you should exclude any part of the tape made by Dean Reese, the most significant being we can't see him, listen to him, and judge his credibility here in the courtroom. Even a madman can sound sane on a tape. But then, when you see him, you know the truth."

Junior stood up but apparently had second thoughts about what he was about to say and sat back down.

"I'm afraid I must grant Mr. Fuller's motion on behalf of the State and admit the tape subject to your inspecting it, Mr. Tuckahoe," the judge said. "I know Reese is not here to cross-examine, and if there were a jury I might hesitate a little more on this ruling. But as you requested, there is no jury. I assure you I am capable of weighing accurately the probative value of the tape. The defense has until Monday morning, five days counting today, to examine the tape and make any further objections at that time. That's plenty of time, don't you think? You may play Exhibit One, Mr. Fuller," Judge McNabb said.

Chip sat down, shaking his head in dismay. My father whispered something to him and then they, like the rest of us, waited to hear the tape.

Junior turned on the machine and Dean Reese's voice filled the courtroom.

"My name is Dean Reese," he said. "I want to set the record straight about what happened to those boys, Turnbow and Johnson, who got killed last week, because I know who they'll try to blame." Reese had a more noticeable twang than most of the people around Tallagumsa. We all talked with heavy southern accents, but his voice had a rough, redneck quality to it that fit perfectly the physical description of Reese given earlier. He sounded like a good old boy.

I dreaded hearing whatever his eerie presence was about to reveal. We'd gone into this trial assuming nothing Reese said would be admitted. How bad would it be?

"This is how it happened, the truth and the whole truth," Reese said. "On the night of August 27, 1963, I was home with my wife, Liz, and our baby, watching TV, when the doorbell rang. It was my friend, Sheriff Newell Hagerdorn. The sheriff's car was out front. Floyd Waddy was sitting in it, waiting. I waved hi to him. 'Wanna go get a drink?' Newell asked me. We spend a lot of time hanging out together. We're buddies, you know. 'Aren't you working?' I asked him. 'Yeah, but nothing's going on,' he said, so I told my wife I was going and went on with them. I thought we were going to a bar to drink, but there was a case of beer in the back seat. We drove around and drank, and after a while Newell asked, did I want to drive. 'Sure,' I said. So we stopped and I got in the driver's seat and Newell took the passenger seat. Floyd stayed in back. I started driving. We all drank beer. 'What do you think about them nigger boys trying to integrate the university?' Newell asked me. 'Not much,' I said. The radio was playing 'Johnny Angel' and I wanted to listen to the song, not to talk, but then Newell said, 'Drive on over to Old Highway 49; they're going to be going that way and we can give them a scare.' We did, and we were laughing and having some fun driving up and down the road, honking and singing, when what do you know, we see a car up ahead, and Newell said, 'Put on the sirens,' so I did. Newell asked Floyd for the shotgun out of the back and told me to pull up alongside the car. I did, we saw who it was, then he shot, twice. I thought he was just trying to scare them, but he hit the one who was driving. Their car swerved and hit a tree and crashed to a stop. 'Shit, man,' Floyd said. 'Quick. Pull over.' So I did. We all got out. The one driving was dead, but the other one got out of the car and began running away. Newell ran after him and shot him, bam, bam, bam, three times, I think. Then Newell ran back, jumped in the car, and said, 'Let's go. Take Floyd home, then I'll drop you off.' And that's it. That's what happened. We dropped Floyd off, then went to my house. I got out and told Newell I'd take the gun and get rid of it. I took it and gave it to Agent Dorr instead."

As the tape played, Judge McNabb's head had fallen forward, revealing the spottiness of his hair transplants. He didn't even look up again when the tape ended. The courtroom was still. Feeling something warm on my chin, I reached up and touched it. I looked at my hand. My lip was bleeding. I must have been chewing on it for some time. I took a Kleenex out of my purse and dabbed at it. Judge McNabb slowly raised his head. His face was pale, and beads of sweat rested on his lip and forehead.

Daddy wrote something on Chip's yellow pad and pushed the pad over to Chip. Chip read it and shrugged.

I turned slightly to look at my family across the courtroom, a few rows behind me. Jane, of course, was no longer there: Earlier that morning the judge had sent her to wait in the witness room. Buck's face was obscured by the handkerchief he was using to wipe his forehead. Eddie looked right at me. Much to my surprise he looked upset and sad. Mother was staring straight ahead, one hand resting lightly on her throat. She appeared to be in a world of her own.

"Mr. Dorr, is that the same statement you heard Dean Reese give on the night of September 5?" Junior asked.

"Yes, it is. Hard to forget that."

"Has anything been added or omitted?"

"No."

"Did you see Dean Reese again after that?"

"No. He died the next day."

"Did you have occasion to talk to anyone else in Tallagumsa during the course of your investigation?"

"Yes, Dean's wife, Liz Reese."

"When?"

"A day or two after he died."

"Can you tell us about that?"

"We dropped by unannounced, as no one ever answered our phone calls. She was hysterical. She had bruises on her legs and a black eye too. She was crying like a wild woman—you know, out of control. She had a little baby there with her, who was crying too. There were clothes everywhere and several open suitcases. She didn't say anything except she blamed us for giving her husband the power to cause so much pain. She was angry and asked us to leave her alone."

"Did the FBI continue its investigation thereafter?"

"No. We closed the investigation mid–September 1963."

"Why?" Junior asked.

"My superior, Carl Best, decided that we didn't have a chance of bringing or winning a case, given the circumstances. Even with the best federal civil rights cases, we often couldn't get indictments out of a local federal grand jury in the South. A conviction was even harder back then. Our policy was to negotiate and persuade as much as possible, to accomplish voting rights and integration with as little violence as possible. Accusing the sheriff of a small southern town of murder wasn't likely to make us too popular. With Dean Reese dead, we didn't seem to have much choice. We could only do so much, and we had plenty of other problems to deal with in the South."

"Did you agree with his decision?"

"I understood it. It wasn't my job to agree or disagree."

"No further questions," Junior said. He walked slowly back to his chair, cracked the knuckles of his right hand, and sat down.

"Are you going to cross-examine, Mr. Tuckahoe?" Judge McNabb asked Chip.

"Yes, sir," Chip said, rising.

"Well, it's almost noon," Judge McNabb said, "so why don't we adjourn for lunch. I have a motion in another matter at one o'clock to attend to. Court is adjourned until two o'clock."

"All rise," the bailiff said.

As we rose, Judge McNabb left the room. I rushed out as fast as I could, pushing past the few people who tried to leave before me. It was starting to drizzle as I walked quickly to my car and drove away.

I had not bothered to go out to the memorial after Ben told me of the defacement but was desperate to see it now. I sped out Old Highway 49 and pulled over at the tree.

A storm was gathering. The sky was rapidly growing dark with distant lightning followed by a roll of thunder every five or so minutes. Behind the tree the corn that had been planted in the spring and grown through the summer was gone. Cows or pigs had been turned out to feed on the stalks after the ears were picked, leaving the fields barren and dusty.

I got out of the car, trying hard not to think of Dean Reese's voice describing that night fifteen years ago. I didn't believe a thing he'd said, but I found his words replaying in my head over and over, as if I'd brought the tape player with me.

The memorial was ruined. Someone had splattered the metal plaque and the stand on which it rested with blood-red paint. Even worse, a big red thick-lipped smile had been painted around the gash in the tree. I couldn't even cry. It was too late for that.

A black storm cloud opened, dropping a torrent of rain. As a lightning bolt landed nearby, I ran back to the car, still fully intending to stay at the memorial for the entire break. After a few minutes, however, the scene Dean Reese had described as having occurred on this very spot seemed to come to life in front of me. Behind the heavy sheets of rain, I watched the boys' car crash into the tree and the sheriff's car pulling over next to it. I squeezed my eyes shut tight for a moment, then sped away, leaving the tree, the memorial, the dead boys, and their murderer behind me.

By one-forty I was back in the courtroom in my seat in the first row behind the empty defense table. I was waiting, trying to concentrate on my throbbing lip to the exclusion of all else, when my father and Chip walked by.

Daddy stopped and put his hand on my shoulder. "Where'd you run off to?" he asked. "We were looking for you at the Steak House."

"I had something I had to do at the house," I lied.

He smiled knowingly.

I'd never been able to lie to him and get away with it.

The spectators filed into the gallery quietly, their voices muted by an almost palpable undercurrent of suspense and expectation.

"How long did Dean Reese provide information to the FBI, Mr. Dorr?" Chip asked when he began his cross-examination of the FBI agent. Chip stood next to his chair. On the table within reach of his right hand were several sharpened pencils, a yellow pad, and a small pile of papers.

"One year, maybe a little more."

"Did you ever bring a case—by that I mean, indict anyone—based on any information Dean Reese gave you—prior to this case, that is?"

"No."

"Did you ever learn anything about the Klan from him, anything that you didn't already know?"

"No."

"Did you feel he was a reliable source of information?"

"We wouldn't have paid him if we didn't," Mr. Dorr said.

"Didn't he ever give you information which turned out to be false?"

"Sure, but that's not unusual. Informants give us what they have, based on what they hear. Sometimes it turns out to be false."

"Didn't he provide false evidence to you in another civil rights case?" Chip asked.

"There was an occasion on which Mr. Reese provided information that turned out not to be accurate information, yes."

"When was that? Before or after the Turnbow-Johnson murders?"

"The spring before, in the murder of a prominent black man in Mississippi, Medgar Evers."

"Didn't Dean Reese purposefully mislead you in that matter?"

"I don't know that to be the case. The information he gave us wasn't accurate, that's all." Dorr, starting to look tired, rested his elbow on the edge of the stand and his chin on his hand.

"But isn't it true that the person who Dean Reese claimed had killed Medgar Evers was the *same person* who'd fired Reese from a garage job in Mississippi the year before?"

"Yes, that's what we discovered."

"And yet you claim his accusation in the Evers case wasn't intentionally false?"

"I just don't know, one way or the other," Dorr said.

"Why did you rely on him for anything after that troubling incident occurred?"

"Objection," Junior said. "The witness hasn't testified the incident was troubling."

"Was it?" Chip asked.

"Yes," Dorr said. "But we needed anything we could get out

of the Deep South in those days. You know, I'm sure, that most people who are willing to inform on other people aren't the most upstanding citizens, but law enforcement needs their help."

"You mean you were desperate?"

"No, I wouldn't say that."

"Let me ask it another way: Would Dean Reese have been your first choice for a reliable source of information?"

"No. But he wouldn't have been my last, either."

"But you had other problems with him, didn't you? In fact, didn't Dean Reese have a reputation for violence and drunkenness?"

"There was some talk along those lines."

Chip picked up a piece of paper from the pile next to his yellow pad. "Didn't you once say, Mr. Dorr . . ."

Junior stood up. "Mr. Reese has been accused today of nearly every sin in the Bible. He is not on trial, however, and I think this collateral attack on him has gone far enough. Could Mr. Tuckahoe just get on with the case at hand?"

"The State can't rely on Reese for its entire case and then try to deny the defense its only avenue for assessing his truth and veracity," Chip said. He looked ready for a fistfight, bouncing slightly off one foot, then the other.

"Dean Reese is not our entire case. Just one little piece of it, as you will see." Junior seemed very smug.

"I doubt that," Chip said.

"You may proceed, Mr. Tuckahoe," Judge McNabb said.

"Didn't you say in 1963 that 'Dean Reese has a reputation for being an extremely unstable alcoholic known for violent and unpredictable behavior'? Aren't those your exact words?" Chip asked, holding up the paper and waving it for emphasis.

"Yes. They are."

"Isn't that why the FBI didn't push this case in 1963? Because it was too embarrassed to go ahead with a case based on the testimony of a drunken liar who killed himself?" Chip asked. "Just as the State today should be embarrassed by this case?"

"Objection," Junior said. "He's arguing his case, not questioning the witness."

"Sustained."

Chip shook his head. His look, like the question he'd just asked, suggested that he couldn't imagine what would motivate anyone to rely on Dean Reese to indict a man for murder.

I just hoped Judge McNabb agreed with that assessment, which required him to disregard the horrors revealed earlier that day by the tape.

"Just one more thing," Chip said. "Wouldn't you agree, Mr. Dorr, that there is less intact evidence today than there was in 1963? After all, not only is your witness still dead, but the gun, the shells, the wadding, and the shot are all lost, and fifteen years have elapsed, fifteen years during which memories inevitably have deteriorated."

"That's true."

"So it's fair to say, isn't it, that this is a much, much weaker case than the one the FBI chose not to pursue in 1963?"

"Objection," Junior said. "This witness is not qualified to comment on the strengths or weaknesses of this case. That is Your Honor's jurisdiction."

"And I'm sure His Honor knows well the only correct answer to that question. I have nothing further," Chip said.

A few minutes later we were outside the courthouse for the afternoon break. The sudden lunchtime storm had left as quickly as it had come. I'd looked for Mother when we left the courtroom but couldn't find her, so I followed Daddy and Chip outside to the ledge around the fountain. Since the day of the courthouse dedication, when Jessie had thrown in her penny, hundreds of others had followed, and the bottom of the fountain was half covered with the copper-colored discs.

For the first time since this mess began, my father looked worried. He pulled a cigar from his shirt pocket, unwrapped it, and then just sat there, too distracted to light it.

"What do you think?" I asked him.

"I don't like it," he said.

"What did you write on Chip's yellow pad after you heard the tape recording?" I asked.

"I wrote the same thing I've been telling all of you this whole time—that Reese was a lying son of a bitch—and I asked Chip if he thought anyone would believe him," my father said.

"Do you, Chip?" I asked.

"I don't know. I sure hope not, but it's a hard call to make. At least now maybe you'll reconsider your position on testifying, Newell," Chip said hopefully.

Daddy shook his head.

Was he telling Chip no, or did I detect the possibility of change, the slightest suggestion that Daddy might finally be fed up with this and be willing to take matters into his own hands and explain away what we'd all just heard?

If not, maybe tomorrow I'd take a Valium or two before I came to court.

CHAPTER NINETEEN

When court reconvened following the afternoon break, Junior called Ray Bartozzi, the FBI firearms identification expert, as a State witness. He was a tall, heavy, middle-aged man with a thick black mustache dotted with gray hair.

"I'll stipulate that Mr. Bartozzi is qualified as an expert in firearms identification, Your Honor," Chip said. "But I move that you not allow his testimony because the gun as well as the shells and shot about which the witness plans to testify are lost in the FBI's storage facilities. The prosecution's case seems to rest entirely on dead men and misplaced evidence."

"Once again, Mr. Tuckahoe, I must deny your motion," Judge McNabb said. "Mr. Bartozzi is here and you can cross-examine him about anything he says on direct. There is no jury to worry about and, as in the case of the tape, I will carefully weigh the probative value of the testimony and the impact, if any, of the missing evidence."

I was beginning to see that my father's tactical decision to waive his right to a jury trial had more negative consequences than I'd understood.

After a few preliminaries, Junior began to question Bartozzi about the case at hand. The witness chewed nervously on his mustache as he listened to each question.

"Were you ever asked as part of your official duties to examine a Winchester Model 21 Custom shotgun and certain shell casings, wadding, and shot?"

"Yes, I was."

"When?"

"On August 30, 1963."

"Tell us about the circumstances of that examination, please," Junior said.

"Special Agent Dorr came to the bureau laboratory on August 30, 1963, with two plastic bags of evidence. One contained five shell casings and two pieces of wadding, and the other contained pellets of shot. Dorr also gave me the Winchester gun. He'd marked and tagged everything, and I added my initials to each piece."

"Why do you remember these events so clearly?"

"Because that gun was a beautiful and very expensive shotgun, and because of the circumstances of the murders we were investigating. It was unusual to have so much physical evidence in a civil rights murder."

"Were you asked to perform any tests?"

"Yes. I was requested to examine the shell casings, the shot, and the wadding, and determine, if possible, whether they had been ejected from the Winchester shotgun."

"Did the items in the evidence bags and the Winchester shotgun remain in your custody from the time Agent Dorr gave them to you until you performed your examinations on them?"

"Yes."

"What happened to them thereafter?"

"I sent them to storage when the case was closed. When we tried to locate them over the last months, we couldn't."

"Is it possible they ever will be located?"

"Possible, but unlikely. We've undertaken a very extensive search."

"Did you make any notes respecting the tests that you performed on the items given to you by Agent Dorr?" Junior asked.

"Yes," Bartozzi said. "I wrote a report, as I always did. Reports were required on every test."

"Do you have that report?"

"Yes."

"Is it necessary for you to refer to that report to refresh your memory as to the tests you performed on the shotgun, the shells, the wadding, and the shot Agent Dorr gave you?"

"Yes, it is."

Junior showed the report to Chip and gave it back to Bartozzi.

"Before we get to the report and the details of the tests, let's get a few definitions out of the way so everyone can understand your testimony, Mr. Bartozzi. Please define a shotgun shell," Junior said.

"It consists of a cartridge case with a brass head and a tube of either plastic or paper, primer—usually center-fire—propellant powder charge, projectiles—usually shot—and wads."

"What is shot?"

"A small spherical mass of round metal, usually made of lead alloyed with other metals. Each shell contains a number of these balls, which are discharged at the same time when fired."

"Can you tell us how shotguns are classified?"

"By gauge. The gauge is the number of spherical balls of pure lead, each exactly fitting the bore, that equal one pound."

"And the wads or wadding?"

"That's the paper or plastic material that keeps the powder and the shot pellets in position inside the shell."

"Is it possible to determine whether a particular shot came from a particular shotgun?"

"No. Unlike other firearms, a shotgun is a smooth-bored weapon. The shot isn't marked by the barrel of the gun the way a bullet from a rifle or a handgun is, thus we're unable to tell what load of shot came from what barrel. We can only tell what number the shot is."

"Is it possible, Mr. Bartozzi, to determine whether a particular wadding came from a particular shotgun?"

"Not usually. We can often determine if the wadding is the same make as that used in a particular gun and we can determine the gauge of the gun from which the wadding came."

"What were you were able to conclude from your examination of the wadding given to you by Agent Dorr on August 30," Junior asked.

"I determined that the wadding was fired from a twelve-gauge shotgun."

"And what were you able to conclude from your examination of the shot Agent Dorr turned over to you?"

"I determined that the shot was number-one shot. The loaded shell in the Winchester Model 21 Custom when Agent Dorr gave it to me was number-one shot also."

"Is it possible to determine whether a particular shell casing was ejected from a particular firearm?"

"Yes."

"How can this be done?"

"By comparing the markings on the casing suspected to have been ejected by a particular gun with the markings on a casing that has been ejected in a test-firing from the same gun."

"Was that done with the shotgun Agent Dorr gave you?"

"Yes, it was."

"What did you find?"

"I was able to match the test casings with two of the shell casings given to me by Agent Dorr based on the firing-pin marks on one and the extractor marks on the other."

"What are the firing-pin marks?"

"A firing pin is the pin that strikes the cartridge primer, or cap, in the breech mechanism of a firearm. The tip of the firing pin left the same irregular impression on the test casings as it had on one of the casings Agent Dorr gave me."

"What are the extractor marks?"

"The extractor is that part of the weapon that removes the shell casing from the chamber after the weapon has been fired. The spring-loaded extractor is forced over the rim of the casing at the instant the shell is loaded into the chamber, leaving distinctive markings. The extractor marks on one of the casings Agent Dorr gave me matched the extractor marks on the test casing."

"As a result of your comparison of the shell casings given to you by Agent Dorr with the casings that you obtained by test-firing the shotgun given to you by Agent Dorr, were you able to form any opinion as to whether the casings were ejected by the Winchester shotgun?" Junior asked.

"Yes, I was," Bartozzi answered.

"What is that opinion?"

"Two of the casings Agent Dorr turned over to me were ejected from the Winchester Model 21 Custom shotgun."

"Thank you, Mr. Bartozzi. No further questions," Junior said.

Chip stood up next to the defense table. He looked down at his yellow pad and read for a moment, then he picked up one of his pencils and held each end with his fingers.

"Weren't there five shell casings in the evidence bag Mr. Dorr gave you?" Chip asked.

"Yes," Bartozzi said.

"You've told us that you believe that two of those five came from the Winchester?"

"That's correct."

"What, if anything, were you able to determine about the other three?"

"Only that they were not fired from the Winchester Model 21 Custom shotgun."

"What kind of gun did the other three casings come from?"

"A shotgun. I don't know what kind."

"Isn't it possible to perform tests on shotgun shells to identify the manufacturer and the type of weapon that ejected them?"

"Yes."

"As a firearms identification expert, don't you regularly determine from shell casings alone the type of weapon that ejected them?"

"Yes."

"And why do you do that?"

"Because if we don't have the gun suspected of being involved in a crime—which is often the case—if we just have the shell casing, then we need to find out what kind of gun it came from."

"Those tests are essential tools of law-enforcement investigation, right?"

"Yes."

"Without them you would be greatly hindered in your work?"

"Definitely."

"In this case were any tests performed on the other three casings, any tests whatsoever from which you would be able to reach any conclusions as to the gauge of the gun involved, the manufacturer of the gun, or any other identifying characteristic?" Chip asked.

"No."

"Why not, Mr. Bartozzi?"

"My assignment was to see if any of the shell casings, the wadding, or the shot came from the Winchester. After I'd made those matches, I had to work on some other more pressing cases. Then when I went back to the three casings you've asked about, I was told not to do the tests, just to pack it all up and send everything to storage, that the case had been closed."

"So you never found out anything about three of the five casings, except that they didn't come from the Winchester?"

"That's right."

"Couldn't the wadding, which you did test, have been shot from almost any twelve-gauge shotgun?"

"That's right."

"And the shot could have been shot out of any shotgun that holds number-one shot?"

"True."

"Now then, Mr. Bartozzi, it's possible those three shell casings you didn't bother to test also came from a twelve-gauge shotgun, isn't it?"

"Sure."

"In fact, you don't know—do you?—whether the wadding and the shot you tested came from the same shotgun as those unidentified shells?"

"No, I don't."

"Couldn't the wadding, the shot, and the unidentified shell casings all have come from the same gun, a shotgun other than the Winchester?" Chip asked.

"Yes."

"You have not testified, have you, that the Winchester Model 21 Custom was used to kill Jimmy Turnbow and Leon Johnson?"

"No, I haven't."

"You couldn't testify to that, could you?"

"No, I couldn't. I testified that it could have been the murder weapon."

"Could have been? Isn't that the same as *maybe* or *perhaps*? In fact, isn't it just as likely that some other twelve-gauge gun—the same gun that ejected those three unidentified cartridges, the wadding, and the shot—was the murder weapon?"

"That's really impossible to answer. I wasn't there."

"Of course you weren't. That's all I have, Your Honor."

Chip sat down and wrapped a rubber band around his pile of pencils. He turned toward me and smiled slightly.

CHAPTER TWENTY

The first witness called by Junior on the second day of the trial was Sheriff Bevins Carter. Bev was in his forties but looked younger. He was slightly pudgy, with skin as smooth and clear as a child's. Most of the time he looked slightly bemused. He took his time walking down the aisle toward the witness stand, physically demonstrating his reluctance to testify against Daddy. Even I understood, though, that he had to do it.

"Were you on duty the night of August 27, 1963?" Junior asked Bev following the name, address, and occupation questions.

"Yes," Bev said.

"Do you recall the events of that evening?"

"It was a right busy night. We had a brawl at that bar used to be over where Clyde's Bar is now. About ten men were throwing each other around the parking lot, and one of them had a knife. I was there awhile, and after that I was at the scene of the murders of Jimmy Turnbow and Leon Johnson."

"Was anyone from the sheriff's office with you at the bar brawl?"

"Two other deputies, Joey Lardner and Doyle Foley."

"Was the defendant, then-sheriff Hagerdorn, at the bar brawl?"

"No."

"Why not?"

"I couldn't reach him on the radio. I tried."

"About what time were you at the bar?"

"Eight or eight-thirty, for an hour or so."

"When you left there, where did you go?"

"Out Old Highway 49 to where the boys' car had crashed into a tree."

"Why did you go there?"

"The dispatcher radioed me."

"Did you see the defendant while you were there, Sheriff Carter?" Junior asked.

"Yes," Bev answered. "Mayor Hagerdorn arrived shortly after I did."

"What, if anything, did he say?"

"After he looked around, he told me to search for any evidence I could find, shells and the like, and he went to call the coroner to come take a look. He also told me to call an ambulance for the bodies. He was very disturbed."

"Did you ever meet Agent George Dorr of the FBI?" Junior asked.

"Yes."

"When was that?"

"In August 1963. August 30."

"Could you describe the occasion of your meeting?"

"He came by the sheriff's office two times that day. He and another agent had come to town to investigate the murders of Turnbow and Johnson. They came by the office to meet with Newell—Mayor Hagerdorn. I was there. That was when we gave the agents the shells, wadding, and shot we'd collected at the scene of the murders. Later they came by when Mayor Hagerdorn wasn't there."

"Can you describe what happened at the second meeting?"

"The agents had a shotgun with them. They asked if I'd ever seen it."

"Had you?"

"Yes."

"Please describe the gun."

"It was a Winchester Model 21 Custom shotgun."

"When had you seen it before that day?"

"Hundreds of times."

"Whose gun was it?"

"Newell Hagerdorn's."

"Did you tell Agent Dorr that the gun belonged to the defendant?"

"Yes."

"No further questions," Junior said. He walked back to his chair and sat down.

"Mr. Tuckahoe, any cross?" Judge McNabb asked.

"Thank you, Your Honor," Chip said, standing up.

"Mr. Carter, when the agents brought the Winchester to the sheriff's office and asked you to identify it, were you surprised to see it?"

"Yes and no," Bev said.

"Please explain."

"Two days before, Mayor Hagerdorn, then the sheriff, had told me the gun was missing. We looked in the sheriff's car and all over the office for the shotgun but couldn't find it. He was pretty upset that it was missing. It was one of his favorite guns. I was surprised the FBI had it, and I didn't understand why they wouldn't give it to me. I still don't understand all this, why he was indicted, how anyone could think he murdered those boys."

"Back on August 30, 1963, did you tell your boss, then-sheriff Hagerdorn, that the FBI had his gun?"

"Soon as the agents left I radioed him and told him what had happened."

"What, if anything, did he say?" Chip asked.

"He said, 'Goddamnit! What is going on here?' I asked him, 'What do you mean?' but he didn't say."

"You testified on direct that he was very disturbed when he got to the scene of the Turnbow-Johnson murders," Chip said. "Is that correct?"

"Yes, he was," Bev said gravely.

"Can you explain that further?"

"As soon as he saw the boys' bodies, he threw up in the field next to us." Bev grimaced. "He organized the gathering of evidence and all, but he wasn't himself. He was pale and shaking all over. I'd never seen him so upset, and I never have since."

"How long have you known Mayor Hagerdorn?"

"All my life."

"No further questions," Chip said.

"I have a few followup questions," Junior said.

"Certainly," Judge McNabb said.

Junior approached the witness stand. "You indicated that the defendant told you he lost his Winchester shotgun two days before the FBI agents brought it to your office for you to identify. Is that correct?"

"Yes, it is."

"What was the date on which the defendant told you the gun was missing?" Junior asked.

"That would make it the twenty-eighth of August, 1963."

"And what was the date of the murders of Jimmy Turnbow and Leon Johnson?"

"August 27, 1963."

"No further questions," Junior said.

Bev left the stand and stopped briefly at the defense table, only to be sent on his way by Chip.

Tim Hogan, the FBI fingerprint expert, was on and off the stand quickly. As in the case of the gun expert, Chip stipulated as to his qualifications. With a few questions, Junior established that at Agent Dorr's request Tim Hogan had examined the Winchester Model 21 Custom shotgun and found on it three sets of fingerprints: my father's, Dean Reese's, and Agent Dorr's.

Chip's cross-examination was similarly brief.

"From your study of the Winchester, can you tell us when the fingerprints were made?" Chip asked.

"No."

"You can't tell us the date on which they were made?"

"No."

"So you don't know when Mayor Hagerdorn handled the gun, do you?"

"No."

"And you don't know under what circumstances he handled it, do you?"

"No."

"The last time he touched the gun could have been months before the murders, isn't that true?"

"Yes."

"Would you be surprised to find a man's fingerprints on his own gun?"

"Of course not," Hogan said.

"There's nothing suspicious about that, is there?"

"No."

"No further questions," Chip said. "Your Honor, I move to strike the testimony given by Mr. Hogan," he said. "It has been held to be reversible error to admit fingerprint evidence where there is no proof as to when the defendant handled the gun where the defendant had legitimate access to the gun. I have the cites here, if Your Honor would consider my motion."

"I'm familiar with those cases, Mr. Tuckahoe," Judge McNabb said. "I am also aware of the line of cases in the State that allow this evidence. You may argue the issue as a question of fact at the appropriate time. Your motion is denied."

The last witness before the lunch break was escorted into the courtroom by the bailiff. Washington Jackson, who appeared to be eighty or more, walked slowly, leaning on a wooden cane for support. He was a small, stooped black man in a shiny navy-blue suit a size too big for him. Completely bald, he carried a hat in his hand. His eyes bugged out behind his glasses, and he never seemed to blink.

"Where did you live in 1963?" Junior asked Jackson after the preliminaries.

"Out on Old Highway 49," Jackson answered.

"What was the address?"

"Wasn't one. I lived with my daughter and her kids in a shack out at Buddy Sheppard's farm."

"Why did you live there?"

"It didn't cost nothing if we helped with the farming."

"Were you employed in August 1963?"

"Yes, sir."

"What was your employment and where was it?"

"The cemetery over to the edge of town. I dug graves."

"Do you recall whether you worked on August 27, 1963?"

"Yes, sir. I worked every day. If I didn't work, I didn't get paid."

"How did you usually get home from work?"

"Walk or get a ride."

"Did you walk home on August 27, 1963?"

"Yes, sir."

"How long did it take you to walk from the cemetery to your home?"

"Two hours."

"What time did you leave work?"

"Six; every day, six."

"What, if anything, did you see on that walk?"

"I was just 'bout home when I heard sirens. I turned around and looked. Way down the road I seen a sheriff's car with the lights going. It pulled up to another car, then there was these shots, the other car hit a tree, and the sheriff's car pulled over. A man get out with a gun. He looked in the wrecked car and then walked around it and shot at a man trying to run away."

"Could you identify the man you saw get out of the sheriff's car?"

"No, I was too far away. He was white. The man who got out of the other car was a Negro. The white man shot him."

"Was anyone else in the sheriff's car?" Junior asked.

"I couldn't tell," Jackson said.

"What did you do?"

"I got home fast and waited there for a few hours. Then I went back up the road after everybody had done left and there was the car crashed into the tree. Nothing else."

"No further questions," Junior said.

I peered over Daddy's shoulder. He was doodling on Chip's yellow pad again. This time he'd drawn a sheriff's car with the star on the door and the light on top. A figure sat at the wheel. Next to the car was a large shotgun and a row of bullets streaming from the gun toward the driver of the car.

"Mr. Jackson," Chip said, standing up for cross-examination, "when did you first tell this story you've just told us?"

"A few months ago."

"Who did you tell it to?"

"Mr. Fuller." The witness pointed at Junior.

"You'd never told the story to anyone before this year, had you?"

"No, sir."

"So for fifteen years you've kept this vision you had a secret?"

"Objection," Junior said. "There's no evidence that Mr. Jackson had a vision."

"Fine," Chip said. "For fifteen years you've kept everything you just testified about a secret. Is that correct?"

"Not a secret, 'xactly."

"Well, why then didn't you tell someone?"

"Nobody asked me."

"You don't think a citizen has an obligation to report a crime he witnesses at or near the time of the crime? You believe you should wait until you're contacted?"

"If you a Negro, 'specially back then, yes, sir."

"Do you know anyone in either Jimmy Turnbow's or Leon Johnson's family?"

"Yes, sir."

"Who do you know?"

"I knows their mamas and most of their brothers and sisters. We go to the same church."

"It's fair to say you are good friends with both families, isn't it?"

"We be friends."

"They're pretty happy about your testimony here, aren't they, Mr. Jackson?" Chip asked.

"I don't know."

"Haven't you discussed your testimony with members of their families over the last months?"

"No."

"Haven't you been in Jimmy Turnbow's mother's house in the last two months?"

"Yes."

"And in Leon Johnson's mother's house in the last two months?"

"Yes."

"And yet you claim never to have discussed your testimony with them."

"We didn't."

"Hard to believe," Chip said.

"Objection," Junior said.

"No further questions," Chip said.

Washington Jackson stood up slowly and looked out around the courtroom with unblinking eyes. If my father hadn't been on trial, I would have believed every word he said.

At the lunch break, I watched Mother leave the courtroom and go down the hallway. She stopped at the witness-room door and knocked. Jane came out; they hugged and walked back in my direction toward one of the exit doors. I ducked into the ladies' room and waited until they and most of the other spectators had time to leave for lunch. Jane was scheduled to take the stand after the break. I knew I was the last person either of them wanted to see at that moment.

* * *

The night before, after the first full day of trial, Jessie and I had been reading *Runaway Bunny* for the zillionth time when my mother called on the phone.

"Bad day, huh?" I said.

"I don't want to think about that right now," Mother said. "I called to talk about your sister. She is very nervous about her testimony tomorrow, her blood pressure is far too high, and I'm worried," she said. "Please, LuAnn. I'm asking you to support her on this. It would mean so much to her."

"She shouldn't testify," I said firmly.

"Oh, don't start that again," she said. "She's six months pregnant, and if she gets too upset she could lose the baby, LuAnn. Don't you care? After all she's been through, try to think of her. You know, she needs you a lot more now than he does."

"I just know what's right, Mother."

"I don't think you have the slightest idea," she said.

CHAPTER TWENTY-ONE

When Jane walked into the courtroom following the lunch break I felt a flash of anger over what she was about to do, as well as concern about how she looked. Her face was so bloated that her eyes, always her best feature, appeared to be no more than slits. She wasn't wearing any of the rings she usually wore; her fingers were too swollen. Her fingernails were gnawed to the quick. She reminded me of the old farm women who came to town for lunch now and again, women who had grown so obese that they couldn't stand without assistance from their husbands or sons.

Jane testified about as I expected, based on what Mother had told me at the Labor Day picnic. She said that Daddy woke her up on the evening of August 27, 1963, and asked her to keep an eye on me, her then-twelve-year-old sister, while he made sure Jimmy Turnbow and Leon Johnson made it safely to the university. He was worried about them, he told her, because of several anonymous threats.

"When did he get home that night?" Junior asked.

"I was asleep, so I'm not sure," Jane said. "Late."

"Did he say anything to you the next day?"

"He said that something terrible had happened, someone had killed the boys. That he'd been at a bar brawl and missed them by minutes. He was pale and upset."

"Were you home on the night of September 4, 1963?"

"Yes."

"Tell us what happened."

"Two men came to the door, identified themselves as FBI agents, and asked to speak to my father."

"Did you get your father?"

"Yes. I called to him. He came in the room, shook their hands, and told me to go on. I went to the kitchen."

"What did you hear after that?"

"I heard the agents say something, and then I heard my father laughing."

"Did you ever discuss that FBI visit with him?"

"Yes. I asked what was going on after they left. He said everything was fine, not to worry. He wouldn't talk about it other than to say that."

"I don't have any further questions," Junior said.

Chip stood up. "You said your father woke you on the night of August 27, 1963, before he went out. Is that correct, Mrs. Newton?" he asked.

"Yes, I was asleep."

"What time was it?"

"Seven or seven-thirty."

"Did you usually go to bed that early?"

"I'd just gotten home from summer school, exams and all, and I was exhausted." Jane's cheeks were starting to turn a little pink even though the courtroom wasn't warm.

"School?" Chip asked. "What school was that?"

Jane's face flushed bright red. She looked startled. The corners of her mouth dropped, and she began to cry softly.

Someone from the other side of the aisle said, "Goddamn you, Newell." It sounded like my mother, but it couldn't be. She never cursed.

I turned to look. Mother's hands were clenched around the top back of the seat in front of her and her face was contorted in anger.

"What school, Mrs. Newton? What courses did you take? What dorm did you live in? Were you in a sorority?" Chip asked Jane.

"Objection," Junior said. "Let the witness answer one question at a time."

"Will you tell us why you were asleep, please?" Chip asked.

"I was exhausted," she said. She stopped crying and got a stubborn look on her face that I knew well from growing up with her. "I was sick with a virus."

"Isn't it true that you never went to college that year?"

"No, that's not true."

"Fine, maybe you went, but didn't you drop out before the year ended and move out of the state? Remember, you're under oath, Mrs. Newton."

Jane turned her attention to Daddy for the first time since taking the stand. On her face was a look of sheer disbelief mixed with absolute fury.

He stared right back, the muscles in his neck tightening as they engaged in a silent battle of wills. His fingers drummed an incessant beat on the defense table.

Jane sat there for what seemed a long time, then slowly turned to Judge McNabb. "Do I have to answer?" she asked.

"I'm afraid so," he said.

Jane's breath grew shallow as she became even more distraught than she'd been after her last miscarriage. What on earth was this about?

She slumped down and began to talk in a whiny, pitiful voice. I had to strain to hear her. "I'd just gotten home from Mississippi where I'd spent seven months at a cousin's," she said. "I had a baby, gave it away before I ever even saw it, and came home to recover. I wasn't doing very well and was on some kind of tranquilizer. That's why I was asleep. Is that what you wanted to know?" she asked, looking up defiantly at Chip. "Now you do."

"And you wanted to keep your child, didn't you?" Chip asked.

"Yes, I did, more than anything in the world."

"Who made the decision about what to do with the child?"

"My father. He made all the decisions then, just like he does now." She looked sharply at Daddy.

He looked down and began to doodle on Chip's yellow pad.

"And at that time you would have done anything to hurt him, wouldn't you?"

"Yes, I would have."

"And isn't that still true? Don't you still blame him for the loss of that child?"

"Yes."

"And you hold him responsible for your having so much trouble bearing children?"

"Yes, I do. The doctor there was a quack. He did something to me, something dreadful. I blamed my father. I hated him!" She began to sob. "I'm sorry, Buck!" she cried, and as her cries steadily grew louder and wilder, Buck rushed up the aisle to Jane.

"No further questions," Chip said.

Buck avoided looking at my father as he wrapped his arms around Jane and helped her walk out of the courtroom.

I was horrified by the news of this baby, my niece or nephew, who was no longer a baby but a child somewhere, aged fifteen, and shocked that Chip would force Jane to testify about her sad experience. Had that cross-examination really been necessary?

I asked my father that question as we walked out after court was adjourned for the day, not long after Jane left the courtroom in tears.

"She shouldn't have testified against me," he said. "You said so yourself, remember?"

"Yes, but . . ." I didn't know where to start.

I kept jeans and a T-shirt, riding hat, boots, and a box of sugar cubes in the trunk of my car for times when I craved a ride on Glory. For a time like this.

I drove out to Miss Edwina's farm, changed clothes in the middle of the barn, and went out to set up the jumps. For over a year I'd hardly jumped at all, certainly nothing over two feet; I decided to try four feet.

Jumping a difficult course requires total focus and in return gives the rider a thrill, a high that is something akin to the exhilaration and intensity of falling in love, just the sort of distraction I so desperately needed at that moment.

Eddie hated my jumping Glory. "It's a stupid way to try to kill yourself," he'd said once. "You could end up crippled. Must be a better way if you're so anxious to end it all." He'd only been half joking. But I wasn't going to die. I'd only fallen a few times in my whole life while taking jumps, and the worst injury had been a broken arm when I was ten.

I set up a course of eight jumps, six at three and a half feet, the last two at four feet. Glory had jumped that high with her trainer, but never with me. I was ready, though. After Jane's testimony, I was ready for anything.

I got Glory from the field. I didn't bother with grooming her, just put on her bridle and saddle and shortened the stirrups three holes. I walked her around the course once, letting her get familiar with it. At the first four-foot fence, she turned and looked at me, as if she wondered what I thought I was doing. "Don't worry about me. I won't interfere," I said, stroking her neck. I hopped on her back.

There are different schools of thought on jumping. One is that each horse has his own jumping speed and pace, and the rider should interfere with the horse as little as possible. The other is that the rider should regulate the horse's stride and pace as well as choose the takeoff spot. To do this, the horse has to be slowed between jumps to a slow canter. Like most people I'd ridden with, I preferred the first approach. My father preferred the second.

As we came up on the first jump, Glory lowered her head, measuring the height and distance of the obstacle. She shortened her stride as she positioned herself for takeoff. I leaned forward, pressed my heels down, and held the reins with my thumb and index finger. Her neck flexed as her front legs left the ground and her hind legs pushed off, pushing me up off her back and farther forward. My hands advanced along her neck. We went over the jump, her head and neck stretching out as her front legs reached for the landing. On landing, her head raised but her neck extended even farther, her hind legs touched the ground, and her front legs started the new stride, a canter to the next jump.

My heart raced as we cleared each jump and cantered to the next. I adapted myself to the rhythm of Glory's every movement. At the next-to-the-last jump, the first of the two four-foot jumps, I looked out and over it, toward Miss Edwina's magnolia trees. Looking at an obstacle sometimes causes involuntary tensing before takeoff, and I couldn't risk confusing Glory on our first four-foot jump together. I felt her hind legs extend and her body reach up and forward. I followed. Together we soared over the jump. After the last jump, we cantered off into the field, then returned to take the course several more times. Maybe jumping was better than falling in love, I thought, especially considering my recent experiences.

When I got off Glory's back, my legs were shaking and my back was sore. Despite predictions of an early fall, the October evening was warm and muggy. A rainstorm earlier in the day had lasted just long enough to raise the humidity to ninety-five percent. My shirt was drenched with sweat. I took off my hard hat and ran my fingers through my wet, matted hair.

I pulled up the stirrups, loosened the girth, and walked Glory in the field to cool her off. When she stopped sweating, we went into the barn, where I hung her saddle and bridle on their pegs. I dried her with one of the old linen cloths I kept in her tack box, smoothed her coat with the dandy brush, and combed out her mane and tail with a metal comb.

By the time I finished grooming and feeding Glory, it was growing dark outside. I left the barn and walked toward the car. A slight breeze had driven off the clouds and the humidity. I looked up. The sky was filling rapidly with stars. I dropped the clothes I'd worn to court and lay down on the grass where I watched the stars pop out, one after the other, until the sky was lit from horizon to horizon.

At the house, I took off my boots in the kitchen and tiptoed into the living room. Jolene was asleep on the couch. I apologized for my lateness. She was understanding as always.

I peeked into Jessie's room.

"Mom," her sweet voice said.

"You still up?" I asked.

"Yes," she answered.

"It's late," I said.

"I wanted you to lie down with me," she said.

I went in. There was no need to feel my way in the dark, I'd been in the room so many times. I lay down in bed next to her. When my eyes adjusted to the darkness, I could see that she had on Eddie's *Star Wars* T-shirt again.

"Sorry I was so late," I said.

"Were you at the Steak House?"

"No. I went to ride Glory. I needed some exercise. What did y'all do?"

"Jolene and I bathed Will and Hank."

"You're a big help, to Jolene and me."

"Then we watched 'Mork and Mindy' and 'One Day at a Time.' "

Shit. I'd forgotten to tell Jolene not to let Jessie watch "One Day at a Time." Lately Jessie had managed to control her distress about Eddie's absence by viewing it as temporary, but whenever she watched "One Day at a Time," where a single mother struggled to raise her children alone, she'd worry anew that her father would never, ever return.

"Do you think Daddy will move back soon?" she asked.

"I don't know what's going to happen," I said. "I hope so, but sometimes things don't work out the way I want. Not lately, anyway."

"Daddy came by today," she said.

"He loves you very much."

"I know."

"We all love you," I said. "Don't you forget that."

We lay there quietly, and in a few minutes she was asleep. I kissed her cheek and lightly touched her hair.

The boys were sound asleep in their cribs. Will lay on his back, his arms and legs wide open, his pacifier tight in his mouth. Hank was on his side. His right hand gripped a fuzzy little gray, black, and white whale that Eddie had given him.

Until midnight, I puttered around the house, successfully avoiding thinking about what had happened in the courtroom that day. Once I went to bed and closed my eyes, though, Jane kept coming back to me: that look of complete betrayal, her flushed, bloated face, her sobs.

I dreamed about a pretty young woman who had been poisoned. I didn't know who the woman was, but hundreds of people were busy trying to figure out what to do about the poisoning. One of the men in the dream decided he had to operate. He put the woman on the dining-room table, where he cut her in half as if she were an avocado, cleaned her out, and sewed her back up. "Good as new," he said. "Otherwise she would rot from the inside out." He explained to her and to his assistants that the procedure had to be concealed at all costs, that no one could ever know. When the woman on the table sat up, I recognized her: it was me.

Saturday morning I called Jane, anxious to talk to her about everything that had happened in court.

My mother answered. "Your sister is in the hospital," she said, her voice shaking. "She might lose the baby."

"Oh, no!" I started to cry.

"It's not surprising. Her health before what she was put through yesterday was bad enough."

"I don't understand why Jane would take the stand when she knew she might have to testify about all that other stuff," I said.

233

"She was subpoenaed, LuAnn."

"I know, but to risk being cross-examined like that . . ."

"She never, ever, thought your father would do that to her," Mother interrupted.

"He didn't do it, Mother. Chip did."

"You absolutely refuse to see what's right in front of your nose," she said in a weary voice.

"You sound exhausted," I said.

"I am."

"I had no idea, Mother. I mean, Jane had a baby! Why didn't anyone tell me?"

"We didn't tell anyone. Even Buck didn't know about that baby."

"Buck! I assumed he knew."

"Now he does. So does everyone else in the world."

"Should I go see Jane?" I asked.

"I don't think that's a good idea," Mother said. "I'm going over to the hospital in a bit. I'll be sleeping over here at Jane's awhile."

"You left Daddy?" I asked, astounded that she would have that much gumption.

"We'll see," she said. "Whether I do that or not, he'll be very sorry for what he did to Jane. I can promise you that."

"What do you mean?" I asked. I'd never heard her sound so resolute.

"Just wait," she said. "Buck's expecting me at the hospital now. I need to go."

"Call me as soon as you know anything about Jane. Please."

CHAPTER TWENTY-TWO

rial reconvened at nine on Monday morning. I had faced the full gamut of emotions since the day I saw the FBI documents at the Steak House. On this last day of the trial, I felt only sadness and fatigue. No matter what happened, my sister was lying in a hospital bed fighting to keep her baby, my husband was living with another woman, my mother had lost all faith in me, and I could not fathom why my father wouldn't tell his story. Was anything worth the price we were all paying?

Judge McNabb entered the courtroom and took his seat. I turned my attention to the man who held my father's fate in his hands.

"Good morning. Our plans have changed for today, ladies and gentlemen. Last night Mr. Fuller, on behalf of the State, paid me a visit. He has moved to dismiss the charges that were brought in the case," the judge said.

The courtroom erupted. From across the aisle came shouts of anger. One black man stood up and screamed, "White mother fucker, you'll die!" He was wrestled to the floor and out of the room by two deputies. Some members of the boys' families cried. Behind me, a few people clapped, others embraced. Several reporters ran out of the room. The rest were writing furiously. My father looked at Chip. Chip looked at my father. Clearly they, like the rest of us, had no idea what was going on.

The gavel came down several times until peace was restored. Judge McNabb continued, "I heard the reasons behind the State's motion and decided to withhold my decision on the motion until you, the public and the press, and I had a chance to hear live the testimony I heard in a summary fashion last night. I think it's only fair to everyone that the record fully reflect all the facts relating to this sad episode in our State's history. This conclusion has been a long time coming, but I believe we will finally be able to close the book on the murders of Jimmy Turnbow and Leon Johnson. Mr. Fuller, you may bring in your witness."

Junior met my eyes as he walked past me out of the courtroom. Seconds later he opened the door to come back in. All eyes were on him as he held the door for someone. In came a woman, a breathtakingly beautiful, self-assured woman in her mid-thirties. She was tall, at least five eleven, with dark brown hair, light makeup, and a glowing tan. Everything about her—hair, makeup, silk dress, even her shoes and purse made of exotic leather—subtly announced style, fashion, and money. No one like her lived anywhere within one hundred miles of Tallagumsa.

"What's the meaning of this?" my father shouted. He jumped up. "I will not have this."

"Mayor Hagerdorn, please sit down," Judge McNabb said.

Ben caught my eye. "Who is that?" he mouthed.

I shrugged. I had no idea, although she did look somewhat familiar. I racked my brain, searching for where I'd seen her before.

When the woman approached my father he grabbed her arm. "You don't have to do this."

She stood for a minute in front of his table. The way they looked at each other took my breath away. There was something deep-seated and strong between them. "Yes, I do," she said firmly. "This has gone on too long. Don't try to stop me, Newell."

She turned and walked to the witness stand. I heard Chip ask my father, "What the fuck is going on?"

"You'll see," my father said, shaking his head in dismay.

"State your name," the bailiff said to the woman.

"Elizabeth Ross Kenney," she said.

She was sworn in and then she sat down.

236

Junior stood to question her. "What is your address?" he asked.

"434 Lakeview Drive, Chicago, Illinois."

"Are you married?"

"No."

"Miss Kenney," Junior asked, "were you once married?"

"Yes, I was."

"What was your married name?"

"Reese. Everybody back then knew me as Liz Reese."

"Your husband was Dean Reese?"

"Yes."

"How long were you married?"

"Two years."

"Until he died?"

"That's right."

"What is your occupation?"

"I am president and CEO of Miss Reese's Pies. My company bakes pies, cakes, and cookies and sells them internationally."

"Do you know the defendant?" Junior asked.

"Yes."

"How long have you known him?"

"Since January of 1963." With the exception of occasional glances at Junior or the judge by Liz Reese (I couldn't think of her as Miss Kenney), she and my father stared at each other as she answered Junior's questions.

"Please describe your relationship."

She took a deep breath and smiled slightly. "We were lovers. I was very young and we were in love. You know how it is when you're young? You think no one ever felt the way you feel, that you'll die without each other. Well, that's how we were."

Like Eddie and I used to be, I thought.

"How old were you at the time?"

"I was twenty-two."

"Do you have any children?"

"One, Camille."

"How old is Camille now?"

"Sixteen."

"Was your marriage to Dean Reese a happy one?"

"No."

"Why?"

"My husband was a drunk, a hateful, mean man. He was violent. I despised him."

"And yet you married him?"

"He hadn't seemed what he turned out to be when we first met. After the first few months of marriage, though, I wanted out."

"Why didn't you leave?"

"I got pregnant and I didn't know what else to do or where to go." She shrugged. "My parents were dead, and my brother lived in Alaska. When Dean moved from Mississippi to Tallagumsa, the baby and I came along."

"Did he ever hit you?"

"Many times."

"When did that begin?"

"A few months after we married. He'd drink, accuse me of things I hadn't done, and hit me."

"Where were you on the evening of August 27, 1963?"

"At the house we rented in Tallagumsa, 209 Third Avenue."

"Was Dean Reese with you?"

"Yes, but he left about seven. He told me he'd be off working all night. I didn't even know where he said he was going. He had a lot of odd jobs, and by then I didn't listen to him anymore. When he left I called Newell, and Newell came over."

"Do you know what car Mayor Hagerdorn drove to your house?"

"His sheriff's car. He always drove it everywhere."

"What happened after he got there?"

"We checked on Camille. She was asleep, then we went into the bedroom, and I was closing the curtains when I heard a loud noise outside. I looked out. Dean had just closed the hood of Newell's car. He drove the squad car away. There wasn't anything we could do. We watched and waited and eventually Dean came driving up with the car, parked it right back where it had been, and got in his own car and drove away. He had something in his hands, but I couldn't tell what."

"Why didn't you report the car stolen?"

"It was a rather awkward situation. We thought we should wait and see what happened. The car came back in one piece, so we figured no harm was done. He was just harassing me and Newell a little."

"When did you learn that Jimmy Turnbow and Leon Johnson had been murdered?"

"Later that night. Newell called me and told me about the boys' murders. Then the next day I heard Dean talking on the phone to someone about it."

"Describe that conversation, please."

"He told someone over the phone that he knew who'd killed Turnbow and Johnson, that he'd been there when it happened, and he wanted to meet with whoever it was on the phone. He left the house, and I called Newell and told him that Dean was up to something. He said I should keep an eye on him. Dean came back that afternoon, drunk, and finally passed out. I went to his car and looked all over to see if I could find what he'd put in it. There was a shotgun in the trunk that wasn't his. He had plenty of guns, but none of them were as nice as the one in the trunk. The next chance I got I called Newell and told him about it. He told me to try to get the gun from Dean's car, that it was his, but the next time I looked the gun was gone. So we waited for whatever happened next."

"What did happen?" Junior asked.

"First, Bev Carter told Newell that the FBI agents had the gun and wouldn't give it back. Then the FBI agents went to Newell's house, I guess it was a week later, and basically accused him of murder. That's when we figured out what Dean was up to. It was the most ridiculous thing. We both laughed at first because Dean was so pathetic, and we couldn't imagine that anyone, especially the FBI, would actually believe a word he

239

said. The idea was absurd. Then we realized that if the gun had been used that night, as one of the agents told Newell, it meant Dean had killed the boys and it wasn't funny at all. It was terrible. He'd been a mean man and a drunk, but I didn't think he was capable of cold-blooded murder." Liz Reese shook her head sadly. "I was so ashamed to even know him."

"Did you talk to your husband about your fears?"

"Yes. Newell didn't want me to say anything to Dean, but I couldn't stand it. I confronted him. First, though, I took Camille to our neighbors so Dean couldn't hurt her. He never had, but I was worried now that I suspected him of murder. I told him I knew what he was doing, trying to blame Newell for a crime he'd committed, and he wouldn't get away with it. I told him I hated him more than ever."

"What did Dean Reese do?"

"He accused me of being in love with a murderer, and asked what I would do when my boyfriend went to jail. Who would take care of me and the baby? Dean told me he worked for the FBI and had for a year, and they respected him. He kept saying that I was in love with a murderer and soon everyone would know my lover was a murderer."

For the first time in the course of her testimony she began to grow agitated. Her words came faster, and the sure look I'd been so impressed with when she came into the courtroom was replaced by one of fear. She pressed herself toward the back of the stand, as if backing off from something. My father closed his eyes as Liz Reese continued to talk.

"Then Dean punched me in the face. I didn't even care what he did anymore. When I told him he couldn't hurt me, he knocked me across the room into the dining-room wall, I guess to prove me wrong. The wall was a horrible green. I remember it so well because I hated the color from the day we moved in. And there I was, thrown up against that disgusting wall. I sort of slid down it, and he kicked me. When I see that color today— you know, some government offices use it, it must be very cheap—I get sick to my stomach." She forced a smile.

"Were you hurt?" Junior asked.

"My eye swelled shut and was black, my nose was bleeding terribly. The next day I had bruises everywhere."

"Did you try to leave the house?"

"First I ran into the bedroom and got my suitcase from the closet. I don't know why I didn't just leave. I think I must have wanted him to understand that it was over, that I really was leaving him at last. He got madder and madder, but I couldn't stand it anymore. I didn't care if he killed me. I really didn't care. Dean screamed and yelled and told me he and I would die together before I'd be with Newell. I told Dean that I knew he had killed those poor boys, that I saw him with Newell's car and his gun, and I wouldn't let him do that to Newell. It was too late, Dean claimed that he'd already told the FBI the whole story and it was on tape. He said they believed him." She frowned. "I couldn't imagine anyone would believe anything he said, but here we are after all these years for that very reason."

"What happened next?" Junior asked.

"Then he threw me down on the bed and tried to kiss me. I kneed him hard and ran into the kitchen, where I got a butcher knife." She spoke so quickly that the words began to run together. "I told him—"

"Could you please talk a bit slower, Miss Kenney?" Judge McNabb asked.

"Sorry," she said, taking a deep breath. "I told him that if he tried to touch me again, ever, I'd kill him, that he disgusted me, that I hated him, and that I would make sure no one believed anything he said. I told him he wouldn't see me or Camille ever again."

"What did he do?"

"What he always did after he hit me. He started crying and apologizing about how he didn't mean to hurt me, how he loved me and would do anything for me. But I told him that I was getting a divorce, and I left. I ran over to Norma's, my friend down the street who had Camille."

"Did you see Dean Reese again?"

"No. When I came back the next day he was dead. Newell came over and we talked about what to do. Finally we decided not to talk about the murders at all, ever, not to tell anyone about what we knew, that the truth wouldn't help anyone. Justice had been done. Besides, we didn't really trust the FBI. After all, they'd paid a crazy person all that time and they'd believed him too. Without the FBI behind him, he wouldn't have had the nerve to murder those boys."

"How long did you stay in Tallagumsa?"

"I left town the next week. It was hard to leave Newell, but I couldn't stay. He couldn't leave. We've kept in touch over the years, but never so much as mentioned the murders. I thought I'd heard the last of it until Newell called a few months ago and told me some reporter was digging into it. We discussed what we should do and concluded it made sense to do the same thing we'd done before—that is, say and do nothing."

"Why?" Junior asked.

"We worried about the consequences to my daughter. She never knew anything about her father. I didn't want her to get to know him this way. Over the years I had painted a very flattering picture of the father she never knew, and I thought she would be devastated if she learned the truth. Imagine growing up in a happy, basically average household and finding out at age sixteen that your father was a monster. Sixteen is a very sensitive age, especially for a girl. And Newell felt very strongly that our past relationship was nobody's business. I agreed. We assumed the reporter would give up."

"When did you change your plans?" Junior asked.

"When Newell was indicted I offered to help, to risk exposure, because it was obvious that the whole thing wasn't going away. But he said no, that the government couldn't prove anything, not to worry. He dug in his heels, positive he'd never be convicted on my husband's word."

"Is that why you denied knowledge of any of these events when I first contacted you in August?" Junior asked.

"Yes."

"Why have you come forward now?"

"Saturday you called me and told me that you had talked with someone who planned to go to the press with the basics of the story I just told you if I didn't testify. So here I am. My agreeing to come gave me time to talk to Camille and try to explain the circumstances to her. I didn't want her reading about her father in the paper or hearing some distorted version of our past, though I doubt that would have been much worse for her than my telling her was. Still, she was better off hearing the truth out of my mouth first and under my terms, if you know what I mean. And after reading the news accounts of the first two days of the trial, I wasn't so sure that the State wasn't successfully proving the wrong person had committed the crime. I was upset about what was going to happen to Newell."

I cried softly during Liz Reese's testimony. My first emotion was one of relief—immense relief that the trial was over and that my father was innocent. I never believed he had killed Turnbow and Johnson, but until I heard Liz Reese's testimony there was always that unspeakable possibility, which I couldn't acknowledge until it was no longer a possibility, that he had done it. On the heels of relief came a strong sense of outrage. Not at Ben, not at Junior, but at my father. How dare he do this to our family? And for what? To protect someone else's family while his own self-destructed. To keep his sordid, pathetic little affair a secret.

Judge McNabb asked Liz Reese a few questions, but I couldn't concentrate. I began to shake all over. All I could think about was how many times over the last months I'd begged my father to tell me the truth. How many times he'd smugly refused. The horrible things I'd said to my sister and mother. The brushoff I'd given Eddie whenever he tried to talk to me.

What a thoughtless bastard my father really was. All he had to do was tell me the truth that day I called him and told him that Ben had the FBI documents. All he had to do was tell the simple truth. Surely at that time the matter could have been settled discreetly. And even if Ben had insisted on going public with the whole story, at least our family would have been spared the

243

worst of living through this torturous nightmare my father had so selfishly created. I hated him.

When Judge McNabb finished questioning Liz Reese, she glided off the witness stand. She stopped at my father's table, leaned over and whispered something to him, lightly touched his hand, then smiled and walked away.

Judge McNabb asked everyone to quiet down for one more minute, dismissed the case, and thanked everyone for being so patient. He was obviously relieved to have the case end without having to make the hard decision himself.

I stood up and walked to the front of the courtroom, pushed open the swinging gate, and went past the bar. My father grinned, showing about as much remorse as a little boy who'd been caught with his hand in the cookie jar.

I couldn't stop myself. I slapped him across his cheek as hard as I could.

The packed courtroom fell silent. Everyone stared at me as I strode out of the courtroom.

CHAPTER TWENTY-THREE

I magine a sixteenth-century navigator on a great ship plying the vast expanse of the Atlantic Ocean. It is a cloudless night, weeks after leaving Spain, and he glances up to take solace from the familiar Pole Star, the brightest star in the Northern Hemisphere, the star on which he and all navigators rely in charting their routes, the star around which the rest of the night sky is arranged and which puts everything into perspective. On that night he looks to its expected location and, not finding it, begins to search the sky ever more desperately. Finally he shakes his head as if to shake loose something lodged there and looks again. The Pole Star is gone. Breathing deeply, he moans and then sobs in utter despair. He is lost, hopelessly lost, and nothing will ever be the same again.

I knew that nothing would ever be the same in my life after that trial. My father had been the one constant in my universe, and had he died I would not have felt any more adrift than I did when the charges against him were dismissed. I would have grieved, longer and perhaps more deeply than most, but I would have survived and gone on about my life without this feeling of absolute disillusionment compounded by a pervasive sense of my own culpability.

At the moment I slapped him and walked out of the court-room, I would almost have preferred my father's death to what he'd revealed about himself by heartlessly covering up his fifteen-year-old love affair.

I spent the first nights and days after the trial in hiding, refusing all phone calls and visits. Jolene covered for me, as always. She even slept at our house—worried, I suppose, about whether I was competent to care for the children should a middle-of-the-night emergency arise. Estelle and Roland ran the Steak House. When I wasn't asleep (my preferred state), I played with Jessie and the twins. My favorite make-believe game with Jessie was one I invented. Four of her Barbie dolls lived on the planet Zygor in a distant galaxy. The dolls were all alone, just the four of them; they took care of each other, and they knew and needed no one.

I realized during my second day at home that the answer was simple. We would move, far away from Tallagumsa, leaving behind the entire experience and, most important, my father. Outside the state, I would never have to meet the eyes of all the people who knew our tawdry secrets. With that decision as a talisman against what I knew everyone must be saying and thinking, I emerged from my house on Thursday afternoon, three days after the trial ended.

The minute I stepped outside I sensed a change in the weather, a sharpening in the air that signaled a change of seasons. A breeze carrying the first gentle touches of fall rustled the still-green leaves.

I drove first to Jane and Buck's, anxious to assure myself about the welfare of Jane and the baby. Jolene had informed me during my three days in hiding that Jane was out of danger, but I couldn't be sure that Jolene wasn't shading the truth to protect my vulnerable psyche.

Jane and Buck's house was in a new subdivision of Tallagumsa called Overlook, a neighborhood of lonely-looking brick mini-mansions, complete with columns, pools, and foyers as big as my house, built in the middle of two and a half acres of barren land. Hundreds of acres of magnificent trees had been bulldozed to build the subdivision. In their place, the developer had planted small, pitiful-looking saplings along the sidewalks and every few hundred feet in the yards.

Buck's silver Cadillac was in the driveway. I pressed the doorbell. Chimes reminiscent of church bells rang for at least a minute before Buck opened the door.

He was surprised and not particularly happy to see me. "I wanted to see how Jane was doing, if there's anything I could do," I said.

"She's better," he said quietly, blocking the doorway.

Buck seemed a shrunken version of himself. He looked pale and exhausted. All his bluster and hot air were gone. To my surprise, I missed them. I wanted him to call me by some movie star's name, or pat me on the back, a little too hard, or criticize my jeans and T-shirt.

"Can I see her?" I asked him.

When he didn't answer, I took his hand and begged, "Please, Buck?"

"Okay. You can come in for a quick visit, but only if you promise not to upset her. That means don't talk about what all's happened," he said sternly. "I know you want to, but don't. She's under doctor's orders to stay in bed and remain calm."

There went my plans to bare my soul and beg for Jane's forgiveness. I understood that I could never have stopped Daddy from letting Chip tear Jane apart on the stand, even if I'd known the truth about Jane's past. But I had taken my father's side, again and again, and attacked Jane for her refusal to do the same, and for that I owed her an apology.

Buck followed me into their bedroom and hovered about like a mother hen, obviously distrustful of my intentions.

When I saw Jane's turtlelike shape lying in the canopied bed I'd always thought more suitable for a junior-high girl, I fought back tears, determined for once to rise above my own self-indulgent sorrow and put her best interests ahead of my needs.

"Hey, Sis," I said, reverting to my childhood name for her. I leaned down to kiss her cheek. Her face was not as puffy as it had been the last time I saw her. She looked relaxed, the strain of the trial replaced, I hoped, by optimism about her future as a mother. Without the usual layer of hair spray, her hair had a soft, girlish look.

"When did they let you come home from the hospital?" I asked.

"Two days ago, when my blood pressure finally came down and the fluid drained out of my face and hands. They were so swollen," she said. "I looked like a balloon, but I feel much better now."

"You look wonderful," I said.

"You want to sit down?" she asked, turning her hand in the direction of a wingback chair covered in the same lavender-flowered material as the bed canopy.

I glanced at Buck. He frowned; clearly he did not want me to get too comfortable. "No, thanks," I said. "I just stopped by for a minute."

"Did you know I probably have to stay in bed the whole rest of the pregnancy?" Jane asked.

"You are a braver woman than I," I said.

"It won't be that bad," she said cheerfully. "I have my knitting and my magazines and those romance books you hate, and Buck can do a lot of the legwork for me." She smiled at her husband. "It's worth it."

"Where's Mother?" I asked.

"She's not staying here anymore. She's home," Jane said.

"Home?" I said, surprised. I'd assumed that once she got as far as Jane and Buck's, she'd never go back to Daddy and the lake house she'd never wanted in the first place.

"Yeah. She went home when I got back from the hospital," Jane said.

After several uncomfortable silences, punctuated only by small talk about my children and the weather, I said good-bye. At least Jane and Buck had let me in the house. It was a beginning. I would miss them when I moved.

My next stop was my parents'. Mercifully, only Mother's beige Buick sedan was parked next to the house. I walked along the wooden walkway to the back of the house, which faced the lake. Two squirrels ran across my path, scared off by my footsteps. Bright sunlight fought its way through the thick, leafy overhang, forming shifting spots of light.

Through the wall of glass, I could see Mother sitting on the living-room floor, pulling clothes out of boxes. She folded the clothes and placed them in three separate piles. Wearing old baggy brown slacks and a pink pin-striped shirt of Daddy's, she hadn't dressed with her usual impeccable care. Her hair hadn't been brushed either. Was she leaving Daddy? What all had happened while I was holed up at home?

"Where are you going, Mother?" I asked, opening the back screen door.

She looked up at me, and a smile lit her face. "Nowhere. I'm sorting through these old clothes for the church collection. I got a call in the middle of the night that Frank, our church janitor, lost his home in a fire. Everything's gone. Bad wiring caused the fire. That's why I look like this," she said, referring to her unkempt hair and clothes. Her voice was hoarse.

"Was anyone hurt?"

"No, but ten people who lived in a two-bedroom house are homeless and without food and clothing. I'm in charge of the relief effort for our church. You want to help me sort through these? I'm washing the dirty ones and sewing the ones that need it."

"Are you sick?"

"My voice, you mean? No, I've just been talking too much, organizing the relief effort and not getting much sleep for the last week."

"Where's Daddy?"

"At his office."

"He's working already?"

"He never stopped."

"I guess I'm not surprised. Nothing fazes him, does it?"

"You can come all the way in, LuAnn," she said. "I won't bite."

I realized then that I had been standing half in, half out of the doorway, with my hand on the door handle. I came inside and closed the door behind me. The country-music station on her radio was playing "Mammas, Don't Let Your Babies Grow Up to Be Cowboys."

"I've tried to reach you every day this week," Mother said. "I've been worried about you. Are you all right?"

"Jolene told me you called. Thanks for worrying about me at all after the way I've acted. I'm physically okay but mentally kind of a wreck. I just couldn't face anyone for a few days, and I'm still not really ready, but Jessie was starting to look at me funny—you know, very concerned—so I got up and left."

"I'm glad you ventured out, but I must say, you don't look well." Mother stood up and set the clothes in her lap on a chair. "Come on in the kitchen and I'll get you some tea. Have you eaten?"

"I don't think I can eat. Every day when I wake up it feels like somebody has grabbed my stomach and squeezed it into a little ball, then kicked it a few times for good measure."

"I'm sorry. I'll make you something light. Maybe that'll put some color in those cheeks." She walked over to me and touched my cheek lightly. "You really do look too thin."

I shrugged and followed her into the kitchen. I doubted I could eat, but it was easier to follow her than to argue.

She prepared the hot tea, handed it to me along with a plastic bear full of honey and started to prepare scrambled eggs and toast. As she worked she hummed something I couldn't identify.

I cupped the tea with my palms, enjoying the cup's warmth on my hands.

When my parents moved out to the lake, my frugal mother had insisted on bringing all the antique furniture from the old house, even though it seemed incongruous in this modern glass-and-wood setting.

The kitchen table where I now sat was the one I'd grown up with, a round oak table with an ornately carved base and two leaves. On the edge across from me was the burn mark I'd made one night smoking when I was a teenager. A high-school junior home alone and experimenting with smoking, I'd left a lit cigarette resting on the table while I put a stack of records on the turntable. I was horrified to find that the cigarette had burned all the way down to the filter, right through the wood grain, leaving an ugly, indented black mark. I never admitted that I was the person responsible for that damage either, but I guess Mother and Daddy must have known all along.

The smell of the butter, eggs, and toast in the air reminded me of even earlier times. "I feel like a little kid who's home from school, being taken care of by her mother," I said. "But—" I stopped abruptly.

"What?" Mother asked. Her back was to me as she cooked over the stove.

"But it seems like lifetimes ago. I just don't remember you and me like this—relaxing together, you know, hanging out. Not after I was bigger, anyway."

Mother turned around, holding the cast-iron frying pan full of eggs in her left hand, the spatula in her right, and frowned slightly as she scraped the eggs out onto a plate. She served me, then pulled out a chair and sat down across from me. She looked at me expectantly.

I thought back over my high-school and junior-high years. "You and I never avoided each other, I don't think," I said. "We just spent less and less time together over the years. It was always Daddy and me, and Jane and you. Why do you suppose that was?"

"I don't really know," she said. "Over the weekend, waiting next to Jane's hospital bed and struggling with the biggest decision I've ever had to make, I thought about you and your sister, how you gravitated toward Newell, and Jane toward me. I can't pinpoint any particular event. All I know for sure is that by the time you were twelve or thirteen that's how our family was divided. Eat something, please." She pursed her lips and watched me, waiting for me to eat.

I picked up the fork and pushed my eggs around. "I feel responsible," I said. I took a bite of toast.

"For what?"

"Everything, including our relationship back then."

"Oh, LuAnn. You were only a child. I didn't even realize the family had split along those lines—you and Newell, and Jane and me—until it was too late. Relationships change gradually. Nothing seems to change day to day, then suddenly everything is different and you can't put your finger on what happened. Just like I didn't realize Newell was in love with someone else until the affair ended."

I dropped my fork. "You knew about Liz Reese?" I asked.

"I wasn't sure *who* she was until the trial, but I knew he had been in love with someone besides me. I finally figured out last week who it had to be, and then I called Junior and told him what I believed had really happened. Then Junior called her and she testified." Mother took hold of the cross she wore on a slim gold chain around her neck and pulled it back and forth against the chain. She appeared lost in thought.

"You!" Choking on the bite of eggs I'd just eaten, I patted my chest, swallowed, and took a breath. "I can't believe it! Does Daddy know it was you who brought Liz Reese back?"

"I told him Monday afternoon, after the trial ended. And I told him I'd gladly do it again and that if he ever hurt one of my children again I'd leave him for good." Her normally complacent tone was replaced by a defiant one.

"How did you know for sure what had happened?" I asked. "How'd you figure it out?"

"It was the only explanation. In the first place, I never believed your father's line that he was behaving like a fool to uphold some great principle—to make the government meet its burden of proof. I know him too well. He would have been the first to say, Hey, I was at work or whatever. It had to be that he didn't want to reveal where he was that night. All I knew for sure was that he wasn't with me or at home. But I also knew he

252

didn't kill anyone. And I knew he was in love with someone else around that time. It was then just a matter of listening to the testimony."

"Did you tell Daddy what you were going to do before you talked to Junior?"

"Are you kidding? I didn't want to give him a chance to talk me out of it. He's a very persuasive man. I don't think he would ever have told the truth if I hadn't intervened."

"What if he were convicted? Surely he would have said something then?"

"He was so sure he wouldn't be, and he was probably right. He was furious when I told him I had convinced Junior to call Liz Reese. He thought I went to Junior to save him. But I told him that saving him had nothing to do with my actions, that I went to Junior because his version of the truth was not acceptable. I wanted everyone else to see what really happened fifteen years ago, especially Jane and you. Newell and I had a fight about it Monday night. He was sitting where you're sitting now, yelling at me."

"What did he say? Why did he put us through it?"

"He thought his election chances were better if the State failed to prove its case than if he told the whole story right up front, and he wanted to protect Liz Reese and her daughter from the past."

"What about us?" I asked. Again I felt about as significant to my father as one of his fishing worms.

"He thought we could take it, he said, especially you. He thinks you're tough. We knew he was innocent, he said, so he didn't think we had anything to lose. He couldn't understand why that wasn't enough."

"I was a wreck, and he knew it! I couldn't take it. He could even have told us the truth and then gone ahead with his crazy trial strategy. Even that wouldn't have been as horrid as the last months have been. He could have told Ben in the beginning and stopped the whole investigation. There are so many ways Daddy could have avoided all of the terrible things we all went through. How could he allow Chip to put Jane through that cross-examination?"

"He assumed she'd never testify, he said."

"But when she did, at that point he should have stood up and explained how the murders really happened. Why did he want so badly to protect Liz Reese?"

"Well, I think he still loves her in a way. At least he feels something intense for her. She was very young during their affair. He says he owed it to her after all she'd been through. And her daughter, Camille, never knew her father. Newell figured she'd be crushed if she knew the truth about Dean Reese."

"So he let me and Jane be crushed instead. We're only his daughters." I shook my head.

"She reminds me of you," Mother said.

"Who?"

"Liz Reese. Both of you are beautiful, smart, assertive young women. Your father's type. I never was."

"So why aren't you leaving him? He deserves it."

"We'll see how your father and I adjust to one another now. It won't be easy, but I'm hopeful."

"Why? He's mean and selfish! I'd leave him if I were you."

"I'm not that surprised, you see, that he did what he did."

"You've always known he was such a monster?" I asked sarcastically. "That's great."

"That's just it. He's not, LuAnn. You idolize him. I know him. You've always worshiped him. I haven't. I'm not saying what he did wasn't thoughtless, even cruel. But my expectations have never been as high as yours, and I can't let my marriage go as easily as some." She looked at me knowingly.

"I haven't let mine go," I said defensively.

"Sure seems like it," she said. "What are you going to do about your marriage?"

I sighed. "This morning I decided to move as soon as possible."

"Move where?" she asked, startled. "And do what?"

"I don't know. Away, that's all. I don't see how I can live here after the trial, and I don't want to ever see Daddy again. It would be easier to leave."

"You are such a person of extremes, LuAnn. You go from one extreme—adoring him—to the other—wanting never to see him again. When you were little you always threatened to run away when life didn't suit you."

"I don't remember that."

"It's true. Whenever you got mad, you'd tell us we would never see you again, pack your Mickey Mouse bag, and walk down the block. This decision is no different, except that it was easier for you to turn around and come home then. If you run away now, will you ever come back, even to visit?"

"I haven't thought that far ahead. I just want to go. That's all I can deal with."

"Maybe it's time you learned to temper your feelings, to see the shades of gray between the black and white. I hoped after this experience you'd be able to see your father for what he was and is: a human being, LuAnn, just like the rest of us. I'm not justifying or defending anything he did. It was wrong. He and I may not make it through all this, but he's your father, he'll always be your father, and you need to work out a relationship that isn't based on fantasy. This is your chance to do that." The more she talked, the weaker her gravelly voice became.

"Leaving is a more attractive alternative right now."

"And what about Eddie? You can't run off and leave Eddie," she said.

"Maybe he'd come too. Who knows?"

"I don't think he wants to leave Tallagumsa. He's happy at the college, and the cartoons he's done here are wonderful. Your children are content. You have the Steak House. Last time we spoke about the restaurant you called it the perfect job. If you throw all that away, don't you think you'd be sorry? Stay and work this through. Come to church with me. That would help you, I know."

"I knew you couldn't go through an entire conversation

255

without mentioning church," I said, smiling.

"But I've been pretty good about it this afternoon," she said, smiling back at me. "Only once in over an hour."

"I know that was hard for you." I laughed. "Maybe you're right. I shouldn't make any rash decisions. But you didn't want me to live here in the first place, remember? Turns out you were absolutely right."

"I didn't want you to live here because I thought you were coming for all the wrong reasons, but now you're here, and I don't want you leaving for all the wrong reasons. You'll have nothing to build a life on, leaving like that. Call Eddie today, why don't you? Call him now."

"Maybe later. What about Barbara Cox? Are they . . . Is he living with her?"

"I have no idea. You're his wife, though, the mother of his children. You go get him."

"Mother, you are too much today. I'm so proud of you." I stood up and walked around the table and hugged her. *"Go get him!* Really."

I put my dish and cup in the sink. "You want some help with those clothes?" I asked.

"That would be lovely," she said.

"Why don't I fix us both some tea first," I said. "Your throat could use it."

Tea in hand, we walked into the living room. She pointed to each pile. "That pile is for the wash, that one to be folded, and that one needs repair. I'll be right back," she said.

She returned in a few minutes and handed me an envelope. I opened it and saw Ben's all-too-familiar handwriting. It was dated two days earlier. Mother sat down on the rug across from me, sipping her tea and sorting. I read the letter.

Dear LuAnn,

How I wish we could have seen each other before I had to leave for D.C., but Jolene intercepted my calls and turned me away at your door. I wanted to wait you out, but the paper demanded my return for the time being. If I had seen you, I would have said good-bye, kissed you, and asked—where do we stand? I am here for you, or there; you tell me where and when and it's done. I suspect you have a fair amount of figuring things out to do now after the trial. *What do you want?* When you know, call or come. Whatever happens, whatever you decide, I miss you and love you.

Ben

I folded the letter and put it back in the envelope.

Mother looked at me, hoping I'd share the contents of Ben's note with her.

"He just wanted to say good-bye," I said.

"That's all?"

"Not exactly."

"Now I get it." Her face fell. "You're thinking of moving to Washington, aren't you?" she asked sadly.

"No! He doesn't have anything to do with my wanting to leave."

Mother looked skeptical.

"Really, he doesn't. That's one thing I'm sure of. He's a wonderful person, but he and I—that was all just another gigantic mistake. When I make mistakes, I make really big ones."

"I agree," she said, smiling.

I put the envelope down and picked up a familiar looking yellow and white plaid skirt. Could it be the one I'd worn in high school? Half the hem was ripped out. I searched through the sewing box and found white thread, a needle, and a thimble. I threaded the needle and began to sew.

Mother stitched up the lining of an olive-green gabardine suit jacket.

We worked together in friendly silence as the October sun began to drop toward the lake. The pile of clothes that needed repair was slowly shrinking.

Soon a car came down the gravel road to the house, and

Mother and I looked up expectantly from our sewing. I steeled myself for my father's entrance. The last time I'd seen him we were in court and I slapped him. What would I do now? What would I say? I wasn't ready for this.

Perhaps I would never be ready, but I knew Mother was right. I had to face him and begin to build our relationship on an entirely different basis: one in which I was his equal, not his devotee; one in which I judged him by the same standards I judged others. I understood for the first time that I had to separate my well-being, success, and happiness from my father's—not by running away but by meeting him head-on.

A car door slammed, and someone walked around the deck. At first, with the glare of the sun behind the person, I had difficulty making out who was at the door. All I could see were cowboy boots and washed-out jeans.

The door opened. It was Eddie. The answer to Ben's question.

I looked at Mother suspiciously.

She smiled and stood up.

"Did you call him?" I hissed.

"Maybe," she said. She walked out of the living room, down the hall toward her bedroom.

Eddie walked in and I burst into tears.

"You aren't going to run out of the room, are you?" he asked.

I shook my head.

He sat down on the floor next to me. We both stared straight ahead, out toward the lake.

"Sewing?" he asked. "Did you give up restaurant life for a career in fabrics?" he joked.

I was too upset to say anything. Tears streamed down my face.

"She told me you were calm—resigned but calm, was what she said. I guess she got it wrong." He rested his right hand over my left and removed the silver thimble from my finger, then he tossed the thimble up in the air and caught it several times.

"Who said that?" I asked, biting my lip and trying to slow the onslaught of tears.

"Your mother."

"What else did she say?"

"That you were thinking about leaving Tallagumsa."

"Don't you think I should? I've made a mess of everything since I got here. Everything. It's better sometimes to start over—a clean slate and all that." I sniffed and blotted the tears on my face with the back of my hand.

"What about me?" he asked.

"What about you?"

"I'm serious, LuAnn. Would you leave here without me? Are you so crazy now that you would even consider that?"

"Well, what would you care? You and Barbara are pretty cozy, living and working together."

"You have no idea where I've been or with whom. You've refused to talk to me, remember?"

"You could have talked to me if you really wanted to."

"You are such an idiot sometimes. I wasn't about to throw myself down on the ground and kiss your feet, but I did try time and again to call you and see you, and you refused."

"Were you living with her or not?"

"You don't have much right to complain if I was, LuAnn, but in fact, I wasn't. I stayed in Barbara's living room a few nights until she left on some school trip. I baby-sat her dog until Labor Day, when she got back to town. Since then I've been at different teachers' houses. Whoever would have me."

I picked up the pair of pants from my lap, scooped the thimble up off the floor where Eddie had put it, and continued sewing a gray patch over the worn-out knee. "I'm sorry," I said, staring at the patch.

Eddie didn't say anything.

I put the sewing materials on the floor and looked over at him. "I said I'm sorry," I said louder.

He turned toward me. "I forgive you," he said, his searching gray eyes reading my feelings. "I know we can make it work out if we both try, LuAnn. What do you say? Are you ready?"

"More ready than I've ever been. I love you, Eddie Garrett," I said.

Then he smiled that smile, wrapped his arms around me, and kissed me.

"Let's go home," he said.

"Why don't you go ahead and talk to the kids? I'll finish these clothes with Mother." I kissed him. We lingered in each other's arms for a few minutes, then he left.

I walked down the hallway in search of my mother. Along the walls she'd hung a gallery of family portraits and snapshots. I stopped in front of the one of Jane and me at the beach after one of our sand castles was destroyed by high tide. In the photograph I am seven, Jane is thirteen. I am sobbing, with my head on Jane's shoulder. Her arms are wrapped around me, consoling a sister who stubbornly refuses to accept the inevitable, a sister who insists on seeing life as she wants it to be, not as it is.

I took a few steps, then paused in front of a snapshot taken at my high-school graduation. In the picture I am striding across the Tallagumsa High School stage wearing my cap and gown. I recalled believing that I had reached the absolute height of maturity at the moment nine years earlier when the principal handed me my diploma. Several feet away one of my favorite wedding day photographs shows me turning away from Daddy and towards Eddie, my hand reaching for my future husband's as the preacher looks on. I remembered clearly just how grown up I thought I was when my father walked me down the church aisle and "gave me away." Finally, near the end of the hallway, there was a photo of me relaxing in one of the tattered armchairs at the apartment in Atlanta. My bare feet are resting on a footstool, and newborn Jessie is in my lap. The corners of my mouth are lifted in a somewhat self-satisfied smile. When Eddie took that picture, I was congratulating myself on the ease with which I'd made the transition from childhood to womanhood.

Now I knew I was wrong. Each and every time. Now at least I had a chance.